"You finally brought me here," she whispered.

He had no idea what happened next, who moved first, but his lips brushed hers, and his body revved straight into overdrive. She tasted like some kind of fruity lip gloss, sweet and sexy. He bent his head, deepening the kiss.

Next thing he knew, she was in front of him on the bike, facing him, kissing him like crazy, and every cell in his body was lit up for her, for Emma… "Emma."

"Mm?" She lifted her head, her eyes glazed, her pink lips curved in a dreamy smile.

He drew in a ragged breath. "What are we doing?"

"Kissing?" Her gaze dropped to his lips.

Desire curled hot and strong inside him. "Shouldn't."

Her cheeks darkened, and her face fell, and dammit, he was an ass. He hauled her up against him and kissed her again, hard. "I didn't mean… hell, Emma. I am completely blindsided right now. But whatever this thing is between us, I am feeling it. Big time."

ACCLAIM FOR RACHEL LACEY

RUN TO YOU

"4 Stars! Readers will love how the lives of the main characters meld together while still maintaining their individual lives."

—*RT Book Reviews*

"There's much to like in this sweet romance, including the strong hero and heroine, the cast of supporting characters and the beautiful mountain setting."

—Bookpage.com

EVER AFTER

"Lacey's Love to the Rescue contemporary series keeps getting better and better...Olivia's foster dogs, her fluffy kitten, and Pete's dog provide delightful diversions while the humans build their own forever home."

—*Publishers Weekly* (starred review)

"4 1/2 Stars! Lacey's latest is filled with huge doses of humor and passion...[Her] modern storytelling style, with its crisp dialogue and amusing banter, will keep readers engaged until the very end."

—*RT Book Reviews*

FOR KEEPS

"Your heart will be captured many times by the genuine scenarios and the happily-ever-after for all, both human and canine."

—HeroesandHeartbreakers.com

"Lovable men and lovable dogs make this series a winner!"
—Jill Shalvis, *New York Times* bestselling author

UNLEASHED

"Dog lovers rejoice! The stars of Lacey's cute series opener, set in Dogwood, N.C., have four legs instead of two, and their happy ending is guaranteed."
—*Publishers Weekly*

"Endearing! Rachel Lacey is a sure-fire star."
—Lori Wilde, *New York Times* bestselling author

CRAZY *for* YOU

RACHEL LACEY

FOREVER

NEW YORK BOSTON

Forever
Hachette Book Group
1290 Avenue of the Americas, New York, NY 10104
forever-romance.com
twitter.com/foreverromance

First Edition: March 2017

Forever is an imprint of Grand Central Publishing. The Forever name and logo are trademarks of Hachette Book Group, Inc.

The publisher is not responsible for websites (or their content) that are not owned by the publisher.

The Hachette Speakers Bureau provides a wide range of authors for speaking events. To find out more, go to www.hachettespeakersbureau.com or call (866) 376-6591.

ISBNs: 978-1-4555-3756-3 (mass market), 978-1-4555-3757-0 (ebook)

Printed in the United States of America

OPM

10 9 8 7 6 5 4 3 2 1

For my wonderful friend and critique partner, Annie Rains. So glad to be on this amazing journey together!

Acknowledgments

Huge thanks to my editor, Alex Logan. I become a better author every time we work together. Also, a big thank-you to the whole Forever team—Lexi Smail, Michelle Cashman, Elizabeth Turner, and everyone else who helped bring this book from my laptop to the shelves. You are the best!

Thank you to my amazing agent, Sarah Younger. I always say it, but it's so true—I don't know what I'd do without you. I am so glad to be a part of the NYLA team.

Author friends: You guys make my day, every single day! Annie Rains, Tif Marcelo, Sidney Halston, April Hunt, everyone on Team Sarah, and all the many other friends I've made along the way—I love you and am so thankful for you all.

Friends and family: You help make it possible for me to live my dream, and I won't ever forget it. Thank you for helping to keep me sane and taking the munchkin off my hands when I need to meet a deadline.

Thank you to Danielle James for your tattoo expertise

and to Tif Marcelo for inspiring the "ketchup scene" in Chapter 1. (Yeah, you remember the one. Haha!)

Also thank you to Vanessa McBride, who donated to animal rescue as part of our Authors for Cats giveaway on National Cat Day in 2015. Vanessa inspired and named Emma's cat, Smokey.

And the biggest thank-you of all to all the readers and bloggers who've bought, read, reviewed, or otherwise supported me along the way. Everyone who has sent me a photo of my book on the shelves or tweeted me to say hello. It's the little things, and I appreciate them all more than you could know. xoxoxo

CRAZY *for* YOU

CHAPTER ONE

Ryan Blake held a bottle of Maker's 46 in his right hand, a tumbler in his left. With a flick of his wrist, he tossed the bottle. It flipped once before landing back in his grip, top down, ready to pour. He filled the tumbler, set a napkin on the bar, and placed it in front of the brunette on the other side. "Bourbon, neat."

"You're good." She picked up the glass and tipped it in his direction. "Not what I was expecting in this little bar in the middle of nowhere."

"I try," he said with the friendly, semi-flirtatious smile he always used on single ladies seated at his bar. She wasn't wrong. The usual clientele at The Drunken Bear had little use for fancy liquor or bartending tricks, but the trio in front of him were tourists looking for a good time, and he'd see that they had one.

"You were just about to tell me about this tattoo." She placed her hand on his biceps, fingering the eagle he'd had inked there after he flew this coop ten years ago.

"That's right." He shifted backward so that her hand slipped to the countertop. He encouraged flirting—it led to better tips and made the night more interesting—but this chick was getting a bit too friendly, considering the diamond band on her left ring finger. "This one was for spreading my wings. Thought I'd fly far away, and yet, here I am back in Haven."

"You're from here then?" one of the other women asked, shamelessly ogling the tattoos on his arms while giving him an eyeful of cleavage.

"Born and raised. Moved around a lot, but I can't seem to shake this place. It's in my blood." Once upon a time, he'd been hell bent on getting as far away from this sleepy North Carolina mountain town as possible. Spent the better part of a decade drifting from place to place, taking with him only what he could carry on his bike. Funny how things came full circle. He picked up an empty pilsner glass another patron had left behind.

"Ryan?"

He turned at the familiar voice to find Emma Rush standing there, one hip propped against the bar, and he damn near dropped the glass. Emma's trademark ponytail and jogging pants were nowhere in sight. Tonight, her blond hair cascaded over her shoulders in shiny waves, her blue eyes sparkled at him from behind a tasteful—yet sexy—amount of makeup, and her red top was tucked into a pair of jeans that fit her like a glove. He swallowed past the sudden dryness in his throat. "Hey, Em. What brings you out tonight?"

"Girls' night," she said with a smile, gesturing to her friend Mandy, who stood by the door talking on her cell phone. Emma slid onto an empty barstool. "I wasn't expecting to see you."

"I'm still here a few nights a week." His new business

venture—Off-the-Grid Adventures, an extreme outdoor sporting facility he'd opened with his good buddies Ethan Hunter and Mark Dalton six months ago—was finally bringing in enough income that he soon wouldn't need to bartend to pay his rent. "What can I get you?"

"Untapped amber ale, please." She watched while he filled a frosted mug. "Thanks."

"My pleasure."

She lifted the mug to her lips and took a long drink. "Damn, that's good," she said with a happy sigh, setting it on the bar.

"Always been more of a pilsner guy myself." He tried not to stare as she licked froth from her upper lip.

"Hi, Ryan." Mandy stepped up to the bar beside Emma.

He leaned back, tearing his gaze from Emma's lips. "Hi."

Emma turned to her friend with a smile. "Ready to get a table?"

"Yep," Mandy said.

"Have fun, ladies."

"We will." With a wave, Emma walked off after her friend, and damn, those jeans cupped her ass like perfection. No doubt about it, Emma looked *hot* tonight. And his thoughts were way out of line. He'd promised Derek he'd look out for his little sister, not drool all over her.

"Your girlfriend?" the brunette at the bar asked, eyebrows raised as she sipped her bourbon.

Ryan cleared his throat and dragged his eyes away from Emma. "Just a friend."

"Mm-hmm." The brunette gave him a look that said she didn't believe him.

He turned to check on his patrons at the other end of the bar, but his attention was once again diverted by Emma— or rather, the preppy-looking businessman she was talking to now. Ryan couldn't make out their conversation, but the guy wore an irritatingly smug smile, and Emma didn't look at all happy to have bumped into him.

Ryan moved down the bar, chatting and pouring drinks as he went, all the while keeping an eye on Emma. She was deep in conversation with the businessman, although the guy seemed to be doing most of the talking. Emma smiled and nodded. She glanced up and met Ryan's gaze, rolling her eyes at him with a smile while her companion kept on talking.

Next thing Ryan knew, the guy had slung an arm around her shoulders, gesturing wildly with his free hand while Emma subtly edged away from him.

Ryan was around the bar and across the room before he'd even realized what he was doing. "Everything okay over here?"

Emma shrugged out from under the guy's arm, but her smile wasn't nearly as warm or genuine as the one she'd given Ryan a few moments ago. "Yep."

"We're fine," Obnoxious Dude answered. "Who are you?"

"Ryan Blake. And you are?"

"Tristan Farrell."

"Tristan and I are...old friends," Emma said.

By old friends, Ryan assumed she meant former flames. And since she clearly wasn't enjoying his company, it was time for Tristan to leave. Ryan crossed his arms over his chest and stared him down, waiting for the loser to get the message. It didn't take long.

Tristan backed up, his eyes darting toward the front door. "Well, it was great seeing you, Emma. Take care."

"You, too." She watched as Tristan left the bar then turned to Ryan. "Forgot how much I dislike that guy."

"He hassling you?"

Her eyes rounded. "No! Just talking my ear off, really. Sorry to distract you from your duties at the bar."

"No problem." Keeping an eye on his patrons was part of the job, although he was probably feeling more protective of Emma right now than the situation called for.

"Right, well...looks like my table is ready." She waved over her shoulder as she walked away.

Ryan headed back behind the bar, turning his attention to the trio of tourists and their mostly empty cocktails. "Any of you ladies ready for a fresh drink?"

As it turned out, they all were. While he mixed their cocktails, he allowed his gaze to roam over to Emma's table. She was deep in conversation with her friends Gabby, Carly, and Mandy, all of whom he knew, none of whom made his gut tighten the way it did every time he looked at Emma tonight.

He had no idea where this had come from, but he had to get over it, pronto. Emma wasn't interested in a player like him, and even if she were, she was off limits. He'd made a promise to her brother when Derek went off to war, and Ryan had no intention of breaking it.

* * *

Emma Rush polished off her beer and set it on the table with a thunk. Was that her third, or her fourth? Didn't matter. She was on the fun side of tipsy and loving it. They didn't usually come to The Drunken Bear for girls' night, but with plenty of local beer on tap, rock music playing, and one of her favorite people tending bar, she was totally in favor of coming here again.

"Hottie at ten o'clock," Mandy said, tipping her beer in the direction of the bar, where an African American man sat on the first barstool, sipping from a frosty mug of beer. Yeah, he was hot, but Emma's gaze shifted past him to the bartender. Ryan was by far the sexiest man in the room, as far as she was concerned.

"He's hot," Gabby agreed, "but he's no Ethan."

"Or Sam," Carly added with a smile.

"Hush, you two," Emma said. "You don't have to rub it in that you both have sexy men warming your beds at night."

"You should go over and talk to him." Mandy nudged her shoulder. "He's delicious, and he looks very clean-cut."

Emma frowned. "Who says I like my men clean-cut?"

Mandy pressed a finger to her lips then laughed. "I'm thinking back on the last few guys you've dated—Daniel the high school teacher, Tristan the accountant..."

Emma scrunched her nose. "Please don't remind me."

Gabby's lips curved in amusement. "There are worse things than dating clean-cut guys, Emma."

"I bumped into Tristan here earlier," Emma told them. "I seriously can't believe I ever dated that guy." He'd done nothing but brag about a promotion he'd gotten at work, hadn't even asked how she was doing.

Carly leaned forward. "Why? What did he do?"

"Nothing really. He's just so self-absorbed and ridiculous." She took a fortifying gulp of her beer. "But here's the thing that really bugs me. I had kind of forgotten about it until I saw him again tonight. Remember back when I was dating him, I told you guys that I had decided to break up with him because he was so boring?"

They all nodded.

Emma felt a flush creep into her cheeks. "Well, the truth is, he dumped me before I had the chance to dump him. And he basically told me *I* was boring. He said I was too predictable and never wanted to do anything fun."

"Well, obviously he doesn't know you very well," Gabby said with scorn in her voice, "because you're lots of fun. I mean, you got me to sign up for an obstacle course race when I was deathly afraid of heights. That was pretty much the opposite of boring."

Emma smiled wanly. "Well, the world's most boring guy thinks I'm a dud, which means—"

"You need to start dating more exciting guys," Mandy finished for her. "You should shake things up, go outside your comfort zone."

"You did tell me last summer you were ready to try something new," Gabby said.

"Yeah, I wanted to quit being such a goody-two-shoes. Obviously, I haven't put in enough effort." Emma took another sip of her beer. "But you know what? I think it's time to step up my game."

"So, what naughty things did you have in mind?" Mandy asked.

An image flashed through her head of kissing Ryan on the back of his motorcycle. "I want a hot fling with someone *un*-boring. I want the opposite of clean-cut. I've never dated a bad boy. Maybe it's time to find out what the fuss is all about."

Mandy clapped her on the back. "Now we're talking. What else?"

"Well, since I probably have no shot at bagging a guy like that, I've also been thinking about getting a tattoo."

"Tattoos are cool," Carly said. "And speaking from experience, I think you should get the tattoo *and* the bad boy."

"I agree," Gabby said.

"Definitely both. We'll help," Mandy said. "And if you're serious about this, let's talk about sexing you up a bit, too."

"Sexing me up?" Emma giggled.

"You look really cute tonight. I know you can dress casually for work, but this is the look you should be going for. We should go shopping!" Mandy's expression brightened at the idea.

"Ooh, I want to come," Carly said. "Let's plan a shopping day. We could go to the outlet mall in Blowing Rock."

Emma sipped from her beer, feeling excitement stir inside her. "Yeah, that sounds fun. Okay, so we'll freshen up my wardrobe. Then how do I get the hot guy?"

Mandy gave her a wicked smile. "That part will be easy. Leave it to me."

"Um...okay, I think." Emma laughed.

"We can start right now, in fact." Mandy was eyeing a group of men at the bar. Dressed in flannel shirts, worn jeans, and boots, they were obviously locals enjoying a few beers after work, some kind of outdoorsy work by the look of them. They were a boisterous group, with lots of laughter and back slaps being exchanged. "I dare you to go ask one of those guys out."

"Are you kidding?" Emma shook her head. "No way."

"They're not exactly bad boys, but this is a good way to get your feet wet." Mandy reached for the bottle of ketchup on their table, dabbed some on her finger, and smeared it on Emma's cheek. "Here's the plan: You're going to walk over to the bar and take that empty seat next to the group of lumbersexuals. Order a drink. Look sexy. First guy to wipe the ketchup off your cheek is the one you're going to flirt with. Your mission is to get him to ask for your number. Deal?"

On the other side of the table, Carly and Gabby were practically bouncing with excitement.

"No way," Emma repeated, even as a little thrill of excitement raced through her.

Mandy gave her a friendly nudge. "We'll be right here for moral support."

"What if the guy who wipes the ketchup off my cheek is a loser? Or ugly?"

"Then give him a fake number. But you have to flirt with him until he asks for it. That's the dare. Go on. Be unpredictable. It'll be fun."

Emma drained her beer and stood from the table. "If this goes south, it's all your fault."

Mandy gave her a friendly shove in the direction of the bar. "Good luck, my friend. Go charm their socks off."

Emma walked toward the group of guys. They were good-looking, for the most part. Definitely rowdy. She slid onto the empty barstool and glanced around for Ryan because she was definitely going to need another beer to pull this off.

He caught her eye, and her pulse jumped like a startled deer. Yeah, she'd had a crush on Ryan for as long as she could remember. He was three years older and had been her brother Derek's best friend in high school. Ryan was the one always getting into trouble, the one her mom hadn't wanted Derek to hang out with and certainly would never have let Emma date.

Not that Ryan would have considered dating her, not back then anyway. In high school, she'd fancied herself in love with him, but looking back now, she realized it had just been an unrequited teenage crush. And then her whole life imploded. By the time the smoke cleared, Ryan had left town.

Now he was back, and as it turned out, her crush on him was still alive and well. Which was really inconvenient right now because he was seriously distracting her from the task at hand. Tearing her eyes from his gaze, she turned her attention to the group beside her.

"Hey there, sweet thing. What are you drinking?" one of the lumberjacks asked, his brown eyes bright, words slightly slurred.

Ugh. What was she doing?

"Want a shot of tequila?" another guy asked, waving a shot glass in her direction.

"No, thanks." She'd agreed to flirt with whoever wiped the ketchup off her cheek, not get shitfaced on tequila.

"Yo, you've got a little something..."

She turned, and Ryan's thumb swiped across her cheek, his rich, cocoa eyes locked on hers, and *oh shit...*

"Got it." He grinned while warmth spread through her skin in the wake of his touch and sparks pinged through her belly. "You need another beer?"

"She was about to do a shot," the drunk guy beside her said.

Ryan's eyes narrowed in Drunk Guy's direction.

"Actually, I need to get back to my table." Emma lurched to her feet and practically ran back to her friends. "Oh my God, you guys. It was *Ryan.*"

Mandy's eyes were wide. "I saw. That was actually kind of hot."

"Deal's off." Emma dropped into her chair, heart pounding like she'd just run laps around the bar.

"Not so fast," Mandy said. "I saw a little zing when he touched your cheek. You said you wanted a hot fling. Ryan could be just the guy to show you a good time."

"No. Nope. Not happening." Emma waved her hands in front of her face. Ryan had never seen her as anything but Derek's tomboyish little sister. No way was she setting herself up for that kind of humiliation.

Carly looked up from her phone, a sheepish expression on her face. "I can't believe I'm going to miss seeing how this plays out, but guess who's waiting outside?"

"Sam?" Gabby asked.

"He got in a day early." Carly was dating Sam Weiss—who also happened to be a super-hot rock star—and he'd been in LA for the past month or so. By the look on Carly's face, she couldn't wait another minute to see him.

Mandy waggled her eyebrows. "Have fun."

"Good luck, Emma. Call me tomorrow." With a wave, Carly headed for the door.

"So where were we?" Gabby asked, leaning forward conspiratorially.

"We were changing the subject," Emma said.

"No, we were just modifying the dare," Mandy said, her eyes gleaming with mischief.

"I'm with Mandy," Gabby said. "The more I think about it, I love the idea of you flirting with Ryan. I saw the zing when he touched you, too. He could be exactly what you need to break out of the boring-guy rut. He's got that whole bad-boy vibe going for him, but underneath the tattoos, he's a really solid guy."

"New dare," Mandy said. "You're going back up to the bar, and you're going to convince Ryan to give you a ride home on his motorcycle."

A thrill ran through Emma at the thought. "He can't. He's working."

"Then obviously you'll have to hang out and keep him company until he's finished."

Emma shook her head. "This is crazy. I'm not going to flirt with Ryan."

Gabby looked thoughtful. "Well, maybe you can work your way into it. You want to shake things up in your life, right? What if you ask Ryan for his help? He teaches rock climbing lessons at Off-the-Grid. That sounds exciting."

Emma blew out a breath. That sounded okay—maybe

even fun. Ryan could definitely help her break out of her rut, even if things stayed platonic between them. "I could do that."

Mandy nodded enthusiastically. "And you're going to start by asking him to give you a ride home tonight."

"But why wouldn't I ride home with one of you guys?" Emma asked.

Mandy grinned. "Because we're going to ditch you."

"Ethan will be here soon to pick me up, but what about you, Mandy?" Gabby asked.

"I'm going to go meet that hottie at the bar," Mandy said, gesturing toward the man she'd been checking out earlier. "Good luck, Emma, and have fun on that motorcycle. Can't wait to hear all about it." With a wink, she sashayed off toward the bar.

"Are you okay with this?" Gabby asked.

Emma shrugged. "Riding on Ryan's bike sounds fun and taking rock climbing lessons does, too. It's a start. I'm making no promises otherwise. I mean, Ryan and I have known each other since we were teenagers. It's crazy to even think about flirting with him."

"I hear you. It could definitely make things awkward between you two if it didn't work out."

"Exactly. Anyway, I'll hang out with you until Ethan gets here."

Gabby smiled. "Sounds like a plan. You know, we talked about new clothes and a hot guy, but that's all superficial stuff. When you and I talked last summer, you wanted to shake things up with your job, too. Have you put your application in yet?"

Emma blew out a breath, shaking her head. No, she hadn't submitted her application for the landscape architecture program at the University of Georgia. "But you're right.

Since high school, I've been saying this was my dream so why haven't I gone after it yet?"

Gabby placed a hand on Emma's. "I can't answer that for you."

"Tomorrow," Emma said. "I'll do it tomorrow. No more excuses."

"I think this is the most important decision you've made tonight," Gabby said.

The jittery feeling in the pit of Emma's stomach said she was right. "And leaving Haven would definitely be the biggest change in my life."

"Well, you wouldn't be leaving forever, just while you get your degree."

Emma shook her head. "Let's be real. If I move to Georgia to get my degree in landscape architecture, there's no reason to come back. I don't have family here, and job prospects are better there. So if I get in, I'm not coming back."

"Oh." Gabby looked thoughtful. "Well, I would definitely be sad to see you go, but sometimes you have to leave home to find yourself."

Emma knew Gabby was speaking from experience. Last year, she had done just that, leaving her life in Charlotte behind to come here to Haven—looking for a haven of her own. She'd found it, and she'd managed to snag the town's most eligible bachelor, Ethan Hunter, while she was at it.

"The program's pretty hard to get into," Emma said. "So if I get in, I'll make a new life for myself in Georgia. If I don't, it wasn't meant to be."

"Sounds like a good plan to me," Gabby said. "I'm proud of you, you know. This is a big deal. I hope you get in."

"Thanks."

The front door opened, and Ethan stepped inside, his eyes

darting straight to Gabby. He looked at her like there was no one else in the room, like the sun rose and set around her. Emma wanted that kind of pure, unconditional love. Someday. In the meantime, she'd settle for a really hot fling. She wanted sparks like the kind she'd felt just now when Ryan touched her cheek and all the toe-curling things that came next.

"Looks like my ride is here," Gabby said. "Are you really doing this?"

Emma glanced over her shoulder at the bar. "Yeah, I should keep an eye on Mandy anyway in case that guy is a creep. If I chicken out on the dare, I'll just take a cab home."

"Okay. Well, good luck. Call me tomorrow." Gabby gathered her coat and stood up from the table.

"Will do."

"Bye." Gabby walked over to kiss her fiancé, and they left hand-in-hand.

Emma lifted her jacket and purse from the back of her chair and walked to the bar. She found an empty stool and slipped onto it. Ryan looked over and met her eyes. The heat of his gaze started a slow burn deep in her belly. He was sexy, no doubt about it. Six-foot-plus of strong, muscular man. Tattoos peeked from beneath the sleeves of his black T-shirt, covering his arms with their stories.

He made his way over, his eyes never wavering from hers. "Yo, where'd Carly and Gabby go?"

"Home with their hotties." She crossed her arms beneath her breasts and leaned her elbows on the bar to give herself a bit of cleavage. "And I need another beer."

His gaze remained annoyingly on her face. "Sure thing. You still drinking Untapped amber ale?"

She nodded. This was *so* not her style, sitting alone at the bar trying to pick up a guy, let alone Ryan. The only thing she'd committed to was asking for a ride home, but maybe she'd flirt just a little, just enough to see if she could get a reaction out of him.

Think sexy, Emma. You can do this...

"Coming right up," he said, still completely professional.

"Thanks." Emma leaned back to check on Mandy, who was currently making out with the man she'd just met. Well, that was fast. Emma had never hooked up with a random guy like that, wasn't sure she wanted to. But then again, wasn't her new motto to shake things up? Be unpredictable...

"His name's Carl, and he's in town for business. He sells vacation rentals," Ryan said as he set a fresh beer in front of her.

"Thanks, and how did you..."

His lips curved in amusement. "That's my job. You didn't think I'd let Mandy make out with a total stranger, did you?"

She shook her head. Of course not. Ryan made it his business to know everyone he served at the bar.

"Be right back." He walked over to three women sitting at the far end of the bar. They were dressed up and drinking fancy drinks, too fancy for a place like this. One of them leaned in, touching his arm as she spoke. Ryan laughed, then rolled up his shirtsleeve to give her a better look at his tattoos.

Emma frowned into her beer. That woman made flirting look easy. She was effortlessly sexy and probably much more appealing to a man like Ryan. A sinking feeling grew in the pit of her stomach as she watched him banter with them. He pointed at the blonde and winked, flashing that irresistible smile. He was flirting. Definitely flirting.

Someone tapped Emma on the shoulder, and she turned to find Mandy standing there, a sheepish smile on her face. "So, um, Carl and I are going to take off. You okay?"

"Yep. Have fun, be smart, and text me later, okay?" Because it made her nervous to see her friend leave the bar with a stranger, whether Ryan had chatted him up earlier or not.

"I'm always smart, and I will." Mandy leaned in to whisper in Emma's ear. "Bonus points if you kiss him. You'll be sitting behind him on the bike. Just stand up a bit, lean over his shoulder, and kiss him. You'll blow his mind." With a wink, Mandy walked to the door, hooked her arm through Carl's, and headed out into the chilly March night.

"Does girls' night always end with everyone leaving with a guy?" Ryan asked from behind her, humor in his voice.

"Not usually." *Only when they're setting me up.* She lifted her beer and took a drink.

He looked at the mug, his eyes serious. "How are you getting home?"

"Not sure. I rode here with Mandy." *Gah.* She was such a chicken.

"I'll call you a cab."

Wait a minute. No, she was still doing this, dammit. She lifted her eyes to his. "Who said I was ready to leave?"

Ryan watched her for a moment, his expression unreadable, then he cracked another easy smile. "Stay as long as you like."

CHAPTER TWO

By eleven, only a handful of people remained at the bar. Ryan poured a scotch on the rocks for a man sitting alone near the door. Based on the way he fiddled with his bare ring finger, Ryan pegged him as either going through a divorce or a man looking to mess around on his wife. Neither option sat well when he caught the dude staring in Emma's direction.

He walked over to her. "Why are you sitting here alone at the bar on a Monday night, Em?"

She looked up at him, her blue eyes bright and twinkling with mischief despite—or maybe because of—the drunken giggle that revealed how much beer she'd consumed tonight. "Because I'm having fun."

He smiled in spite of himself. "Wouldn't have pegged you as the type."

She gave him a funny look. "Well, I'm trying to broaden my horizons."

"Hang tight," he told her, then went down the bar to settle up with the trio of tourists. They left him a sweet tip before heading out into the night. He wiped down the bar as he made his way back to Emma. "You ready for me to call you that cab?"

"What time are you off?" she asked.

"We close at midnight."

She leaned closer, and her floral scent teased his nostrils. "Any chance you could give me a ride?"

"It's pretty cold out there, and I only have my bike. You'd be more comfortable in a cab." And so would he, because the sight of her here at the bar, all that silky hair loose around her shoulders and the sexiest hint of cleavage showing at the neckline of her shirt...it was doing all kinds of weird things to his mind. Like making him fantasize about her on the back of his bike, her arms around his waist. Her lips on his. Emma in his bed, screaming his name.

"I've always wanted to ride on a motorcycle," she said softly.

"You've never..."

She shook her head, a wicked smile curving her lips. "So what do you say, will you be my first?"

Ah, hell. *Derek's little sister.* He repeated the words in his head until he'd dragged his mind out of the gutter. "You're not dressed to ride."

"I only live a few miles down the road. I'll survive."

This was a terrible idea. He should insist she take a cab, for his own sake if not for hers, but..."All right then, if you don't mind waiting around while I close up."

"Not at all. It's kind of fun hanging out at the bar by myself. A couple of guys have even flirted with me. Maybe I should let my hair down more often. What do you think?"

He thought those guys were too smooth for a woman like Emma, and if the cheater by the door tried to put a move on her, he might "accidentally" spill a drink in the douche's lap.

"I think you're beautiful however you wear your hair, but it does look really nice tonight."

She sat up straighter. Yeah, he hadn't expected to hear himself say that either.

"Thanks."

He grabbed a cloth and rubbed at a water ring on the bar top, more as a distraction than out of necessity.

She leaned closer, those blue eyes hitting him like a punch to the gut. "I'm trying to shake things up this year, not be so much of a goody-two-shoes."

He blinked. "Say what?"

"I want to have some fun." She smiled, not the practiced take-me-home-tonight smile he received from so many women every time he tended bar, but a warm, honest smile that seemed somehow much sexier. "I'm thinking about getting a tattoo. And I want to sign up for rock climbing lessons when you start up for the season."

His brain got fuzzy somewhere around the mention of a tattoo. "Oh, yeah?"

She nodded, tucking a lock of hair behind her ear. "It looks exciting."

"Almost as good as a ride on my bike." And dammit, he was flirting.

"You could bring all kinds of excitement into my life," she said with a giggle, reminding him that she was borderline drunk.

"Water for you until we close," he said, plunking an empty glass on the bar in front of her, which he filled from the tap.

She grumbled but took it without protest.

Ryan ventured down the bar to check on the cheater by the door and the other lone couple still remaining. The couple paid their tab and left, leaving only Emma and the cheater. And luck must have been on Ryan's side because that guy paid up, too, and headed out into the night.

"I've never been the last one at the bar before," Emma said, watching as he cleaned up.

"The place is dead tonight. Monday night outside of tourist season."

"Can I help?" she asked as he placed dirty mugs into the dishwasher beneath the counter.

"Nope, but I do appreciate you keeping me company." He hadn't paid much attention to her when they were kids, but grown-up Emma was pretty cool, even if she was totally messing with his head tonight.

She chattered away while he cleaned up the bar. Jason, the manager, swung through and flipped the sign on the door from OPEN to CLOSED. Emma went to the restroom while Ryan finished up in back.

"Who's the chick?" Jason asked. "She doesn't look like your usual type."

"Emma Rush," Ryan answered. "She's an old friend who needs a ride home."

"On your bike?" Jason looked skeptical, and for good reason.

Because Ryan didn't often give a chick a ride without hoping to get laid afterward. "Only ride I've got. I've known Emma since she was a kid. She's just a friend."

"Whatever you say, man." Jason slapped him on the shoulder and headed for the back door.

Ryan turned to find Emma in the doorway, a funny smile on her face. "It might sound better if you said you'd known me since *we* were kids, instead of since *I* was a kid."

"Same thing, isn't it?" He zipped his jacket and led the way toward the back door.

"As long as you're not still thinking about me like I'm

twelve," she said with a wink as she pushed the door open ahead of him. She wore a blue jacket now, not nearly thick enough to keep her warm on his bike. It was mid-March, and the temperature tonight had dipped into the forties.

He glanced at her ass. Yep, she was definitely all grown up now. "You sure you want to do this? If Mark's still up, I could get his keys and drive you home in his SUV."

"I'm positive I won't freeze to death in the time it takes you to drive me home."

"All right then." It was cold tonight, but he'd always found it exhilarating to feel the icy rush against his body as he rode. Emma might regret her decision later, but she was right; she wouldn't freeze to death in the time it took to get her home. "You got gloves?"

She pulled a pair of black gloves out of her pockets and slipped them on.

He led the way around the corner and down two blocks to the renovated building he, Ethan, and Mark had bought condos in last year. Ethan's condo was noticeably empty these days as he spent more and more time at Gabby's place.

Emma walked up to the Harley and rested her hand on the handlebar. She turned to look at him with a gleam in her eyes. She really did want to ride on it. Well, he'd be damned. Maybe he'd underestimated her.

He unlocked the door to his first-floor unit and grabbed the spare helmet he kept for just this occasion. Except usually the woman riding on the back of his bike was someone he was either sleeping with or hoping to sleep with. *But this is Emma.*

"You ready?" he asked as he held it out to her.

"You have no idea." She took it with a smile and slid it onto her head.

And...*fuck*. The combination of the skintight jeans,

jacket, and his helmet on her head was too much. He'd never been able to resist a woman dressed to ride, let alone a woman on his bike. Which meant he was crazy to give her this ride.

He handed her a pair of glasses, then put on his own helmet.

"What are these?" she asked.

"Eye protection." His slid his pair into place. Too bad they did nothing to obscure his view of Emma, because damn, she was turning him on big time right now. Those jeans... "All right, wait for me to give you the all clear, then you're going to put your left foot on the peg, grab my shoulders, and climb on."

"Okay." Excitement danced in her eyes.

He mounted the bike, settled himself, and cranked the engine. It roared beneath him with barely leashed restraint. This bike was his pride and joy, the first thing of value he'd ever bought for himself. He'd worked his ass off for this beast and never regretted a single penny he'd spent.

Once the engine settled beneath him, he gave Emma a nod. As she swung into place, her hands settled on his waist, searing his skin even through all the layers of clothing. No doubt about it, she was going to be his undoing tonight.

* * *

Whoa. Emma closed her eyes and let out a shriek as Ryan guided the bike onto Main Street and picked up speed. The cold wind whipped her face, taking her breath away. Beneath her, the engine rumbled and roared like a wild thing. *Holy shit.* She was on the back of Ryan Blake's bike, and it was amazing.

The wind bit through her thin, knit gloves, hitting her

fingers with an icy blast. Actually, every part of her was freezing, but she didn't care. She wrapped her arms more firmly around Ryan's waist, anchoring herself to him so she didn't tumble off the back of the bike, and somehow her hands slipped beneath his jacket. *Ahh*. That was better. Toasty warm, and also...her hands were on his T-shirt. Even through her gloves, she felt the hard contour of his abs, and nope, she wasn't cold now.

And this was absolutely freaking amazing.

She hung on tight as he guided them over Haven's twisting mountain roads, deserted at this hour. Overhead the moon shone like a beacon, illuminating the night in its soft, silvery glow. The roar of the engine and the slap of the wind against her face shocked her senses. It was thrilling, invigorating, so completely different from riding inside a car.

She'd never have done this if Mandy hadn't dared her, and now she felt like her eyes were open for the first time in years. *This* was what she needed. Somewhere along the way, as she sat at the bar talking to Ryan, she'd realized she was having fun, *really* having fun. And she wanted more. She wanted it all, every last wild and crazy fantasy.

All too soon, her building came into view. Ryan cut the engine and guided them quietly into the driveway, coming to a stop behind her silver Toyota RAV4.

"Don't worry," she told him. "I share this place with students. They're probably still up, but if not, I've suffered through enough of their late-night parties that they'd sure as hell better not complain about a little motorcycle noise." She rented the front half of this multi-unit cabin. The back half had two apartments, both occupied by college students.

He turned his head to look at her, so sexy in his helmet and riding glasses. "So how was it?"

"Even better than I thought it would be." She gulped for

air. His lips were way too close to hers, and she was still a little bit drunk on beer and a whole lot drunk on her first motorcycle ride. Mandy's words echoed in her ears. *Bonus points if you kiss him. Just stand up a bit, lean over his shoulder, and...*

Emma leaned forward, her chest sliding up his back as she tipped her face to his. Holy hell, she had completely lost her mind, but she was going for it. Every nerve in her body went haywire.

Clunk. Her helmet smacked into his, drawing her up an inch short of his lips.

Ryan sucked in a breath, his dark eyes locked on hers.

She froze. Oh God, this was so embarrassing! She was pressed against him, her hands still on his waist, her face so close to his, so awkward, so obvious she'd been about to kiss him. Foiled by the stupid helmet.

"Emma." His voice was low, his face a blank mask behind his glasses.

"Um—" Well, now the moment was ruined, and she felt like a total idiot. She scrambled off the bike, pulled off her helmet and glasses, and turned her back to him.

He came up behind her, put a hand on her shoulder, and spun her to face him. "What just happened?"

She just shook her head, crossing her arms over her chest.

He stared at her for a long second, looking so disreputably rumpled she almost went for it again—this time without helmets to get in the way.

"You had too much to drink tonight."

"I'm not drunk." Or wait—maybe she should have let him think she was. That might be less embarrassing, and it's not like she was totally sober, after all.

His gaze slipped to her lips. "It wouldn't be a good idea." And there it was. She absorbed the sting of his words.

"Oh. You don't—I mean, I get it. Those other women at the bar are a lot more—"

"Emma," he interrupted her, his dark eyes nearly knocking her off her feet with their intensity, "it's got nothing to do with them. You're...any guy would be lucky to kiss you, but I can't." Something flickered in his expression. It almost looked like desire...for her.

Whoa. "Why not?"

A muscle in his jaw flexed. "You know why."

She jabbed a finger at him. "Don't you dare bring up my brother right now."

"I promised him I'd look out for you. I specifically promised him that I would *not* take advantage of you."

"Well, that's insulting because I wouldn't call anything that happened tonight you taking advantage of me. And that was over ten years ago, Ryan." She paused as hot tears pressed against the backs of her eyes. "Derek's gone."

The words hung between them, crisp and cold. Ryan had been there beside her at Derek's funeral. He'd always been there for her. But he didn't want to be *with* her. And it hurt even more than she'd feared.

His eyes shone with regret. "And I can never get his okay on this."

* * *

Emma woke up the next morning to the ding of an incoming text message, followed by another, and another. Her head ached, and *ugh*, her pride stung even worse. She pressed a hand over her eyes with a groan. A heavy weight plopped onto her chest, knocking the breath from her lungs.

"Meow."

Emma peeked through her fingers at the gray cat perched

on top of her, regarding her from wide blue eyes. "Morning, Smokey."

She shifted the cat to the side so that she could grab her cell phone off the nightstand. The screen showed five new text messages, all from her friends.

Rumor has it you did indeed catch a ride on Ryan's bike, Gabby said.

Details. We need details! from Mandy.

I've got fresh cinnamon buns. Come and get 'em, and let's gossip, from Carly, who owned A Piece of Cake bakery and made the best cinnamon buns Emma had ever tasted.

I'm in, Gabby texted.

Be there in thirty. Emma, wake up! from Mandy.

I'll be there, she texted. But the details are less exciting than you're imagining. I'm going to need extra frosting, Carly.

Then she rolled out of bed. Smokey meowed again as she hopped victoriously onto Emma's pillow and sat, lifting a paw to wash her face.

"You are such a diva," Emma muttered as she headed for the bathroom. She stepped into the shower, submersing herself in the hot spray. Forty-five minutes later, she walked through the doors of A Piece of Cake, finding her friends already gathered at the counter, drinking coffee and munching on cinnamon buns.

She scowled. "You could have at least waited for me."

"You're late. Long night?" Mandy gave her an assessing look, one eyebrow raised.

"More like too much beer." She rubbed her forehead as she sat on an empty stool. "What happened with you and Carl?"

"Eh, he turned out to be a dud," Mandy said with a shrug. "But we want to hear all about your night with Ryan."

"Extra frosting," Carly said, passing a plate across the counter with a cinnamon bun dripping with gooey white goodness. She set a steaming cup of coffee beside it.

"You're the best." Emma inhaled the rich aroma of cinnamon and French roast, feeling her system starting to perk up already.

"So?" Gabby asked. "What happened?"

Emma held up a finger. She took a big, fortifying sip of her coffee and popped a forkful of sinfully delicious cinnamon bun into her mouth. Once the sugar and caffeine had taken effect, she turned to her friends. "Ryan gave me a ride home on his bike."

"And?" Carly asked.

"Was it amazing? I've always wanted to ride on a motorcycle," Gabby said.

"It was great." A shiver of excitement snaked down her spine as she remembered the feel of the bike beneath her, the wind in her hair, the moon illuminating them like a scene out of a movie.

"Just great?" Mandy gave her a look that said, *We want more.*

"It was fantastic. Is that better?" Emma shook her head. "You guys really pushed me last night, and you know what? I loved it. I had so much fun hanging out at the bar, and riding home on Ryan's bike was the most fun I've had in ages."

"So why the extra scoop of frosting?" Carly asked, leaning her elbows on the counter.

"Because between the dare, the beer, and the motorcycle ride, I completely lost my mind, and I kissed him. Or I *tried* to kiss him." She pressed a hand over her eyes as her friends squealed in surprise.

"Did you kiss him or not?" Mandy asked.

"I went for it, but at the last moment, we bonked helmets instead." She cringed.

"That sounds kind of adorable," Carly said, a wistful note in her voice.

"It wasn't. It was awkward and embarrassing." For a moment right before their helmets bumped, she'd been so sure he wanted to kiss her, too. "And then he gave me some speech about how he'd promised Derek he'd never take advantage of me."

"Really? He promised Derek he wouldn't go after you?" Mandy looked surprised.

Emma nodded. "Which was reasonable at the time. I was fifteen and as innocent as they came, and he was an eighteen-year-old troublemaker who had no business anywhere near me."

"But Derek never came home from the war," Gabby said softly.

"That was twelve years ago," Emma said. "Things change. We're adults now."

"What are you going to do?" Mandy asked.

Emma took another bite of her cinnamon bun. "Easy. I'm going to pretend it never happened."

"But you do have feelings for him?" Carly asked.

Emma spluttered. "What? No! Like, of course he's hot, and I'm sure the kiss would have been great, but feelings? No. No way."

They were all staring at her. Gabby's mouth dropped open.

"Whoa," Carly said. "You totally do."

Emma felt her cheeks start to burn. "Don't be ridiculous. I do not have feelings for Ryan Blake."

"Ever hear that saying about 'the lady doth protest too much'?" Mandy said.

"Cut it out, seriously." Emma gulped from her coffee and scorched her throat, making her sputter again.

"Interesting. Very interesting." Mandy tapped her fingers against her lips. "Well, I'd say last night's dare was a success. Now we have to keep the momentum going. You need an excuse to see him again."

"I'm seeing him in a couple of hours," Emma mumbled, still coughing. "I'm going out to Off-the-Grid to talk about spring landscaping."

"That's right," Mandy said. She and Emma both worked at Artful Blooms Landscape Designs and often helped each other out on projects. "But you need something more interesting than work. You need to get back on his bike or—"

"Remember last night how you said you wanted a tattoo?" Gabby asked. "Ryan used to manage a tattoo parlor. It would make perfect sense for him to take you."

Emma choked down the last bite of her cinnamon bun. "After last night? Definitely not."

CHAPTER THREE

Ryan arrived at Off-the-Grid, bleary-eyed and buzzing with restless energy. The temperature this morning barely topped fifty degrees, but he didn't care. He needed some quality time on the rock face before work to clear his head. He went into the closet for his Patagonia jacket and hat. No gloves. He needed full contact with the rock to climb.

Back outside, he hiked down the path through the woods, letting the exercise get his blood pumping. Fifteen minutes later, his favorite climbing spot came into view. Last night's motorcycle encounter with Emma had left him off balance. She'd been drunk, but what was his excuse? He shook his head as he gripped the base of the rock and hauled himself upward.

He didn't have one. Never should have happened.

He'd wanted to kiss her. *Really* wanted to kiss her. Would have kissed her if the damn helmets hadn't gotten in the way. And now he had to figure out how to stop thinking about her in those jeans, wearing his helmet, on his bike...looking so goddamn sexy and windswept by the light of the moon. Because just thinking about it was turning him inside out.

The truth was, he'd been feeling unsettled for the last six months or so, almost since he'd returned to Haven. He'd picked up a few women right after he got back in town, but not in months now. And now, every time he closed his eyes, he thought of Emma.

He pulled himself up on top of the rock and sat, looking out over the forest. Around him, the trees buzzed with activity. Birds sang. Squirrels leaped from branch to branch. Ryan felt like the King of the Jungle up here. He'd missed this during his years on the road, missed having a place where he belonged. A part of him had always envied Derek for knowing what he wanted out of life. Ryan had felt more adrift than ever after his friend enlisted. But he had Off-the-Grid now, and no way was he going to fuck this up. Finally, he climbed down and hiked back to the office, ready to tackle the day ahead. He went in through the back door.

"There's someone here to see you," Ethan called from the reception area.

Ryan glanced at the clock. It was just past ten, and already his stomach was grumbling for lunch. Clearly he'd gotten up too early this morning. Or gone to bed too late last night. Or a combination of both. "A vendor?" he asked. He wasn't expecting anyone today other than...hell, Emma was scheduled to come talk about spring landscaping in an hour.

But Ethan was shaking his head. "Don't think so. Looks like a teenager to me, but he asked for you specifically."

"Might be looking for a rock climbing lesson."

"Could be. I'm heading out on the zip-line course with a group. Be back in a couple of hours." Ethan headed for the door.

Ryan walked through the reception area and out the front

door to find a kid standing there, hands wedged in his pockets, shoulders hunched, watching Ethan lead the group of tourists down to the zip-line course. Late teens maybe. Asian. He glanced at Ryan, then his eyes darted back to the zip-line group. They'd never met, and yet something about him was oddly familiar.

"I'm Ryan Blake. Can I help you?"

The kid looked at him again. He swallowed hard. "My name's Trent. Trent Lamar."

Trent. Ryan felt like he'd been slammed backward. It couldn't possibly be. After all these years...

Trent shoved his hands farther into his pockets. "I, um, I think I might be your brother."

Ryan hadn't known his baby brother's last name after the adoption, but *shit*. He didn't know who Trent's father was—or his own for that matter—but he knew his brother had Asian heritage. "Nah, man. I'm sure of it."

"Really?" Trent eyed him warily.

"Yeah." Ryan pulled him in and clapped him on the back. Then they stood there, staring at each other. Ryan found himself uncharacteristically at a complete loss for words. Trent. *Hell.* "I can't believe it. How did you find me?" Because he'd spent years, half a lifetime, searching for the half brother he hadn't seen since Trent was an infant.

"My parents told me your name." Trent looked away.

Yeah, Trent's adoptive parents had been total assholes, to Ryan anyway. They'd labeled him a bad influence and cut him out of his brother's life after the adoption went through. "Let's go inside where we can talk." Ryan led the way to his office and closed the door behind them.

Trent sat in the big chair in the corner, fidgeting with his hands in his lap. "I tried to look you up online a few times, but I never found anything. Then, a few months ago, I saw an article about this place. It had your name and your picture, and when I saw it was in Haven, I knew it had to be you."

"I looked for you, too. I never stopped," Ryan said as emotion welled up, squeezing his chest. He'd moved around for the last ten years looking for his brother. Trent was the only living blood relative he had, and it had been like a knife slowly twisting in his gut knowing his brother was out there somewhere. "So where'd you grow up?"

"Outside St. Louis," Trent said.

His brother had grown up halfway across the country. Ryan still couldn't quite believe Trent was sitting there. He looked like a pretty okay kid, baggy jeans and overstyled hair like Ryan had noticed on a lot of the local teens. Trent's hands were soft, like he spent more time in front of an Xbox than out roaming the woods as Ryan had done at his age. Still... "So your parents—they're okay? You're happy?"

Trent shrugged awkwardly. Yeah, typical teenager. "They're all right, I guess."

"But you had a good childhood?" Because Ryan had always wondered, hoping that Trent had grown up in a stable, happy home. Their mom had OD'ed when Trent was just a baby, sparing him most of the chaos that had surrounded her. As a healthy infant, he'd been adopted quickly. Ryan, eleven when their mother died, had remained in the foster care system until he aged out at eighteen.

"Yeah," Trent said. "It was good."

"I'm glad. So you're what... eighteen now? Are you in college?"

Trent shook his head. "I started college last fall, but it just wasn't for me. I dropped out and came looking for you."

Shit. If he'd ever found Trent, Ryan's goal had been to get into his adoptive parents' good graces so that he could stay a part of his life, and now he was proving a bad influence before they'd even met.

Fate had a really fucked-up sense of humor sometimes.

* * *

Emma arrived at Off-the-Grid for her eleven o'clock meeting with Ryan with her head held high. She might be mortified about how last night ended, but he never needed to know it. She stepped out of her SUV and smoothed her hands over her Artful Blooms logoed jacket and khaki pants. Last night's almost-kiss aside, right now she was here to talk business. And if she'd left her hair down again today, well, that was because of the chilly weather, not because Ryan had said it looked beautiful. Okay, maybe it was a little bit about Ryan. Or a lot.

With her iPad in hand, she pulled open the front door and walked inside. Ryan—coming out of the kitchen while stuffing a candy bar in his mouth—nearly ran right into her. He pulled up short, his eyes settling on hers with an intensity that sent sparks ricocheting around in her belly.

"Sorry." He wore a black fleece pullover with Off-the-Grid's logo on it and a pair of worn jeans. And he smelled delicious, a combination of some kind of manly aftershave and chocolate—courtesy of the candy bar.

"No problem." She clutched the iPad against her chest. Okay, so internally she was definitely not playing it cool right now, but she was reasonably sure her face remained impassive. She'd perfected the art of hiding her feelings years ago. "I thought we should walk the property together first so we can make sure we're on the same page with landscaping. Then I'll put together an estimate and some virtual mock-ups that I'll e-mail you in a day or so."

A muscle in his cheek twitched. Apparently he hadn't expected her to launch right into business after the way they'd left things last night. "Okay."

She turned around and walked back out the front door with Ryan at her heels. "I assume most of what we're looking at will be here around the main building and out along the road by the sign."

"Yeah. We want something eye-catching, maybe some nice, bright colors, especially out by the road, but it needs to be low maintenance. We don't have any money in the budget for grounds keeping this year so Ethan, Mark, and I have got to be able to keep it up ourselves."

"Okay. I was envisioning some beds along the walkway here, maybe African daisies. They come in pretty purples and yellows, and they're hardy."

Ryan shoved his hands in his pockets and rocked back on his heels. "Long as you stick to the budget, we don't much care which plants you pick. Just don't stick us with a bunch of hot pink roses or anything." He cracked a smile.

"I'll keep your manhood intact, don't worry." She grinned, leading the way around the side of the house. "I can put in some flowering bushes around the edges of the field. If there's room in the budget, are you interested in reseeding the grass, too?"

"Sure." Ryan was still watching her intently.

Every time she glanced over and caught him staring, she felt a jolt of awareness. Did he feel it, too? Or was he just uncomfortable about the fact she'd almost kissed him last night? They walked together to the sign by the road and discussed the options there. Then he led her down the path to the ropes course.

"We need to add something to hide that drainage ditch back there," he said, pointing.

"Done." She tapped it into her notes and marked the spot on the digital rendering of Off-the-Grid's property on her iPad. "I can get some inexpensive shrubs in here that will hide the ditch and even look pretty while they're at it."

"Great." His brow wrinkled. "Em—"

She looked away. If he had something to say, he was just going to have to come out and say it. She'd already made a big enough fool of herself.

"About last night..." He gave her a pleading look.

She cocked her head, pressing her lips together.

He chuckled. "You aren't going to help me out here, are you?"

She shook her head with a smile. "My mom always said I was the stubborn one."

"That makes two of us." He took a step closer. "Look, it's not that I wouldn't enjoy kissing you, but—"

"Please, stop right there." She cringed, pressing a hand over her eyes.

He peeled her hands away, holding them in his. He met her gaze, his eyes warm and rich as the earth around them. "I like you a lot, and that's the problem. We're friends, and I don't want to mess that up, okay?"

She blew out a breath. What the hell could she say? "Look, I drank a lot of beer last night, and that motorcycle ride? Well, it was awesome, and I got a little carried away, but let's just pretend that I hopped off your bike and went straight inside after, okay?"

He stared at her for a long moment, his expression so intense it was all she could do not to squirm. Then he cracked a smile. "'Kay."

Relief loosened in her chest. "You'll still teach me rock climbing, though, right?"

"Course."

"And maybe take me to get a tattoo?"

He looked pained. "Em—"

"If you won't take me, I'll have to go by myself, and I might choose a crappy place." Which was so not true. She would research the hell out of it before she let anyone take a needle and ink to her body, but Mandy was right. It would be so much more fun if Ryan went with her.

Heat flickered in his eyes. "What is this all about?"

She tugged her bottom lip between her teeth. "Look, last night started as a dare, but it turned out to be really fun—other than that one part we'll never speak of again."

"A dare?"

"I was complaining to my friends about how I'm tired of being so boring—"

"Not a word I'd ever use to describe you, Em." Something in his tone made her feel all warm and mushy.

"But I've always been the dependable one, right? I was the world's most well-behaved teenager. It wasn't a fun time for me." Understatement of the century. She'd buried her whole family before she turned twenty. "But last night made me realize I'm ready for a change. So what do you say, will you help a girl out?"

He turned away. "I'm not that guy anymore. I can't be responsible for corrupting you."

Corrupting her? Was he serious? She kicked at a clump of weeds growing across the path. "God, Ryan. It's not like I asked you for advice on how to become a stripper."

He squeezed his eyes shut. "Please promise me that you won't."

"Who should I go to on that one then? There was that one girl in high school who everyone said—" She broke off when she caught sight of the look of horror on his face and doubled over in laughter.

He scrubbed a hand over his jaw. "You're messing with me now."

"What's up with you today? You're not usually this serious." In fact, he wasn't acting like himself at all, and if this was what it was going to be like between them now, all because she'd tried to kiss him last night...

"It's not about last night," he said as if he'd read her mind. "Let's start with the rock climbing lessons and take it from there."

"Deal." She stuck her hand out.

He took it, his big, warm hand enveloping her small, chilly one, and *whoa*, more sparks.

"So when do we start?" she asked, reluctantly tucking her hand into the pocket of her jacket.

"Another week or two, once the weather warms up."

"I'm not cold."

He stared at her for a moment then shook his head and started walking back toward the main building. "You're trouble, Emma Rush."

She fist-pumped the air. "Exactly what I was hoping for. See? You're helping me out already."

* * *

The Harley roared beneath him as Ryan hugged the mountain roads outside Haven. The wind whipped at his face and filled his lungs, cold and crisp. He could taste spring in the air, see it in the green buds on the trees along the roadside.

He'd been back in Haven almost a year now. Sometimes, it felt like he'd never left. So many things were the same, like these roads and the invigorating mountain air. Some things had changed, though. *He'd* changed. He wanted to make something of himself at Off-the-Grid with Ethan and Mark, something permanent and worthwhile. And now, with Trent here, it seemed more important than ever. He wanted to be someone his little brother could look up to.

When the Lamars had first begun the process of adopting Trent, Ryan got suspended from school for vandalism and was looking at time in juvie. So once the adoption had gone through, they'd moved away with him, and Ryan never heard from them again.

He'd never known his dad so the one-two punch of losing his mom and then his brother had sent Ryan into a predictable downward spiral. He'd met Ethan and Mark in a group home, all of them wards of the state. The three of them had become thick as thieves, raising hell but also forming a bond, a brotherhood that had lasted into adulthood.

Those guys, and now Trent, were all Ryan had in this world.

He turned onto Mountain Breeze Road and gunned the engine, headed back into town. He was on his way to meet Trent for burgers at Rowdy's, but he'd needed a long ride to blow off some steam and cool his head first.

Except every time he let his mind wander, he was remembering the feel of Emma's arms around his waist when he'd driven her home last night, her sweet, floral scent, the way she'd crawled up his back and tried to kiss him. She'd gotten her wish all right—he was definitely not still thinking about her as the tomboyish kid she'd once been. Nope, he had seen the sexy, grown-up version of her, and he liked it, a little too much.

But he didn't like that she'd asked him for help changing her image. Because now she was doing exactly what she'd accused him of: She was still seeing him as the hell-raiser he'd been back in the day. And he was not that guy anymore.

He couldn't afford to be that guy, not if he wanted to stay part of Trent's life.

He roared past Off-the-Grid, waving at Ethan and Gabby standing by Ethan's red Jeep, then grimaced when he saw what they were doing. "Yo, get a room!" he yelled.

Ethan flipped him the bird.

Shaking his head, Ryan followed Mountain Breeze Road to its end, then swung a right onto Main Street. As luck would have it, he rolled into an open spot right in front of Rowdy's. Trent stood out front, hands shoved into the pockets of an oversized gray hoodie with MISSOURI COLLEGE written in big letters on the front and a black knit cap pulled low over his ears.

He couldn't have looked any more like an awkward teenager if he'd tried.

Ryan pulled off his helmet and glasses. "Hey."

Trent's eyes were almost as big as his face. "That's a sweet ride. It's yours?"

Ryan nodded as he swung off the bike. "Hungry?"

"Yeah."

Inside Rowdy's, their waitress showed them to the table Ryan and his friends usually occupied—off to the side with a view of whatever game was on the big-screen TV over the bar. The place occasionally lived up to its name on a Friday or Saturday night, but at six o'clock on a Tuesday, it was a perfectly respectable place to bring his teenage brother for a burger.

His brother.

Ryan shook his head as he looked at the skinny kid across from him. "Still can't quite believe you're here."

"My folks are super-pissed." Trent said it with the kind of smug satisfaction Ryan might have felt at that age. Today, it twisted uncomfortably in his gut.

"They know you're here?"

Trent nodded.

"You got plans? Going home? Back to college?"

His brother shrugged. "Thought I might hang here awhile, if that's cool with you."

"It's definitely cool with me, man, as long as you're not using me to piss your parents off." Ryan gave him a hard look.

Trent lifted a shoulder. "Don't care either way."

"How are you paying for all this?" Ryan asked.

"I've got a credit card," Trent said. "Just charging stuff until I get a job."

Their waitress came over, and they ordered burgers, chocolate milkshakes, and a plate of cheese fries. It seemed like appropriate chow for the occasion. While they ate, Ryan learned that Trent had been a business major for the short time he'd been in college before he dropped out to try his luck as a dubstep DJ. Ryan managed to keep his opinion on that decision to himself.

But in doing so, he realized something. Trent's parents had always seen him as a bad influence. If Ryan was able to convince his brother to go back to college, he might finally win them over. Now that Trent was legally an adult, he didn't need his parents' permission to visit, but Ryan didn't want to play it that way if he could help it. He was a decent human being, dammit, and he wanted them to see that. He wanted a permanent place in his brother's life, and it would be so much easier if the Lamars weren't constantly trying to push him out of the picture.

He glanced up to see Ethan and Mark coming toward their table.

"We heard there was a family reunion happening without us," Ethan announced as he and Mark dropped into two empty chairs at the table. "I'm Ethan Hunter. We're practically related, too, since I consider both of these guys to be my brothers."

Trent just stared, but his eyes had gotten really wide again.

"Mark Dalton," Mark said. "Don't mind him. He hit his head a lot when he was a kid."

Ryan shook his head with a laugh. "These two idiots are my business partners. We own Off-the-Grid Adventures together, but yeah, as kids we were foster brothers. They're my family here, which makes them extended family of sorts for you, too."

"Oh. Okay." Trent gulped from his milkshake.

"You should come out tomorrow. I'll take you for a ride on the zip-line course." Ethan, with his unruly shock of blond hair and easygoing smile, was the fun-loving adventurer of their group.

Trent's eyes lit with interest. "Cool."

"It's way cool," Ethan told him, digging into their plate of cheese fries. "So how long are you in town?"

The kid shrugged. "Awhile, I guess."

"Need a place to stay?" Ethan asked.

"Yeah."

"I've got a place," Ethan said.

Ryan slapped the table. "Your condo? That's perfect."

His friend nodded. "I was thinking about renting it out soon anyway. I'm basically living at Gabby's house now. She's my fiancée," he told Trent.

"You'll need a job, too," Ryan said. "We can always use some extra help at Off-the-Grid, long as you don't mind getting your hands dirty."

Trent definitely looked interested. "Yeah. That sounds great."

"We're all really glad you're here," Ethan said.

Mark nodded, always a man of few words. He'd left the Army last year after getting blown half to pieces in Iraq. A deep scar creased his right cheek, but the other scars—the ones you couldn't see by looking at him—might cut even deeper. He'd never told them what happened, but Ryan assumed it had been bad.

"Do you have a lot of family back in St. Louis?" Ryan asked. It was flat-out weird knowing so little about his brother or how he'd grown up.

"Yeah, I guess. I'm an only child, though...I mean, for a while I thought I was. Once my folks told me about you, I started trying to find you."

"You know he never quit looking for you either, right?" Ethan said, his expression serious.

"Yeah." Trent fiddled with his milkshake.

"You're welcome to stay with us here in Haven as long as you like," Ryan told him. "You have family here now, too."

* * *

Emma took a deep breath and clicked on the big, red Submit button in the middle of her screen. There. She'd done it. She'd officially applied for college. She'd taken the first step toward fulfilling her dream of owning her own landscape design business.

Moving to Georgia to get her degree was phase two of her "new Emma" plan. Phase one involved cutting loose and having fun while she was still here in Haven. And she planned to have a *lot* of fun. Just not at this exact moment because, right now, she was borderline late for a meeting.

She closed her laptop, grabbed her purse, and headed for her car. Ten minutes later, she was hustling across the town square, careful not to lose her footing in the damp grass. Her bosses, Lucas and Mary Pratt, the owners of Artful Blooms Landscape Design, had asked her to meet them here, which meant this was probably a pretty big project, and she didn't want to make a lousy first impression on the potential new client by being late.

Tucking a loose strand of hair behind her ear, she picked her way around a puddle. Last night's rain had drenched things, but in her line of work, a solid soaking could be a blessing, too. It saturated deep down into the soil, which was great for the plants. She caught sight of Lucas and Mary on the far side of the square, talking with several well-dressed people. She was pretty sure one of them was Lorraine Hanaford from the Haven Town Council. And the guy in the gray suit looked like—*gulp*—Terrence Clemmons, the mayor of Haven.

What in the world? She usually got called in to consult with homeowners or small business owners looking to spruce up their landscaping.

Emma smoothed a hand over her hair as she approached the group.

"Emma!" Mary gave her a warm smile, waving her over. "We're so glad you could join us."

"Sorry I'm late," Emma said.

"We just got here a few minutes ago ourselves," Lucas told her.

Mary made introductions. In addition to Lorraine Hanaford and Terrence Clemmons, the other two men in the group were James Daniels from the Town Planning Committee and Donald Ray with the architectural commission.

Emma shook hands with everyone. What in the world was she doing here? Uncertainty swam in her stomach.

"The town has recently approved a memorial to be built

here in the town square honoring our local men and women who have given their lives serving their country," Mayor Clemmons told her.

"Oh, wow." Emma clasped her hands in front of herself. "That sounds wonderful."

"Mary and Lucas have done fantastic work for us in the past so we brought Artful Blooms in on the project," he said.

"And Lucas and I will be backing you up, but we want you to lead the project, Emma," Mary told her, her eyes shining with affection.

"Me?" Emma breathed. This was a big project, a huge responsibility, and much more public exposure than she'd ever had in the past. This was the kind of work portfolios were built on.

Mayor Clemmons's dark eyes were kind. "Your brother Derek's name will be on the memorial, of course. When Mary and Lucas suggested you, we thought it especially fitting that you would be the one designing the memorial garden."

Emma pressed a hand to her heart. "I'm really honored, you guys. I don't know what to say."

"We're very humbled by your brother's sacrifice and the other men and women whose names will be memorialized, and we know that you will do them proud."

"Thank you." Although her connection to Derek made her a little uneasy. Had she gotten this job on her own merit or only because her brother died in Afghanistan? Either way, she was going to throw herself into it full force and make sure no one regretted choosing her.

They talked for a few more minutes before the town representatives headed back to their offices. Lucas and Mary lingered to go over some preliminary details. Emma was already so indebted to them both. They'd hired her when she was a teenager with no family, no money for college, and desperate for work. She'd always loved to be outside and get her hands dirty so helping to install their landscape work had been a perfect way to earn a paycheck.

Over the years, she'd discovered she really loved landscape design and had worked her way up to managing her own projects. Lucas and Mary planned to retire at the end of the year, which was one of the reasons she'd finally taken the plunge and applied to the program at the University of Georgia. She would need a new job when they retired, and she'd always dreamed of opening her own landscape design business. A degree would be a good first step, plus a new beginning, leaving Haven behind.

Emma looked at the empty stretch of grass in front of her, the space she'd just been tasked with filling. Butterflies flapped around in her belly.

"The Town Planning Committee is rather well known for being difficult to please," Mary said. "Don't be discouraged if it takes you a few tries to come up with a design they like."

"Really?" It felt like one of those butterflies had just lodged in her throat. What if she screwed this up and didn't come up with a design they liked in time?

"They're an eclectic bunch," Lucas said. "They'll be expecting something traditional but unique."

"Traditional but unique," Emma repeated. "I can do that."

"And Lucas and I will be here to back you up anytime you need us." Mary rested a hand on her shoulder. "Maybe you and I can get coffee later this week and go over some ideas?"

Emma sucked in a breath and nodded. "I'd like that."

"This might be our last project together," Mary said, a hint of sadness in her tone. "You'll give us a beautiful new addition to the town commons before you go off to college."

"I hope so."

"You will." Mary nodded. "It's true what they say: When one door closes, another one opens. The end of Artful Blooms will be the beginning of something new and beautiful for all of us. You're beginning the next step in your career, and Lucas and I will enjoy the luxury of retirement."

"Yes." Emma could barely speak past the lump in her throat. "What do you guys have planned after you retire?"

"Just booked a trip to Paris this fall," Lucas said. "Always wanted to visit Europe."

"And we plan on spending a lot more time with the grandkids." Mary smiled at her husband, then at Emma. "Which might bring us out your way."

"Oh, that's right!" Emma had completely forgotten that Lucas and Mary's daughter Beatrice and her family lived outside Atlanta. "Maybe we can get together when you visit Bea and the kids."

"That's a definite." Mary pulled Emma in for a warm hug. "You're like family to us, Emma. That won't change when Lucas and I retire."

"I know." Emma swallowed past the knot in her throat because truthfully, she *didn't* know, not for sure. People promised to stay in touch, but in her experience, once life carried them in separate directions, they rarely did. And Lucas and Mary had come to mean so much to her. The thought of losing touch with them...it hurt. A lot.

Mary brushed back a silver lock of hair. "Well, we're running late to another appointment. I'll call you later about coffee tomorrow."

After Mary and Lucas left, Emma walked to a bench along the edge of the square and sat, elbows on her knees, just staring at the ground. Derek would have turned thirty this year. She didn't let herself dwell too often on the "what ifs" of life, but sometimes . . . sometimes she wondered what he would be like now. Would he still be in the military? He'd barely reached adulthood when he died. She had no idea what kind of man he would have become.

A good one, though. He'd always had his priorities straight.

"You okay?"

Ryan's voice filtered through her thoughts, and she looked up. He stood a few feet away, hands shoved into the pockets of his jeans.

"They're going to build a memorial here," she said.

"And Derek's name will be on it." Ryan sat beside her on the bench.

She nodded. "And I'm going to design it."

"No shit?"

"Mary and Lucas know the mayor, and I guess they pulled some strings for me because of Derek."

Ryan nudged her shoulder with his. "Or maybe they recommended you because you're their protégée, and they knew you'd do a kick-ass job on the project, you ever consider that?"

She managed a small smile. "Maybe a little bit of both?"

"Maybe, but heavy on the talent, not so much about pulling strings. So how do you feel about it?"

She straightened, her heart beating faster. "I'm psyched. This is a huge opportunity for me, and I'm really proud to help honor Haven's fallen heroes."

"That's my girl." He looked over at her. "You interested in another ride?"

"Um, yeah." She couldn't keep the *duh* out of her tone.

He smiled, a sexy smile that did all kinds of fluttery things inside her chest. "Got someplace I want to show you."

CHAPTER FOUR

$\mathcal{R}$yan guided his bike down Spring Glenn Road, trying desperately to cool his head. Emma did this thing when she rode with him where her hands somehow wound up underneath his jacket, resting flat against his stomach. Other women had ridden this way, but none of them had left him feeling so distracted, so *hot*, that he was having trouble keeping his mind on the road, and it didn't belong anywhere else while he was riding.

It was probably foolish bringing her here. He hadn't been out to the bluffs in years. Not since Derek's death. But once upon a time, he and Derek had owned this place—in the most unofficial sense. They'd scaled the bluffs for kicks, trying to out-badass each other, to see who could take the riskiest route to the top.

And when they got there, they'd cliff-jump, plummeting fifty feet into Crystal Lake. Then they'd climb out, shake themselves off, and do it all over again. Back then,

Emma would beg them to let her tag along, but they never had.

Somehow, he felt he owed it to her now.

The access road looked different than he remembered. It was wider than it had been and paved. He eased the bike up the road and stopped at the top, overlooking the lake and bluffs. There were a lot more houses around now than there had been then. But the bluffs...they looked the same. They rose from the water, towers of sheer rock. Even now, the sight gave him a thrill.

Emma shifted closer behind him, her chest pressed to his back. "Where are we?"

"Derek and I used to come here a lot. Thought you might like to see it."

She didn't say anything, but her arms tightened around him. He held in a groan. Her hands on his stomach had gone from distracting to flat-out arousing, and that was not a good state to be in while straddling a bike. But he couldn't bring himself to move, to break the connection.

"Is this where you guys went cliff-jumping?" she asked.

"Yeah."

"You finally brought me," she whispered. Her hands rested just above the waistband of his jeans, and he was practically holding his breath, silently hoping she'd slide them south, even while his brain wrestled with his dick, reminding him this was *Emma*. He could feel Derek's shadow here like a physical presence.

He motioned for her to hop off the bike. She lifted off her helmet and stood behind him, leaving him without the feel of her chest against his back, her arms around him, and her hands...

She swung her right leg over the bike, stumbling as she hit the ground. He reached out and grabbed her arm to steady her. Instead of hitting the asphalt, she fell against him. Her blue eyes widened, her lips parted, and *hell*.

He had no idea what happened next, who moved first, but his lips brushed hers, and his body revved straight into overdrive. She tasted like some kind of fruity lip gloss, sweet and sexy. He bent his head, deepening the kiss.

Next thing he knew, she was in front of him on the bike, facing him, kissing him like crazy, and every cell in his body was lit up for her, for Emma. *Emma...*

She moaned, scooting closer, her knees pressing into his thighs, and it was all he could do not to reach down and hook her legs over his so that she could slide all the way home. But—

"Emma."

"Mm?" She lifted her head, her eyes glazed, her pink lips curved in a dreamy smile.

He drew in a ragged breath. "What are we doing?"

"Kissing?" Her gaze dropped to his lips.

Desire curled hot and strong inside him. "Shouldn't."

Her cheeks darkened, and her face fell, and dammit, he was an ass. He hauled her up against him and kissed her again, hard. "I didn't mean...hell, Emma. I am completely blindsided right now. But whatever this thing is between us, I am feeling it. Big time."

"Me, too," she said, sounding breathless.

"Let's walk. I have someplace I want to show you, and then we need to talk."

She grimaced. "Unless *talk* is a euphemism for kissing..."

No, they definitely needed to talk, but he was never going to be able to think straight with her in his lap, her knee mere inches from a certain, very hard part of his anatomy. He slid his hands up her sides and lifted her off the bike.

Emma grumbled in protest as he set her on the ground.

"Let's walk, and then we'll talk."

* * *

Emma pressed her fingers against her lips as she followed Ryan down a path into the woods. *That kiss.* Holy shit. Her pulse was still racing, her knees still weak. The chemistry between them combined with the rumble of the motorcycle beneath them was altogether the hottest thing she'd ever experienced.

Her little crush on Ryan Blake had just exploded into something a whole lot more, and she had no idea what would happen next. He wanted to talk, which didn't sound terribly promising, but unless she'd totally lost her mind, she was pretty sure *he* had kissed *her*, not the other way around. Which meant...well, it meant he was attracted to her, whether he liked it or not.

And that knowledge alone was enough to rock her world.

"So how serious are you about living a little dangerously?" Ryan asked, tossing her a wicked smile.

"Totally serious—oh shit." She stopped dead in her tracks as they came out on the bank of a rushing stream spanned only by a fallen tree trunk lying about five feet above the icy water.

"Looks like the bridge is washed out," he said. "Feeling adventurous?"

"Um...yeah, sure. Why not?" She'd just kissed Ryan. She was invincible right now!

"The water's not deep. Sure would be cold, though." He stepped onto the trunk and walked out over the rushing water.

The trunk was wide, the bark worn smooth across the top where countless other people had crossed. Spreading her arms for balance, she followed Ryan across to the other side.

"You still come here a lot?" she asked as they hiked up a steep incline, headed she presumed for the top of the bluffs, where he and Derek used to cliff jump.

"Not since Derek left." He extended a hand to help her over a large rock in their path.

"And how many times did I beg you to let me tag along?"

"A lot," he admitted with a laugh. "You were persistent."

"Not persistent enough."

"No offense, but this was kind of a 'no chicks allowed' zone for us. Maybe the right girl could have convinced one of us to come up here and fool around under the stars, but..." He drifted off with a shrug.

"Derek's dorky little sister didn't stand a chance," she finished for him.

He chuckled. "Pretty much."

But she sure as hell stood a chance today. Now that she'd kissed him, she wanted to do it again. If she got into the University of Georgia, she'd be leaving town in the fall anyway so who cared if it didn't work out between them? She wouldn't have to stick around to face the fallout.

They hiked in silence for the next few minutes. The terrain had gotten steeper, and although she was a fairly experienced hiker, she let Ryan boost her up and over a few large rocks in their path.

"So what's the deal with this dare?" he asked.

"Oh, that. Well, my friends were trying to help me shake things up a little at girls' night, but I had so much fun, and it kind of got me thinking. If Derek had known he'd die so young, would he have done anything differently? If something happened to me, would I be happy with the way I've lived my life so far?" She shook her head. "I've been holding back, doing what's expected of me, just going through the motions."

"So what is it that you want?" he asked, his cocoa eyes locked on hers.

"Excitement." Her voice sounded breathless...maybe because the trail had steepened again. "Like...whoa." She paused as they came out at a little overlook, the cliffs dropping straight down below them to where the lake twinkled like a beautiful sapphire. "Like *this*."

"Just wait," Ryan said, nudging her on. "You ain't seen nothin' yet."

"Did you guys really jump from here?" Because the very thought made her light-headed.

"A few times," he said. "But usually we jumped from up there." He pointed to another spot above them, and *holy shit*, that was absolute insanity.

"That is crazy."

"It's an adrenaline rush like no other." He gave her another wicked smile.

Her heart thumped hard against her ribs. "Take me."

Ryan's eyes darkened, and oops, yeah, she should have worded that better.

"Up there," she said as her cheeks warmed. "Take me up there."

"Planning on it."

Okay, now everything sounded dirty, but maybe that was just because her hormones were still dangerously out of control from their kiss. She fell into step behind him, panting from the climb.

He led her up what might have been considered a path or could have just been a scrape of dirt between some rocks. Together, they scrambled toward the summit of the bluffs. Her blood was pumping, her adrenaline flowing. Hiking was fun, but heading for the one place that had been off limits throughout her childhood with the man who'd occupied her teenage fantasies? Now, *that* was exciting.

Ryan took her hand, hoisting her up beside him. They stood on a big rock as the world fell away in every direction. It was dizzying and thrilling and amazing.

"Wow," she whispered.

"Forgot how much I dig this place." Ryan had a blissed-out look on his face as he took in their surroundings.

She peered over the edge toward the lake, glittering in the sunshine so impossibly far below. "You really jump from up here?"

"Oh yeah." He said it with the cocky confidence of a man who'd done this and so much more. "Your brother and I have scaled every inch of these cliffs and jumped off every available surface. It's a rush."

"I can see why." She tightened her grip on his hand as she looked down. She wasn't afraid of heights, but...*whoa.* "Maybe I'll try it this summer once the water's warm."

"Em—" His brow bunched.

"Will you stop with the overprotective act?" She gave him a friendly nudge.

He captured her fist with his free hand, drawing it against his chest. "Can't."

Her breath caught in her throat as the low rumble of his voice vibrated through her fingertips. "I'm going to jump."

He groaned, casting his eyes toward the cloudless sky above. "You're killing me here. Okay, but just know I'm going to try my damndest to talk some sense into you between now and then, and don't you dare jump without me if I don't succeed."

"I'd rather jump with you anyway."

He looked down and met her eyes, scorching her with the heat of his gaze. She gulped.

"It's time for us to have that talk," he said.

She scrunched her nose. "I'm trying to have fun, Ryan, and this does *not* sound fun."

He chuckled. "Maybe not. Look, I have no idea what's going on between us all of a sudden, but here's what I do know: I fuck up relationships. I sleep with women, but I don't date them. And you're too important to me to risk losing you when I inevitably fuck it up."

She fought to keep her face impassive. "Are you always this romantic?"

He groaned. "Hell, Emma. I'm just trying to be honest."

Her inner hopeless romantic wrestled with the new, cooler, more adventurous Emma. "Chill out, Ryan. I never asked you for a relationship. I just wanted you to help me have a little fun this summer." And now that she'd made out with him, she knew exactly what kind of fun she wanted, but she'd had enough rejection from him to last a lifetime.

"I am totally down with that." He grinned. "As your *friend*, you're welcome to go for a ride with me anytime you like."

"Okay." Except her hand was still on his chest, and nothing she was feeling toward him at that moment could be defined as friendly. But whatever happened next between them, it had to come from him.

* * *

Ryan desperately needed to get his hands off Emma before he completely lost his mind and kissed her again, but to let go of her now would make him look like even more of an ass than he already did. "I'm just trying to do the right thing. For Derek. For you, and for me."

She gave him a long look then stepped backward out of

his grasp. He'd been half expecting her to sucker punch him the way she'd been looking at him a minute ago so it caught him completely by surprise when she smiled. "I know."

Huh. That was easier than he thought it was going to be.

Emma looked down at the lake sparkling below them. She let out a little laugh and twirled around on the rock, making his breath catch in his throat.

"This summer," she said, pointing a finger at him, "we're jumping. Or I am anyway. You can suit yourself."

"If you jump, I'm jumping with you." In the meantime, he was just glad to be back on semi-solid ground with her. He wouldn't put it past her brother to come back from the grave and give his sorry ass a ghostly kicking if he ever hurt her.

She shimmied down the rocks ahead of him to the path below. "Thanks for bringing me," she said when he'd joined her.

"I have a feeling you're going to make me regret it."

She grinned at him over her shoulder. "Oh, I fully intend to."

$\mathcal{C}$HAPTER FIVE

$\mathcal{U}$m, this is a lot harder than it looks." Emma clung to a knob on the rock face as her fingers burned and her legs shook. Ryan had made it look so easy when he'd demonstrated the climb for her before he'd hooked her up in a harness. Now that she'd left the ground, the rock seemed sheer and daunting, determined to pitch her backward onto the ground.

"You're overthinking it," he said from below her. "Move your right foot across to the ledge there with the inside edge of your shoe. Remember to angle your legs so that your hips stay close to the rock. If you stick your butt out, gravity's going to pull you right down."

She brought her body closer to the rock and turned her head to give him a look. "Do you talk about all your clients' butts?"

He grinned, looking so at ease there with his harness on, holding on to the belay rope to catch her if she fell. And at this rate, chances were high that she'd need catching.

"I might choose my words more carefully with a client I don't know well, but the overall message is the same. Keep your body close against the rock or gravity will do its thing."

Gravity was trying awfully hard to do its thing right now. She slid her right foot over, feeling blindly for the ledge he'd said was there. Her toes connected with a ridge barely wider than her big toe. "That's not wide enough to hold me."

"Sure it is. You're wearing climbing shoes. They'll grip just about anything."

She shifted her weight onto her right foot, keeping her belly pressed against the rock, and sure enough, it held. Her fingers were about to give out, though, and she'd only made it about three feet off the ground. "I suck at this."

"Not even a little bit. Learning to climb takes time and patience. Keep your weight in your feet or your arms will tire out. You want to be using your hands to steady yourself, not to hold yourself up."

"Um . . ." She was pretty sure if she loosened her white-knuckled grip on the rock, she'd tumble right off.

"Trust your shoes, Emma."

She loosened her grip with her left hand, reaching up with her right for a crease in the rock above her head. The shoes held.

"Atta girl," Ryan encouraged from below. "Now look for your next foothold."

Feeling rejuvenated now that her fingers weren't about to fall off, she scooted her left foot over to another little ledge and stepped up. And—

"Oh no!" She toppled backward off the rock.

Her stomach flopped, prepared for the fall, but the harness caught her, and she swung against the rock face, bumping her shoulder on it. "Shit."

"Happens to everyone," Ryan said as he lowered her to the ground. "This was your first fall. Won't be your last."

"Good to know." She gripped the rock and hauled herself back up. The first few moves were easy, and it didn't take her long to get back to the spot where she'd fallen. After a few false starts, she found her next foothold and shimmied her way up a few more feet, finally daring to take a glimpse over her shoulder. "Hey, look! I'm finally far enough up to actually need the harness."

He laughed. "You're doing great."

Then she looked up and realized the top wasn't even in sight yet. She let out a groan.

"Don't expect to get there on your first day. I started you on the easy end of the rock, but this baby is still a beast. It makes victory that much sweeter when you reach it."

"If you say so." She scooted her left foot toward a new ledge, missed, and fell . . . again.

Her stomach dropped in that disorienting moment between losing contact with the rock and the reassuring yank of the harness behind her thighs.

"I've got you," Ryan said.

Umph. She winced as the harness dug into her legs, but yeah, he had her. In every way that counted. He stood there, so solid and strong as he eased her to the ground.

"You ready to call it a day?" he asked.

She shook her head, even though her arms were trembling with fatigue. "I'd rather end on my own terms."

He nodded. "Sure thing."

She grabbed the rock and stepped up, wincing at the ache in her forearms.

"You're going to be sore in some interesting places tomorrow," Ryan commented.

"Fabulous." She glanced over her shoulder at him, and

their gazes locked. His eyes got all dark and smoldery while her insides heated up. Oh, how she wished she would be sore in *those* places tomorrow, instead of her forearms and calves.

Ryan cleared his throat. "So, I hear Ethan and Gabby and a few other people are going to Rowdy's after work tonight."

"Yep." She boosted herself up, scraping her belly on a jagged edge of the rock in the process. It had been almost two weeks since she and Ryan had kissed on his motorcycle. They'd seen each other a handful of times since and kept things totally professional—on the outside at least. Inside, she was still tying herself up in knots for him, but he'd played the friend card so now the ball was in his court.

And she got it—really, she did. Having sex could and probably would totally mess up their friendship. Ryan was practically family, and she had precious little of that to spare. She hauled herself up to the point where she'd fallen, then went one step higher. "I'm going to jump."

"Brace with your feet and keep your knees bent," Ryan said.

"Okay." She jumped, ready this time for the familiar catch of the harness. Her hands were shaking like crazy, the muscles in them completely spent. Ooh yeah, he was definitely right. She was going to be sore tomorrow.

She touched down, and Ryan unfastened the harness from around her legs and waist, allowing her to step out of it. He worked quickly and professionally, but still the warmth of his fingers through her thin knit pants left her feeling hot and restless.

"So what did you think?" he asked as they started hiking together back toward Off-the-Grid's main building.

"A lot harder than I was expecting it to be."

"The most worthwhile things in life usually are," he said with a smile. "And I'm not kidding, take some ibuprofen and a hot bath before you go to bed tonight. You're going to be sore in muscles you don't even know about yet."

She could already feel the truth of his words in her aching limbs. "Will do."

"So, I'll see you at Rowdy's later?"

"Yeah, I'll be there."

* * *

Ryan settled back in his chair and took a long drink from his beer. To his right, Trent was deep in conversation with Ethan, chatting excitedly about some new DJ technique he'd tried out. The kid had some kind of software on his laptop that let him mix and dub tracks, and he spent hours each day messing around with it.

Ryan respected Trent's enthusiasm for his craft, but he needed to get an education, too. Or at least hold a steady job. Since he'd hired him at Off-the-Grid, Trent often showed up late or spent excessive amounts of time in the break room playing around on his cell phone. The kid was bright as the day was long and funny as hell, but he needed to grow his ass up. Pronto.

"How are you liking Haven so far?" Gabby asked Trent with a warm smile.

The kid shrugged. "It's pretty cool. There's this club in Silver Springs that's eighteen and over."

Ethan grinned. "Oh yeah? The Music Factory's still around?"

Trent's head bobbed. "Yeah. I've been hanging out there most nights."

"Most nights, huh?" Ryan turned his head to give his little brother a look. No wonder he had trouble getting to work on time.

"Yeah. The DJ last night was totally sick. She played this new mix that was seriously, like, the coolest thing I've ever heard."

"This why you dropped out of school?" Ryan asked. "To spend every night at the club?"

The chatter around the table stopped as everyone tuned in. Trent scowled. "Music is my passion. College is *so* not relevant to me right now."

Ryan wondered when he'd quit being the troublemaking kid and started being the adult wanting to smack some sense into the troublemaking kid. "Then find classes that are relevant. Music classes. Business classes. Becoming a DJ means going into business for yourself."

Trent just shrugged and chugged the rest of his Dr Pepper.

Ryan glanced across the table. Emma caught his eye and smiled. Her hair was down again tonight. She'd worn it down almost every day since that night she'd hung out at the bar, the night he'd given her a ride home. The night she'd first started messing with his head.

He'd settled them safely back into the friend zone. No harm, no foul. Except just being near her made him hot. Her smile did weird, warm, and fuzzy things to his insides. And the image of her climbing up that rock face this afternoon was etched forever in his brain, her sweet ass in his harness and her victorious whoop just before she'd jumped off and let him bring her down...

He had it bad for Emma Rush, which was absolutely ridiculous. He needed to get her out of his head. He fucking needed to get laid, but no other chick had caught his eye in far too long. No one could when he only had eyes for Emma.

She had on a bright blue top tonight, with a silver necklace that dipped into her cleavage, and it was taking every bit of his self-control to keep his eyes on her face.

"I think it's great that you're so passionate about DJ'ing," she said to Trent.

"Thanks." Trent blushed, shooting Ryan a wary look.

"I do, too," he said with a sigh. "I just don't want you to have regrets, that's all."

Mark, seated to Ryan's left, had remained quiet throughout the exchange, but his dark eyes were watchful. He'd enlisted after high school, let the Army iron out his kinks and make him into a man. Maybe he could have a chat with Trent about his priorities sometime.

"So, um, the DJ last night...her name is Iris," Trent said, as stars practically began to dance in his eyes. "She let me hang out in the booth with her, and after they closed for the night, she let me mix a few tunes on her equipment. The manager said he'll let me play for an hour next Tuesday night, see how it goes."

"Really?" Emma's eyes were wide, her pride palpable. "That's so amazing, Trent. This could be your first break!"

Trent bounced in his seat. "It's just an hour, but maybe if it goes well, they'll let me mix again. Maybe it could turn into a regular gig for me."

"We'll all come to hear you," Emma said. "Right, guys?"

"Of course!" Gabby was grinning from ear to ear.

"Wouldn't miss it," Ethan said. "Haven't been to that joint in years." He turned toward his fiancée with a smile. "Got a few moves to show you on the dance floor, sweetheart."

"Likewise," Gabby said. "I used to go clubbing in Charlotte, you know."

Ryan turned to his brother. "And this Iris, she's a friend?"

Trent fiddled with his glass. "Yeah. A friend. She's cool."

And he was obviously crushing on her. Which was okay, but... "How old is she?"

"Twenty-two."

Ethan gave him a fist bump while Ryan bit his tongue. He was Trent's brother, not his father, and he needed to act like it. He took a deep breath and let it go. "Can't wait to hear you play."

"You mean it?" Trent looked at him with a new light in his eyes.

Emotion socked Ryan in the gut. "Yeah, man. Of course."

"And we all have an excuse to go dancing." Emma wiggled in her seat with a smile.

The thought of Emma on the dance floor in a cute dress hit Ryan with an entirely different kind of punch to the gut, the kind that let him know he was in big trouble where she was concerned.

* * *

"So what's the deal with you and Ryan these days?" Gabby asked as she and Emma stood together in front of the mirror in the ladies' room at Rowdy's, touching up their lipstick.

Emma lifted her shoulder. "No deal. Just friends."

"Really? Because that kiss on his motorcycle sounded hot. I thought it was going to be the start of something for you guys."

"Yeah, so did I, but he was afraid of messing up our friendship if we took it any further." Emma ran her fingers through her hair, smoothing a few fly-away strands. "Honestly, he hasn't so much as looked at me funny since, and it's been weeks. Obviously there was a spark, but I think he's moved on."

"And you?"

Emma fidgeted in front of the mirror. "I got kind of infatuated with the idea of a thing between us, but I think it's time for me to move on, too."

Gabby was silent for a moment, her lips pursed. "Actually, I think you're right. We need to set you up on a date. It'd be good for you, plus if Ryan *does* have feelings for you, it'll totally make him jealous."

"Got anyone in mind?" She'd never been fond of blind dates, but maybe Gabby was right. She needed to quit pining after Ryan and put herself back in the game.

"No, but let me think on it." With a wink, she led the way back to their table.

Emma spent the next fifteen minutes thinking about her conversation with Gabby, and the more she thought about it, the more she liked it. She'd get herself a hot date, maybe even a couple of hot dates. She was *so* done with waiting for Ryan to make a move he was never going to make.

"I think we're going to head out," Gabby said, gathering her jacket as Ethan stood from the table. "See you guys at Off-the-Grid tomorrow."

Emma would be there installing flowers along the walkway, and yeah, it was fun that she'd get to see everyone. With Trent working there and her landscaping gig, right now she saw her friends at Off-the-Grid more often than anywhere else.

Mark said his good-byes, too, and headed for the door, with Trent following close behind.

Emma looked across the table at Ryan. "I guess we should get going, too."

He nodded and stood, resting a hand on the small of her back as they walked toward the front door. Outside, the weather was cool but not cold, the stars above shimmering in the cloudless night sky.

"You did great today, you know," he said.

"Thanks. I had a good teacher." She turned her head to smile at him, and *gah*, the sight of him there beside her in the dark, his eyes twinkling in the moonlight, was too sexy for words.

His hand lingered on her back as he walked her to her car, parked a hundred feet or so down Main Street. It felt so natural because it was Ryan and she'd known him forever, but at the same time, it felt so romantic, like she expected him to lean in and kiss her when they got to her car. Like he was *hers*, and not just her friend.

But when they got to her car, he tucked his hands into his pockets. "Night, Em."

"Good night, Ryan. See you tomorrow."

With a nod, he strode off into the darkness. Shaking her head at herself for the ridiculous warmth flushing her body, she got in her car and drove home. Inside her apartment, Smokey waited, perched on the back of the couch, meowing loudly as soon as Emma was through the front door.

"Hello to you, too," Emma said. With her bright blue eyes and extremely vocal nature, Smokey might have some Siamese heritage, but her steel gray fur gave nothing away for certain.

Emma liked having someone there to say "hi" to when she walked in the door. Usually, she enjoyed having the place to herself with only Smokey for company. Sometimes, though, like tonight, she felt lonely and restless.

It was only eight o'clock, and she wasn't tired. She was in the mood for company, for conversation. Except Gabby was home with Ethan, and Carly was home with Sam. She texted Mandy to see if she wanted to come over and watch a movie, but Mandy replied that she was "otherwise occupied" tonight.

Dammit.

All her friends were getting laid tonight. Except her.

Feeling even more restless and with a serious side of sexual frustration, she remembered Ryan's advice about the hot bath. Her muscles were already grumpy so she started the water running, then went into the kitchen for a glass of wine. A few minutes later, she sank into the hot bubbles and all her troubles melted away.

For a few minutes anyway. That nagging feeling of loneliness just wouldn't leave her alone tonight. She missed her mom, dammit. The emotion rose up so suddenly and unexpectedly that, before she knew it, she was sobbing into her bubble bath.

She put her wine down on the edge of the tub, buried her face in her hands, and cried until she'd run out of tears. She and her mom had been so close. Her dad had taken off before she was out of diapers so it had always just been the three of them: Emma, Derek, and their mom. But while Derek was off dare-deviling with Ryan, Emma's closest friend had been her mom. They'd done everything together, gone shopping, to the movies, even gossiped about boys.

When a drunk driver ran her off the road when Emma was just fifteen, she'd felt like her life had ended, too. Derek, who'd just turned eighteen, enlisted and went off to boot camp. Emma had gone to live with her friend Clara Mackenzie and her family. She was so grateful to the Mackenzies for taking her in when she'd had nowhere else to go, but she'd never felt like part of their family. She'd always felt more like a guest in their home.

Then, just two years later, Derek died, too, lost in a helicopter crash in Afghanistan.

Emma hiccupped and blew her nose. Then she downed the rest of her glass of wine and dried her eyes. *Enough of that.*

Still feeling lonely and unsettled, she went into her bedroom, changed into her pajamas, and started flipping through channels on the TV, looking for something to watch, preferably something lighthearted and funny. She settled on an old episode of *Friends*. It was one of the episodes where Monica and Chandler had started sleeping with each other but were hiding their relationship from the rest of the group.

Would it be that way if she and Ryan hooked up?

Stop it. This was ridiculous. It was time to quit fantasizing about Ryan Blake. She'd spent the better part of her life lusting after him, and it should have become obvious to her years ago that it was never going to happen.

But he kissed me.

And then he went right back to treating her like a friend. So now it was time to find herself someone new to fantasize about. She needed a man, someone who hadn't known her since she was a kid, someone who could give her the kind of excitement and companionship she was sorely lacking right now.

Sniffling past the last of her melancholy, she grabbed her phone and clicked on the Tinder app. She'd created a profile last year. It was fun swiping through photos of available guys. Of course, she'd never actually gone on a date that way, but hey, this was her year to step outside her comfort zone. She looked at the photo she'd chosen for her profile, a silly snapshot of her with her hands in the dirt, planting a rosebush, taken by Mandy, if she remembered correctly. Eh. It was cute, but maybe she'd ask one of her friends to take a sexier picture of her tomorrow. She spent a few minutes updating her profile—while Chandler hid Monica beneath the bubbles in their bath to protect their secret relationship—and then, taking a deep breath, she switched her Tinder status to active.

Boom.

Take that, Ryan. Maybe the man of her dreams would

click on her photo any minute now. Or at least a bad boy to give her the hot fling she'd been lusting after. Ha. She was so ridiculous. Giggling at herself, she started swiping. Left to pass. Right to like. If a guy she "liked" also liked her photo, they were a match and could start chatting. And if all went well? A date.

Left. Left. Left...She made it through at least twenty guys without anyone catching her eye. Was she just picky or were the pickings slim these days?

Next up was a tattooed man posing on a motorcycle. Todd Pierce, age thirty-five, from Silver Springs. He wasn't all that attractive, and the ponytail wasn't doing anything for her, but just for fun, she swiped right. Still giggling, she took a screenshot and texted it to Mandy.

Then she got back to business. By nine thirty, she'd swiped right on five guys. She wasn't too hopeful about any of them, but she made a pact with herself that she *would* go on a date in the next week. Her phone pinged with an incoming text message. Hoping it was Mandy, she closed Tinder.

What time are you coming out tomorrow? It was from Ryan.

She scowled, annoyed that her heart beat faster just at the sight of his name. Ryan was one of the most organized people she knew. Surely he'd written down their appointment. Ten, she wrote back.

That's what I thought. Just making sure.

Sure you're not checking up on me? She meant it as a joke, but the silence that followed her words hung heavy in the air. She squirmed, picturing Ryan in his bed, wearing nothing but boxer briefs...No, strike that, wearing nothing at all...

Just going over tomorrow's schedule, he answered finally.

Ugh. Why did he have to be so annoyingly platonic where she was concerned? Okay, well, if that's it, I need to get back to some very important business. She pulled up the screenshot she'd sent Mandy, the one showing Todd Pierce the biker with the Tinder logo clearly visible, attached it to her message, and hit Send.

What the hell? His reply was instantaneous this time.

Gotta go. In search of a hot date. See you tomorrow at 10.

Her phone rang. Ryan. A funny quiver took hold in her stomach. "Did you call to offer dating advice?" she answered.

"What's this about?" His voice sounded low and scratchy and so friggin' sexy.

Annoyed with her traitorous body for practically melting at the sound, she let out an exasperated sigh. "I need a man, Ryan. It's been a *long* time. Know anyone?"

"Em—"

"What? We're just friends, right? Don't friends help friends find dates?"

He exhaled into the phone. "You're going to need to ask one of your girlfriends for help with this one."

"Then why did you call?" she asked, frustrated because Ryan was the only man she wanted, and the one man she couldn't have.

"I don't know." He sounded as frustrated as she felt.

"I'm hanging up now," she whispered.

"That's probably best."

And with a click, she ended the call.

CHAPTER SIX

*R*yan was going to lose his fucking mind. He'd just caught Trent up on the ropes course smoking a joint when he was supposed to be repairing a line damaged by a fallen tree limb after last night's thunderstorm. And Emma... *Emma*... was on her hands and knees in the dirt potting plants and gossiping with Mandy about the men she'd contacted last night on fucking Tinder.

There was no logical explanation for the fact that he felt like a goddamn Neanderthal at the thought of her going on a date with someone else. No explanation except that he was a damn fool because he was so hot for Emma he could barely see straight when he was around her, yet he'd been the idiot who insisted they remain just friends.

"Lookin' good," he said, stopping a few feet away from where they were busy planting some kind of purple and yellow flower in the beds Emma had built around the front perimeter of Off-the-Grid's office building.

Emma looked over her shoulder at him. "Do you like them?"

"Yeah. They look great." They definitely brightened up the side of the building, but not nearly as much as Emma's presence did.

"So what did you think of Todd Pierce?" Mandy asked, sitting forward on her knees.

"Who?" Ryan asked, drawing a blank.

Mandy rolled her eyes dramatically. "Emma said she sent his photo to both of us. She's thinking about asking him out. What do you think?"

Ryan bristled, remembering the photo of the ponytailed loser on the cheap foreign bike she'd texted to him last night. "I think..." *The only motorcycle she ought to be riding is mine.* "I think that guy looks like bad news."

Emma gave him a dirty look. "I'll be sure to keep that in mind."

Dammit all. He ought to be cheering her on because, if she started dating someone else, it would let him off the hook for turning her down. He went inside to his office and typed the loser's name into the search engine. A mug shot popped up from the local news website. Todd Pierce had been arrested last week for drunk and disorderly at the Rusty Bucket, a bar in nearby Silver Springs.

* * *

Emma and Mandy washed up and headed into town to the deli for lunch.

"Have you thought about what you're going to do after Lucas and Mary retire?" Emma asked while they waited for their sandwiches.

Mandy had worked at Artful Blooms for about three

years. Before that, she'd taught Zumba at the fitness center. Before that? Emma wasn't sure, but Mandy was definitely a Jill of many trades. "Not sure. I might see if any of the other landscape firms in the area are hiring. I really do enjoy it."

"I hope you find something."

"I will," Mandy said, looking unconcerned. "Let me see your phone."

"Why?" Emma asked as she typed in the code and handed it over.

"I'm checking out some more hot guys for you." Mandy pulled up Tinder and started swiping photos.

"Hey!" Emma made a grab for the phone.

"Chill. I have good taste. If I pick someone you don't like, just ignore them."

"Hmph." Emma sat back with a sigh. Well, maybe she'd have better luck letting someone else pick out her next date anyway. It wasn't as if she'd done a very good job on her own so far.

"Ooh, I like him. I *really* like him." Mandy held the phone out so that Emma could see. A rugged-looking man with longish hair and intense blue eyes was on the screen.

And yeah...he was hot. Not someone Emma would have ever picked out for herself, but... "Definitely. Swipe right."

"Oh." Mandy's eyes widened, and she held up the phone. "He had already liked you so you're an instant match."

"Are you serious?" Emma snatched the phone out of her friend's hand. Sure enough, Rugged Hot Guy—real name Joe Relka—showed as a match on the screen. A button below his picture invited her to start up a chat with him.

"You going to ask him out?"

"No way. Not yet anyway." Emma clicked through the photos in his profile. In addition to his close-up, there was a snapshot of him hamming for the camera out in the woods, pointing over his shoulder toward a black bear visible in the background. "Okay, I'll send him a message. What should I say?"

"Ask him if he still has all his fingers and toes."

"What? Why on earth would I ask him that?"

"The bear." Mandy gestured toward the phone. "You've got to mention the bear. Be interesting. Make him laugh."

"Hmm." Emma typed out, Are all your dates this furry? Then she hit Send before she could chicken out.

Mandy reached for the phone, snorting with laughter when she saw Emma's message. "Perfect."

Emma giggled as she reached for her Diet Coke.

"Dude, this is addictive," Mandy said after she'd swipe-liked five more guys for Emma. "I'm totally setting this up on my phone. Maybe we can have a Tinder double date."

"That's assuming I get a date."

Mandy gave her a look. "Are you kidding me? You're fun and adorable. They'll be lining up. And meanwhile, you're driving Ryan crazy."

"You think so?"

"Did you see the look on his face when I asked him about Todd Pierce? I thought smoke was going to start coming out of his ears."

"I can't believe you did that anyway. I was never actually going to go out with Todd Pierce and certainly not after you found his mug shot."

"Sure did get a nice reaction out of Ryan, though, didn't it?" Mandy looked smug.

Their sandwiches arrived, and Mandy handed Emma's phone back to her. Emma took a bite of her turkey club and chewed through her thoughts. "Well, maybe I'm partly do-ing this to make him jealous, but he's made it pretty clear he wants to keep us in the friend zone so, unless he makes a move, I'm going full steam ahead with Tinder."

"That's the spirit," Mandy said, sipping her iced tea. "We'll definitely get you a Tinder date. I'm going to swipe some more guys for you after we finish eating."

And she did. By the time they made it back to Off-the-Grid, Mandy had added eleven guys to Emma's "liked" list. They spent the afternoon planting bushes along the edges of the ropes course. Then Mandy headed out to get ready for a hot date of her own.

Emma slid her phone out of her back pocket and checked Tinder. Joe Relka had replied. I usually prefer them clean-shaven, followed by a winky face. Want to come over to my place tonight and show me? Emma scrunched her nose in distaste. What a perv. She deleted Joe Relka from her list. Moving on...

Oh, she had another match! It was a guy she'd liked last night. His profile picture showed him in outdoor gear. Blond hair. Beard. Not hard on the eyes. Not even a little bit. And he had a really nice smile. For the first time, she felt an actual tingle of excitement over the idea of going on a date.

Take that, Ryan.

Grinning, she shoved her cell phone back into her pocket. She spied Trent on a platform overhead, full attention on his own phone. "Hey, Trent," she called.

Trent glanced down at her, that shock of straight, black hair hanging in his eyes. He needed a haircut badly, but she suspected the 'do was considered cool among his circle of friends. "Hi," he said with a wave.

"What've they got you working on up there?" she asked.

"Oh, uh, I'm getting rid of a downed branch."

Hmm. Looked more like he'd been playing games on his phone. Emma liked Trent a lot and wanted more than anything for Ryan to bond with his newly found brother, but Trent might be in need of a swift kick to the seat of his pants if this was how he spent his days at Off-the-Grid. She was extremely curious to see him play at the club next week, to see if he truly had talent as a DJ or if it was just another excuse to avoid school.

"Need some help?" she asked.

"Nope. I'm good." Trent shook his head furiously as he set to work tugging at one of the lines overhead.

"Okay then. Good luck." Emma walked toward the main building to freshen up before she headed home. Ryan's bike was still parked out front.

The door to his office was slightly open, just enough for her to catch a glimpse of him seated at his desk. She slipped past his door and into the bathroom at the end of the hall. She used the facilities and spent several minutes at the sink, scrubbing dirt from her hands and arms. When she opened the door, Ryan stood in the hallway, leaning against the doorway to his office. "You're not going out with Todd Pierce."

She sucked in a breath. "That's none of your business."

Ryan kept his eyes on hers, looking all macho and protective. "You made it my business when you texted me his picture. He's bad news."

"You don't even know him." Her stomach quivered from all the butterflies flapping around inside it.

"I looked him up." His voice was low and gravelly.

"You did?" The hallway seemed to constrict around them, pushing them closer together. Her heart was about to pound out of her chest.

"The guy's got a record, Em." His brown eyes burned into hers.

"I know. I looked him up, too."

He raked a hand through his hair. "And you're still going on a date with him?"

"Who said anything about a date?" she asked, trying desperately to look nonchalant even though her body was totally short-circuiting from all the chemistry in the air between them.

Ryan's expression was intense and unflinching. "Mandy said you were thinking of asking him out."

Emma wasn't sure if she'd moved or if he had, but she was standing way too close to him now. Close enough to see the gold flecks in his dark eyes and feel the warmth of his body on hers. "She was trying to get a rise out of you. Did it work?"

He scrubbed a hand across his jaw and shook his head with a smile. "Guess it did. Whatever is and isn't between us, no way I'm going to stand back and watch you go out with a criminal. You're too good for that."

This time she knew she'd taken another step closer, going up on tiptoes to glare right into his eyes. "And in case you weren't paying attention, I'm trying to be *less* good. I'm tired of boring, clean-cut guys. I want excitement, and adventure, and"—she put a hand on his heavily inked biceps—"tattoos. I want a guy who pushes me out of my comfort zone and gives me the kind of mind-blowing sex I've only read about in romance novels."

Ryan's pupils had dilated until his eyes were black, and the look in them said he wanted to give her all those things and then some. Her hand was still on his arm, her breathing erratic as lust burned its way through her belly. They stood that way for several wild beats of her pounding heart.

"Dammit, Emma," he rasped, sucking in a deep breath. He only used her full name when he was rattled. She'd noticed that over the course of the last month.

Dammit indeed. He wasn't going to kiss her, and she was so frustrated she wanted to scream. Instead, she lifted her hand from his biceps and jabbed a finger against his chest. "You don't get a say in who I do or don't date."

His big, warm hand closed over hers, flattening it against the firm expanse of his chest. "I damn well do. Your brother would turn over in his grave if I let you date a guy like Todd Pierce."

There he went, playing the Derek card again. "If he were here, he wouldn't be able to stop me any more than you can."

* * *

"You can't possibly—" Ryan heard voices a moment before Mark and Ethan turned the corner.

They stopped dead in their tracks and stared.

Ryan looked from the guys to Emma as the hallway sizzled with a heavy silence. He was acutely aware that Emma's hand was on his chest, still engulfed in his. And they were standing way too close. For one long, awkward moment, they just stared at each other. Then she scooted backward, mumbled a hasty good-bye, and headed for the door.

"Whoa," Ethan said once she'd gone. "You and *Emma?* Where the fuck did that come from?"

Ryan shook his head. "Not what you're thinking."

"I know what I saw." A wide grin spread across his buddy's face. "You two were looking at each other like you were about two beats from jumping in the sack together, and while I totally did not see this coming, I kind of dig the idea of you guys together."

Mark nodded in agreement, looking suspiciously as if he was fighting a smile of his own.

"We are not together," Ryan said, pushing past them to go get a drink from the water cooler in the lobby. "In fact, we were arguing about her choice of men on Tinder."

"You hear this?" Ethan said to Mark.

Mark shook his head with a smile. "I hear it. Don't believe a word of it."

"I've got to go secure the equipment for the night, but this definitely calls for beers at Rowdy's later," Ethan said.

"Agreed." Mark headed for the door.

Ryan, finding himself completely tongue-tied where Emma was concerned, followed them out, headed for the ropes course to see if Trent was still there getting rid of that downed branch. He found the kid seated on the rope bridge, feet dangling, cell phone in hand. He wore ear buds, his head bobbing to whatever music he had going. The hand saw lay discarded on the bridge beside him.

Ryan's temper reared up like an angry beast. He wasn't a stickler about work. He and the guys goofed around plenty, but they also worked their asses off out here. Maybe hiring his brother had been a mistake because now he was going to have to give the kid a lecture, and he'd rather Trent learn this lesson from an employer who wasn't also the brother trying to find a way back into his life for good.

He stopped below the rope bridge and looked up, waiting for Trent to notice him.

"Oh, hey," Trent said finally, shoving the phone and ear buds into the pocket of his hoodie. "I just finished with that branch. Took me all afternoon."

"Shouldn't have taken more than an hour or so," Ryan said, shoving his hands into his pockets.

"Oh, uh..." Trent shrugged awkwardly.

"You know we don't have any rules about cell phones out here, but every single time I've come out to check on you today, man, you've been goofing off. You smoked weed while you're on my dime. If you were anyone but my brother, I'd have fired you on the spot." He kicked at a rock on the path and sent it soaring toward the woods.

Trent straightened, temper sparking in his dark eyes. "Well, don't let that hold you back."

"Come down from there so we can talk." Ryan grabbed the downed branch Trent had disentangled, carrying it to the edge of the clearing to toss it into the woods. He needed to watch himself right now because a healthy portion of his current mood had to do with what had just gone down between him and Emma, not Trent.

By the time he'd gotten rid of the branch, Trent had climbed down from the rope bridge, saw in hand. "I don't need your charity. If you want to fire me, go ahead and do it."

"I don't." Ryan scrubbed a hand over his jaw. "I don't want to fire you at all, but you've got to start pulling your weight around here. And if I ever catch you lighting up out here again, you're done. Are we clear?"

"I could get a job somewhere else," Trent said, his chin up.

"You could, but I think you'll find that working out here beats the pants off busing tables or ringing up groceries at the supermart." Ryan paused. "I *want* you to work here, Trent, but you've got to do the job I'm paying you for."

His brother deflated some then, tugging his beanie lower over his ears. "Fine." He headed off in the direction of the house.

Ryan watched him go, pulsing with frustration and restless energy. He debated going for a climb, but he'd have to go back to the house and get his gear, and by then the guys would be ready to hit Rowdy's. He'd just have to endure their ribbing about Emma and hope a few beers would be enough to make it bearable.

He had to get a handle on himself where Emma was concerned. If he could just hold her off long enough, this attraction between them was sure to fizzle. She'd find someone new, and he'd hook up with another woman—and he and Emma could go back to being just friends. Because if they slept together? Forget it. That would change everything, and he'd never forgive himself if he fucked up their friendship because he was thinking with his dick.

Thirty minutes later, he, Ethan, and Mark were seated at their usual table, a pitcher of beer and a platter of wings between them, and—ribbing or not—Ryan felt his tension leaking away after a few good laughs with his buddies.

"So back to this thing with Emma," Ethan said after they'd moved on to their second pitcher.

"There is no thing," Ryan answered, reaching for another wing.

"We definitely saw something," Mark commented. "And it's not the first time I've seen it. There's been kind of a vibe between you two lately."

"It was the first time I saw it," Ethan said. "But I'm telling you, if we hadn't walked in and interrupted you..."

Ryan shrugged. "Maybe there was a vibe, or whatever. But that's all it is, and all it's going to be."

"Why's that?" Mark asked.

"Yo, we're talking about *Emma* here." He shook his head, taking another gulp of his beer.

"Is this about Derek?" Ethan asked.

"Yeah, partly. I made a promise before he went off to war that I'd look out for her, and more specifically, that I wouldn't go after her."

Ethan raised an eyebrow. "Yeah, that made sense when she was fifteen, but you're both consenting adults now."

Pretty much what Emma had said. "Doesn't change the

fact that she and I have been friends, practically family, since we were kids. If I sleep with her, sooner or later things will go south and she'll end up hating me."

"That a common problem you have?" Mark asked drily.

"No, but I don't date chicks like Emma. I just hook up. You know, keep it casual. Emma's not a casual, hookup kind of girl, and I won't take advantage of her."

"You have a point there." Ethan bit into another wing. "But on that note, when's the last time you did hook up with someone?"

Ryan took a drink from his beer to avoid having to answer that question.

"Not sure I've seen you with a woman since I got back in town," Mark said. "Other than Emma, of course."

Ryan shrugged. "I've been busy, between Off-the-Grid and tending bar..."

"Too busy to get laid?" Ethan's eyebrows arched.

Ryan snatched a wing from the platter and bit into it.

Mark glanced across the table at Ethan. "It's worse than we thought."

Ethan nodded. "I can't remember the last time I saw you with a woman other than Emma either. Damn. I had no idea you were this hung up on her. How long's it been, man?"

Too fucking long. Ryan finished eating his wing, flipped Ethan the bird, and lifted his beer.

"Interesting." Ethan took a drink from his own beer. "So why are you so sure you couldn't have something real with her, something more than a hookup?"

Ryan took another drink from his beer. "Emma's got this thing right now where she's trying to shake things up. She wants to get a tattoo and date outside her comfort zone. I think it's a dare her friends put her up to. But this isn't who she is, and sooner or later she's going to come to her senses."

"You sure about that?" Ethan asked with humor in his eyes.

Ryan grimaced. "She's looking up guys on Tinder... shady guys. I don't know how to stop her."

"I know how." Ethan was laughing now.

Even Mark was grinning from ear to ear.

"Yo, I'm not sleeping with Emma. You assholes are supposed to back me up here."

CHAPTER SEVEN

Ryan had a problem. A big, fucking problem.

A problem he'd spent the last hour jogging the twisting streets of Haven trying to tame, but it was no use. His sexual frustration had reached epic proportions. He'd given Emma her second rock climbing lesson earlier today, and an hour spent staring at her ass in that harness was more than a man could take. Right now, he was coiled so tight he was about to jump out of his own skin. After that first night on his bike, the night they'd almost kissed, he'd set a ground rule for himself: no fantasizing about Emma.

Fantasizing about her would only make him want her even more, and he needed to get her out of his head as fast as possible so he was *not* going there.

Problem was, since that night, he couldn't get off without thinking about her. He'd tried every distraction he could think of, but as soon as he got down to business, his mind filled with images of Emma, imagining her on his bike... beneath him in bed... her hand on his dick...

And *fuck it*.

He hadn't had any relief now in a long, fucking time.

But he'd come to pride himself on his self-control, and he'd get through this. His attraction to Emma would fade soon, as long as he didn't give in to it. It had to. Any day now, some other chick would catch his eye, and he'd make up for lost time.

In the meantime...

He jogged until his body was spent then went home and took a long, cold shower. At least he was bartending at The Drunken Bear later tonight. That ought to provide a healthy distraction from Emma and his libido.

* * *

Emma reached for her beer and took a lengthy sip. Across the table, her date did the same. Calvin Rocha aka Outdoorsy Bearded Guy from Tinder flashed her an easy smile. They'd messaged with each other for a few days, so when he asked her to dinner at The Drunken Bear, she'd happily accepted. Okay, maybe she'd been partially motivated by her hope that Ryan would be tending bar tonight so he could see firsthand that she was serious about dating. That she'd moved on. She'd even worn one of the new dresses she'd bought on her very successful shopping spree with the girls last weekend.

But Ryan wasn't here.

And Calvin was sweet... but her heart wasn't in it.

"So what do you do for work?" she asked, offering him what she hoped was a cheerful smile.

"I'm a wildlife rehabilitator," Calvin said, brushing his blond hair out of his eyes. "I work at the Bear Tracks Institute in Silver Springs."

"Oh, that's so cool. What kinds of animals do you work with?" This time, she knew her smile was genuine because, *aww*, he worked with wild animals! That was really amazing and also kind of adorable.

"Pretty much anything you find in the Smoky Mountains National Park. We've got orphaned bear cubs, deer, raccoons, snakes. I'm rehabbing a red-tailed hawk right now. Came in with a broken wing, but she's almost ready to fly again." He reached for his burger.

"That is really amazing. Wow."

"It's pretty cool, yeah," he answered, a smile crinkling his brown eyes. "No two days are ever alike, that's for sure."

"I like that about my job, too." Emma reached for her own burger and took a big bite. The more she got to know Calvin, the more she liked him. They had things in common, and he was really cute, not to mention a perfect gentleman. The only problem was, she didn't *like* him. There was no spark, not for her at least. But she totally wanted to set one of her friends up with him.

"I could give you a tour of the facility if you're interested," he offered with another easy smile.

"I'd love that."

"You'd like Nancy. She's one of our bear cubs. Cute little thing, but watch your back because she's a pickpocket. She lifted my cell phone last week and prank called my mom."

Emma laughed so hard she almost snorted beer up her nose.

"She's a character, all right." Calvin's brows bunched. "I'm pretty sure the bartender is throwing some major shade our way. He your ex or something?"

Emma glanced at the bar, and her gaze collided with Ryan's. It zapped her system with a ridiculous burst of heat and sparks. So he was here tonight after all. But instead of feeling giddy about rubbing his nose in her date with Calvin, she just felt mad. Because she couldn't even enjoy her date, and it was all his fault. Well, her fault really for letting herself get so hopelessly hung up on him, but right now, it felt better to blame him for her misery. "Oh, um, something like that."

"He needs to chill," Calvin commented, taking a big bite out of his burger.

"Yeah, he really does. I'm sorry. I didn't know he'd be working tonight." Which was technically true, but now she felt terrible for hoping he would be, because she hadn't considered that it might be awkward for Calvin. What a disaster. She shot Ryan a pointed look.

He glared back at her, the heat of his stare enough to make her body sizzle. She felt it even after she'd turned her attention back to her date, a tingling feeling on the back of her neck that let her know Ryan was watching.

Which made her even angrier. If he didn't want her dating other guys, if he was *jealous*, then he needed to quit acting like a big baby and do something about it. And if not? He needed to butt the hell out of her dating life and stop acting like an overprotective ogre.

"So what do you like to do for fun?" Calvin asked, seemingly willing to ignore the situation with Ryan.

They enjoyed the rest of their meal together, or Calvin seemed to anyway. Emma tried her best, but she was completely distracted by Ryan's presence and the annoying prickle of his gaze on the back of her neck. Which meant she was thinking about Ryan instead of her date, and that was just ridiculous. Next time, she'd insist on going somewhere other than The Drunken Bear.

Maybe a change of scenery would help, or maybe her mind would be on Ryan regardless. And that was pathetic.

And it sucked. And it made her want to strangle him...or kiss him...or *something*.

"This was really nice," she said as Calvin walked her to her car after dinner. She fiddled awkwardly with her keys. *Shit*. Was he going to try to kiss her? Because...

But Calvin shoved his hands in his pockets, offering her an apologetic smile. "I had a great time. And I'd love to give you that tour at Bear Tracks if you're interested. But before I take you to dinner again, you've got to work out whatever's between you and the bartender."

Emma's cheeks flushed hot despite the cool evening breeze. She ducked her head and blew out a breath. "Yes, you're right. I'm so sorry."

"No worries," Calvin said, turning to walk away. "Call me if things change."

"I will. Thanks, Calvin." She got in her car and sat there for a few minutes, fuming. This was so ridiculous. She'd just ruined a perfectly good date with a perfectly nice—and not at all boring—guy because of Ryan.

Ugh.

She thumped her fist against the steering wheel, and then—because clearly she'd lost her mind—she stormed back inside The Drunken Bear, heading straight for the bar. Ryan looked up, the intensity of his gaze slamming into her like a tidal wave.

She walked straight to him, leaning in with her elbows on the bar, so mad she felt like slapping him. "You're an asshole."

He blinked, seemingly at an uncharacteristic loss for words. His gaze scorched her, and for a moment, she thought he was going to reach right across the bar and kiss her. But of course, *that* didn't happen. Instead, he took a step back, and his gaze shuttered. "You're right. I am."

Now *she* blinked. She'd been itching for a fight, and since he wasn't giving her one, she had no idea what to do. "Do me a favor and keep your nose out of my dating life from now on."

He nodded. "Fair enough. But take your next date somewhere else."

"Oh, that's a definite."

"Em—"

"Just don't, Ryan." She looked up at the ceiling, mortified to feel tears stinging the backs of her eyes. *Why this man? Of all the men in the world, why this one?*

In an instant, his hand snaked out and covered hers. "I'm sorry. Really." And when she met his gaze, she saw the truth of his words in his eyes. He was sorry, whether for ruining her date or for not dating her himself, she wasn't sure. In the long run, what did it matter?

Ryan could never be more than her friend, and the sooner she got that message through her thick skull, the better, for everyone involved.

* * *

Ryan walked inside The Music Factory at nine o'clock on Tuesday, feeling like he'd just stepped back in time. The place looked exactly the same as it had when he, Ethan, and Mark had frequented the place as teenagers: scuffed wood floors, dim lighting, and techno music pumping, even at this relatively early hour.

He spotted Trent in back, dancing enthusiastically with a group of kids that looked about his age, maybe a little older. At least he was making friends, and they didn't seem like a bad crowd. And Trent had made a real effort since their chat last week to start pulling his weight at Off-the-Grid.

"Oh my gosh, I haven't been here in ages," Emma said from behind him. "It looks exactly the same."

"Yep," Ethan agreed.

"I'm not surprised," Gabby said with a laugh. "This place looks straight out of the nineties."

"Probably haven't updated a thing since it opened in the late eighties," Ethan said, hooking an arm around her shoulder. "Really cool that Trent's playing here, though."

"Yeah," Ryan said.

"You want to dance?" Ethan asked Gabby.

"How about a drink first?" she said. "Emma?"

Emma nodded and followed them toward the bar. Ryan walked toward the back to say hi to his brother. Trent spotted him and gave him a nod. Was it uncool for his thirty-year-old brother to come over? Ryan didn't care.

"Yo," he said as he walked up to the group.

"Hey." Trent paused his energetic bopping to make introductions. "This is my brother, Ryan. Ryan, this is Jax, Ellis, Marco, Marina, Nico, and Emerson."

The kids waved and said hello. Then Trent moved closer to Ryan. "That's Iris over there in the DJ booth." He pointed out a woman with jet-black hair and heavy makeup. "I'll be going up to join her in about fifteen minutes."

"Can't wait to hear you play," Ryan said.

"Spin," Trent said. "I'm going to spin."

"Right." Score one for the uncool older brother. "Can't wait to hear you spin. Ethan, Gabby, and Emma are at the bar."

"No Mark?"

Ryan shook his head. "Not really his scene, but you know he supports you one hundred percent."

Trent nodded. "Can't quite picture him here. It's okay."

"Good luck." Ryan cracked a grin. "Break a leg up there."

"I'll try my best," Trent said with an answering grin, then resumed his wild bouncing to the techno beat.

Ryan made his way to the mostly empty bar, sliding in next to Emma. Not many people came out this early, let alone on a Tuesday night. The four of them were by far the oldest people in the room, maybe the only ones old enough to drink.

"I feel ancient," Emma whispered with a giggle, as if she'd read his mind.

"Liquid courage," Gabby said as she passed out shot glasses.

Ryan took one. They raised their glasses together and drank. He felt the familiar burn of whiskey slide into his stomach. To hell with liquid courage, though. Given the way Emma looked tonight, in a short pink dress, her blond hair in loose curls over her shoulders, he needed the opposite of courage to keep his hands to himself.

He'd almost lost it the other night when she'd come to The Drunken Bear on a date. If she'd been trying to get a rise out of him, it had worked. Big time.

"You're awfully quiet tonight." Emma turned toward him, still smiling. Her blue eyes danced with the lights flickering behind them.

He shrugged. "It's pretty loud in here."

She rolled her eyes. "Don't be an old fogey. You're going to dance with us, right?"

Dance with Emma? *Hell.* He was screwed. "Yeah. I can dance."

"I remember you having a few moves of your own." She bumped her hip against his with a laugh. "This is going to be so fun. I'm glad Trent gave us an excuse to go dancing tonight."

"Yes," Gabby agreed. "I'm ready to get my groove on."

At the back of the room, they watched as Trent made his way up to the DJ booth. He took his place next to Iris and slipped a set of headphones into place.

"I think that's our cue," Emma said, grabbing Ryan's hand.

"Aw, he looks so important up there," Gabby said as she took Ethan's hand and followed them onto the dance floor.

Ryan had no clue what song was playing, but it had the familiar techno bass thump he associated with club music. It vibrated in his chest once they'd reached the dance floor, commanding his body to move to the beat.

Emma clapped her hands and spun, and *fuck*, her skirt twirled when she moved. Desire coiled in his belly, tight and hot. Gabby had settled into the beat, her arms around Ethan's neck. Ryan felt a little bit awkward dancing alone. He would have far preferred a woman in his arms, but touching Emma would be way too dangerous tonight so he kept his distance and watched her dance.

"Ladies and gentlemen," a woman's voice announced over the music. Ryan looked up to see Iris speaking into a microphone from the DJ's booth. "We've got a special guest DJ in the house tonight. In fact, tonight is his very *first* gig, and I think you're going to be blown away when you hear what he's got in store for you. Just eighteen years old out of St. Louis, Missouri. Give it up for DJ Chillax."

The crowd—such as it was—burst into applause, whooping and cheering for his kid brother. *Chillax?* Ryan grinned to himself, adding his own voice to the noise.

Trent stepped up, looking right at home with his headphones on, one arm waving to the beat while he mixed music with the other. Ryan had no idea if he was any good, but he looked good, and the music sounded pretty cool. Everyone was dancing.

That's my brother, he wanted to shout. Spinning tunes at eighteen years old. Okay, maybe not worth dropping out of college for, but Ryan got it now. He did. Trent was passionate about his music, and it showed. Ryan found himself bouncing on his feet, moving to the beat as he watched his brother work.

Then Emma twirled into his arms. "Dance with me."

CHAPTER EIGHT

Emma closed her eyes and let the rhythm move her feet. Dancing was so much fun. Why had it been so long since the last time she went out like this? The whiskey had given her just enough of a buzz to help her shed her inhibitions and let loose.

The beat changed, and she recognized a popular dance song from the radio.

"I love this song," Gabby said.

Emma opened her eyes to see her friend dancing happily with Ethan, their bodies bumping into each other in the casual way of people who're already intimate on every level. Ethan seemed at home on the dance floor, busting a move as Gabby laughed with delight.

Emma spun toward Ryan, also moving easily to the beat although less enthusiastically than the more outrageous Ethan. Ryan wore his trademark black T-shirt and dark-washed jeans, and he looked so damned sexy she wanted to smack him—because it simply wasn't fair for him to look so good. Not when she was trying her hardest to get over him and move on.

She moved closer, and his hands settled on her hips.

"Trent looks great up there," she said, glancing up at the teen in the DJ booth. Trent's head bounced to the music as he worked the equipment.

"What?" Ryan dipped his head closer to hers.

She leaned forward. "I said, Trent looks great up there."

"Yeah, he does."

Somehow she'd rested her hand on his chest when she leaned in, and now her face was way too close to his for any reason that didn't involve kissing. She glanced up into his mocha eyes, glittering now with the multicolored lights pulsing around them. *Oomph.* Desire shot through her, hot and bright, settling into a restless ache inside her that throbbed like the music around them.

"I need a drink," Ryan said. "You?"

No, actually she'd rather smack him for ruining the moment, but... "Okay."

Reluctantly, she followed him to the bar. They ordered beers and sat side by side on two barstools, watching the crowd on the dance floor. It had grown since they arrived. The place was hardly packed, but it seemed like a decent crowd for a Tuesday night.

Ryan took a drink from his beer then leaned in so that she could hear him over the music. "So how was your date?"

"You really want to know?" She raised her eyebrows at him.

He grimaced. "No, but I'm trying here."

She grinned, unable to help herself. "Well, since you asked, it was lovely. Calvin's a great guy."

Ryan took a long drink from his beer. "So what happened to Todd?"

"Who?" she blurted out, a moment before she remembered the motorcycle-riding, drunk and disorderly dude she'd supposedly planned to go out with. "Oh, right. He was okay, a little dull for my taste."

Ryan gave her a skeptical look. "So dull you forgot his name?"

She shrugged, taking a drink from her own beer. "I've been on so many dates in the last week, it's hard to keep track."

Ryan's fingers clenched around the pilsner glass in his hand. "That so?"

"So many bad boys to choose from," she said, sliding a look in his direction to gauge his reaction. She was *so* toying with him right now. She'd messaged with a couple of guys through the dating site's online system, but she'd only been on the one date. None of the guys she'd met so far on Tinder were half as sexy or interesting or...*badass* as Ryan.

The look on his face said he might just sucker punch any guy he caught so much as looking in her direction. "Bad in what way?"

"Oh, you know..." She leaned in closer. "Rough around the edges, especially in the bedroom."

Ryan sucked in a breath, his expression gradually softening from deadly to wary. "You're messing with me now, right? Please tell me you're messing with me."

She grinned. "I'm messing with you."

He exhaled, casting his eyes toward the ceiling as he shook his head. "I have no idea what to do with you, Emma Rush."

"That makes two of us." She spun her barstool toward him, and her thigh brushed his. "If you want the truth, Calvin *is* a great guy, but he said he won't take me out again until I've resolved things with you."

Ryan froze with his beer halfway to his mouth. He set it back on the counter with a heavy clunk and rubbed a hand over his brow. "Fuck."

"Pretty much my thoughts exactly."

He looked at her then, his expression heavy with regret. "I have no idea how we got here."

"Me either," she said, deciding to play it casual. "But I'm going to keep dating. This year is all about experimenting and trying new things for me. I want to have fun."

"I'd say you're doing it," he said, polishing off his beer.

"I'm off to a decent start anyway." She chugged the rest of her own beer and grabbed his hand. "Come on, let's get back out there before Trent's hour is up."

She led the way to the dance floor, where she found Gabby and Ethan still dancing not far from where she'd left them. She fell back into the groove, moving to the beat.

Gabby grabbed her hand and leaned in to whisper in her ear. "Where did you and Ryan go?"

"To the bar."

"Oh." Her friend looked disappointed. "I was hoping you guys were off making out somewhere or something."

I wish. "Nope, not happening."

"Hey, any word from the University of Georgia yet?" Gabby asked.

Emma shook her head. "I think it's still early, but I've been checking my mailbox like crazy." Now that she'd finally taken the plunge and applied, she could hardly wait to find out for sure. She got all jittery with excitement every time she opened her mail.

"Well, I'm keeping my fingers crossed for you."

"Thanks," Emma said.

She and Gabby danced together until Trent came back down from the DJ booth. They all lavished him with praise, and Emma noted with a smile that Ryan looked particularly proud. The teen blushed and got adorably awkward while they congratulated him, but he was puffed up like a peacock by the time he made it over to his group of friends still dancing in back.

Not long after, Gabby and Ethan said their good-byes. Emma was too buzzed to drive herself home right now, and besides, she was having fun, so she kept dancing. Ryan stayed, too, probably more out of protectiveness than a desire to keep dancing.

"This isn't going to be like the night you hung out at the bar until closing, is it?" he asked, leaning in.

She shook her head. "I don't think it would be wise to get on your bike in this dress."

His gaze dropped to her skirt, and his eyes darkened. "Definitely not advisable."

"Besides, I drove myself tonight. I just need to dance off that last beer."

Somehow his hands were on her hips again, and she was about to lose her mind from that simple contact. She kept moving to the beat, resting her hands on his shoulders as they danced. Had the music gotten louder, or was it just her pulse pounding in her ears?

All around them college-age kids were bumping and grinding. Couples were making out. The lights had gotten dimmer, and the music was definitely louder now that the time had ticked past eleven o'clock. She twirled in Ryan's arms, and their hips bumped. His fingers bunched in the fabric of her skirt, hauling her up against him. She let out a startled gasp, looking up just in time to see his lips slam into hers.

Oh. She closed her eyes, her lips parting beneath his. Ryan's kiss was hot and explosive and electrifying. His tongue thrust against hers, drawing a needy whimper from her throat. They were still swaying to the beat of the music, his hands fisted in her skirt. The lights above the dance floor dazzled her eyes when she peeked up at him, blurring her vision.

Each stroke of his tongue lit flames inside her, blazing straight to the fire burning low in her belly, an aching need that grew until it threatened to burn her up. *Holy shit.* Ryan's kiss was like him: big and powerful and just a little bit rough.

And she never wanted it to end.

Someone jostled her from behind, and she stumbled against Ryan's chest. She slid her arms around his neck, anchoring herself more securely against him. Someone else slammed into them, knocking them sideways.

Ryan tore his mouth from hers, and she grumbled in protest. He gripped her hand in his and tugged her after him. She followed him off the dance floor and down a hall in back, even more dimly lit and still pulsing with music. There he pressed her against the wall, lowered his head to hers, and kissed her again, hard.

She slid her arms around his back, drawing him in closer, his big, hard body pressed against hers. His tongue was doing all kinds of magic things that heated her up until she felt like she might melt on the floor in a big puddle of need if he let her go.

Ryan. She slid her hands down his arms, greedy with the freedom to finally touch him, to run her fingers over his tattoos. His skin was surprisingly soft beneath her fingers. He let out a low growl, nipping at her bottom lip while his hands did some wandering of their own. Next thing she knew, his fingers were skimming up the backs of her thighs, palming her butt, pressing her more firmly against him.

"You drive me absolutely crazy, you know that?" he whispered against her lips, his words sending a thrill through her.

"Good," she gasped. Because she'd never been this crazy for anyone, ever. No one but Ryan had ever made her feel anything this powerful, this all-consuming, like she just might combust if he didn't kiss her again.

"Promised myself I wouldn't do this," he said as he brought his lips back to hers.

"I won't tell," she whispered as he kissed her. They kissed until she was seeing stars and his chest heaved against hers. The rhythmic boom of the bass from the dance floor seemed to echo the frantic pounding of her heart.

"I see fucking red just thinking about another guy touching you." In the dim light of the hall, his eyes glittered, deep and dark as the night sky.

"I don't want anyone to touch me but you."

He crushed his mouth against hers. "No matter how hard I try, I just can't get you out of my head."

"Same." She went up on her tiptoes, bringing their bodies into alignment. They kissed again, raw and greedy and desperate.

"I can't stop needing you, needing *this*." He clutched her closer against him, a note of desperation in his voice.

"I don't want you to. Please, Ryan, stop holding back."

Her words seemed to unleash something inside him. His muscles bunched like a tiger about to pounce, his fingers gripping tighter on her butt. "So just how bad do you want to be?"

She felt his hard length straining the front of his jeans, and *oh my God*, this was really happening. "So bad," she whispered.

His hand slid around to cup her through her panties, and

she let out a squeak of pleasure. He stroked her through the thin cotton, and she moaned into his mouth.

"Here's your first lesson." His gruff words were a whispered promise as his fingers slipped inside her panties. Her body was already on fire from his touch, from his kisses, from the rhythm of the music that seemed to be driving them closer and closer to the edge.

She whimpered, clinging to him as his fingers stroked her toward oblivion.

"Forget those guys on Tinder," he growled into her ear.

"Done." Her voice was nothing but a whisper as desire coiled hot and tight inside her. She'd never wanted those guys anyway. She'd only ever wanted Ryan.

Ryan.

"Come for me, Emma." His thumb scraped across her center and sent her flying.

She buried her face on his shoulder as the orgasm ripped through her, knocking her senseless. When she'd finally come back to herself, she lifted her head. "Whoa."

Ryan's eyes blazed into hers, hot and fierce. "You were right. Bad looks good on you."

* * *

Ryan smoothed Emma's skirt down and took a step back. She looked all flushed and rumpled, still glowing with pleasure, and he wanted her so bad it hurt. His dick was screaming to get inside her, which wasn't going to happen—not tonight anyway—but one thing was for damn sure: There was no more pretending this thing between them wasn't happening.

It was fucking happening.

Emma was his, and he was hers, and there was no way

either of them could keep on pretending otherwise. Not after tonight.

She glanced around as if just becoming aware of their surroundings, the dim hallway leading back to the pool tables—which were closed during the week—where he'd just gotten her off right here in public. And it had been hot as hell.

She sucked her bottom lip between her teeth and looked at him, her eyes still glossy and dazed. "That was…*bad* in the very best way."

Hell yeah, it was. "Let's be clear. You and me? Still a bad idea. But if bad's what you're looking for…"

"It is," she said quickly. "I want you, Ryan."

He wasn't sure he'd ever wanted anything as much as he wanted Emma. "Right now, it's time for you to go home. We'll figure this out tomorrow." When his dick wasn't hard as granite, and he had enough blood left in his brain to think this through properly.

"Oh." She looked disappointed.

"I'll walk you to your car." He drew her up against him for one last kiss, and she melted in his arms all over again.

Dammit. He might not ever get his head back on straight where Emma was concerned.

He took her hand in his and led her back through the bar area to the dance floor. They paused to say good-bye to Trent—still dancing energetically with his friends—then walked outside into the cool night. Emma hadn't brought a jacket so she hustled him toward her silver RAV4. When they got there, she went up on her tiptoes to kiss him again.

"Thank you, for tonight," she whispered. "It was… amazing."

He nodded. "Drive safe."

He watched as she got into her car, started it, and drove

away. The night around him seemed to echo with silence after the blasting noise of the club. He walked slowly toward his bike, parked around the side of the building.

Brussels sprouts. Sauerkraut. Blue cheese. Green tomatoes.

He ran through all the nasty foods he could think of as he stood beside the Harley, waiting for the pressure in his dick to ease enough that he could climb on without causing himself serious pain. He eased himself gingerly onto the seat and cranked the engine.

He went straight home, but it was still a hell of an uncomfortable ride. He didn't let himself think of Emma again until he was safely inside his condo.

Emma.

He was still hard, still aching for her. The truth was, he hadn't been with a woman in at least six months now. Had he been lusting after Emma for that long? She was the only woman he could conjure up in his fantasies, the only woman who made him hard.

And he'd punished himself long enough, denying his fantasies of her. In fact, maybe his sexual frustration was part of the reason he'd let himself go tonight.

Well, there was at least one problem he could fix. He headed for the shower, desperate for relief, the memory of Emma's pleasure still buzzing in his blood. In this case, the reality had definitely been better than the fantasy. Now that he knew what she sounded like when she came? The beautiful glow on her skin after he'd sent her flying? He'd never fucking forget it.

He cranked the shower up nice and hot then shucked his clothes. His dick stood urgently at attention, refusing to be ignored. Cursing under his breath, he stepped beneath the shower's steamy spray.

Emma...

He remembered the soft sounds she'd made as he touched her, how hot and wet she'd been when he slid his hand inside her panties...His dick surged, throbbing in time with the wild pounding of his heart. He reached for the bar of soap and slicked his palm then gripped himself. As he tightened his fist, he imagined Emma there with him in the shower, urging him on.

"You're so big, Ryan. I'm getting so wet just watching you." In his filthy mind, that's what she'd say. He pumped his fist up and down his shaft, tugging harder as the aching need grew more intense. He could almost feel the heat of her stare, and the fantasy of her watching made his dick harder still. He closed his eyes and braced his free hand against the wall, his head bent, the shower beating down over his shoulders.

"Come for me, Ryan," Imaginary Emma whispered in his ear.

His balls drew up tight against his body, and he tensed, then release pulsed through him, hot and fierce. He stood there, head bowed, gasping for breath for several long seconds. But even now, his yearning for Emma never lessened. If anything, it grew stronger. And the next time he came, he wanted to be inside her.

CHAPTER NINE

Whoa. Emma lay in bed, her body still humming with satisfaction. Had she really let Ryan put his hands up her skirt right there in the back hallway of The Music Factory? Yes, she had, and oh, had it been worth it. If this was what it felt like to be bad, she never wanted to be good again.

Who's in for cinnamon buns in the morning? she texted to her friends. I have a major dare update to share.

OMG, Gabby replied. This better be good! You guys were so obviously hot for each other on the dance floor tonight.

Oh, it's good. She inserted a winking emoticon and several flames. I'll spill all the deets tomorrow around 8?

This ignited a flurry of texts from Gabby, Carly, and Mandy, all of whom promised to be there tomorrow morning at eight to hear her news. Emma set her phone on the nightstand, turned out the light, and crashed almost as soon as her head hit the pillow, with Smokey snuggled in beside her.

She awoke the next morning with memories of Ryan still dancing in her mind. Holy shit. That really happened. Nothing boring or predictable about anything she'd done last night, and she liked it. She *loved* it. No use trying to deny it any longer. It wasn't just a wild and crazy fling she wanted.

She wanted Ryan.

And there was no way she was going to let him push her away again. It still sent a hot thrill through her when she remembered the way he'd touched her, the harsh possessiveness of his words when he'd told her to forget about other guys.

Oh, they were forgotten all right.

And her body ached for him to touch her again. She wanted more. She wanted *everything*. And she was going to have it, dammit.

She showered, dressed in jeans and a long-sleeved tee for work, and headed to A Piece of Cake to meet the girls. Carly had fresh cinnamon buns and coffees waiting.

"Please tell me you hooked up with Ryan last night," Gabby said with a huge smile as she slid onto the seat next to Emma's.

"Define 'hooked up,'" she said with a grin.

Mandy came up behind them, her eyes wide. "Holy shit, Emma. Tell us everything."

"We were at The Music Factory last night to hear his brother DJ—which is a whole other story because I'm so proud of Trent—but after everyone else left, we were still dancing, and somehow dancing turned to kissing, and—"

Gabby gasped.

"He took me down this hall in back, and holy crap, you guys..."

"What?" Mandy asked. They all leaned in, hanging on her every word.

"Well, let's just say, *things* happened." Emma felt her cheeks getting hot.

"Things?" Mandy repeated with a laugh. "What kind of things?"

Emma glanced around the bakery, but no one else was nearby to overhear her naughty confession. "Well, his hands were up my skirt, and he's *very* good with his hands. And...he's a dirty talker...and—"

"Oh my God!" Carly squealed.

Mandy sat back with a wide smile. "Now *that's* what I'm talking about. Way to go, my friend." She raised her hand and slapped a high five with Emma.

"And then what happened?" Gabby asked.

"Then he sent me home and said we'd talk about it today."

"Like I said in the beginning," Mandy said, "Ryan Blake is a sheep in wolf's clothing. He's the perfect guy for you to experiment with, Emma, because he's a gentleman at heart."

Emma knew Mandy was right, which meant she had to watch out where Ryan was concerned. She'd spent most of her life wanting him, and once she had him, she'd have a hell of a time not falling head over heels in love with him.

A few hours later, she was back out at Off-the-Grid, overseeing several seasonal contractors as they reseeded the grass in the field behind the house while she finished up the flowers she was planting along the walkway.

Ryan came sauntering out of the building, looking all badass and sexy, and she practically swooned into the begonias. "Got a minute?" he asked, his expression masked by his sunglasses.

"Sure." She stood, wiping the dirt from her hands.

"Let's walk." He led the way down one of the many paths into the woods on the property, looking for all the world like he was just out for a casual stroll, like he was the same Ryan he'd been her whole life until last night, when he'd kissed the daylights out of her and given her an orgasm in the back hallway of The Music Factory.

"Beautiful weather," he commented as they walked.

"Yeah." She chewed her bottom lip. He'd better not be planning to act like last night never happened because—

"So here's the thing," he said once they'd rounded a corner, firmly out of sight from anyone else on the property.

"Yes?" she asked hopefully.

"The thing is . . ." He blew out a breath, shaking his head. "I have no idea what to do about this thing between us."

Nervous laughter bubbled out of her, and she slapped a hand over her mouth. "Me either. So maybe we should quit overthinking it and just see what happens."

He pushed his glasses up on his head and took her hands in his. "Promise me, Em. Promise me that whatever happens, we won't let it ruin our friendship, okay?"

She nodded, as her heart flopped in her chest. "I promise. We can just be friends with benefits, or whatever, in the meantime."

His expression grew more intense, and he tugged her in close. "I'm not sure there's anything friendly about the way I'm feeling about you right now."

Her heart started pounding, and heat pooled in her belly. "That makes two of us." Although standing here in broad daylight at Off-the-Grid, it did indeed sound kind of surreal to be talking about hooking up with Ryan.

"And no guys from Tinder," he said, his expression fierce.

"No one but you." She hoped he couldn't hear the absolute truth in her words. Then she narrowed her eyes. "Same goes for you."

"I never mess around, Emma," he said, looking so protective and loyal it made her chest hurt. "If I'm with you, I'm *only* with you."

"Okay then." She tried to hide the big mushy mess that was her heart behind a casual smile. "What will we tell everyone else?"

"Let's play it by ear," he said. "Right now, I think we're doing way too much talking."

"Agreed." She leaned forward and pressed her lips to his.

Next thing she knew, she was plastered against his chest. His hands had found their way into her back pockets while his mouth devoured hers. "Wow," she said when they'd finally come up for air.

"Yeah." He looked just as dazed as she felt. "You are blowing my mind right now."

She grinned. "Thanks, I think."

"So what now?" he asked, for once looking at a loss.

Yeah, this was slightly awkward. Last night, beneath the strobing lights of the dance floor and fueled by alcohol, they'd been possessed by their need for each other. But here, in the bright sunshine, while both of them were technically at work? It wasn't as if they could just fall into bed together.

"Well, I was thinking...I've decided on my tattoo. Will you take me to get it done?"

He was quiet for a moment. Then he nodded. "If you're sure it's what you want. I used to manage a place in Charlotte. The guys there are top notch. They did most of mine."

She traced her fingers over a tribal design that wrapped around his wrist. The reality of getting a tattoo—namely, the pain from the needle, but also the idea of it being on her body forever—was still slightly terrifying, but this was something she'd always wanted to do. And having Ryan take her felt beyond perfect. "I like yours. So Charlotte, huh?"

He nodded. "We could go this weekend."

Charlotte was at least a two-hour drive from Haven.

Maybe they could spend the night, too, but right now that still felt a bit too forward to mention. "It's a date."

"So what are you getting?"

"A poppy." She smiled when his brow furrowed. "It's a flower. You knew I had to get a flower, right?"

He looked down at her dirt-stained hands. "Yeah. A flower definitely suits you."

"The red poppy symbolizes loss, especially those lost at war. And I want to have an anchor woven into the stem to symbolize hope."

He stared straight into her eyes, and his expression made her sizzle from head to toe. "That's perfect. Really perfect."

* * *

Ryan scraped a hand over his chin as he followed Emma back toward the main building. Holy shit, this thing between them had taken on a life of its own. Bringing her to Charlotte to get a tattoo would be a turning point, that much was for damn sure.

Trent pulled into the parking lot in his little Kia sedan, and Ryan headed his way. Emma beat him to it.

"You were so fantastic last night," she gushed as soon as Trent had stepped out of his car.

"Thanks." He tugged at his cap with a shy smile.

"You really have something there. I could feel it," she said. "And it seemed like everyone else was really enjoying your music, too. I think this could be the start of big things for you."

Ryan wasn't so sure about that. Sure, the kid had a passion and talent for DJ'ing, but was that really a viable career? Seemed more like something someone might do for a few years until a real job came along. And that was fine, as long as he got his education so that he'd have it to fall back on.

Emma gave Trent a big hug before she headed back to the flowers she'd been planting when Ryan had come out and interrupted her.

"You did great last night," Ryan said. "Made me real proud."

"Thanks." Trent ducked his head.

"I thought maybe you and I could work together out on the ropes course today."

"Keeping an eye on me?"

"Nah." Not entirely anyway. "Just thought we could spend some time together."

"Okay. Cool."

"I need to test out all the connections before we open the course for spring and summer activities," Ryan said as he led the way down the path.

"So who uses it?" Trent asked.

"Companies can do team-building exercises or groups can rent it for a party or event, but one of us has to be there leading the exercises and supervising. It's not open for free play, 'cept for us, of course." He winked, and Trent grinned.

"It's fun being here, working outside. Never did much of that in St. Louis."

"You live in the city?"

"Suburbs."

"Play any sports?" Ryan asked.

"Does the Wii count?"

Ryan laughed as he shook his head. He and his brother had almost nothing in common. Didn't matter, though. "I thought we could start on the tires and work our way around the course."

"Okay. What am I looking for?"

Ryan showed him how to spot structural wear on the tires and on the ropes supporting them. He and Trent sat side by side on tires, swinging slightly as they felt along the ropes for any signs of decay or wear.

"Did you know your dad? Or mine?" Trent asked suddenly as he examined the rope overhead.

"No. Mom went out with a lot of guys. I'm not sure if she even knew."

"Oh." Trent shrugged. "I kind of wonder sometimes, you know, about my heritage."

Ryan had wondered, too. "I've tried to remember seeing her with an Asian man, but I don't. Our mom was...Well, you're probably lucky you don't remember her."

Trent kept his eyes on the rope. "What was she like?"

Ryan took a deep breath. "She loved us. I mean, she was never abusive or anything like that. But the drugs, the alcohol...it took a toll. She was always looking for her next fix. She just couldn't break free of the cycle."

"Did she try? You know, for us?" Hurt gleamed in his younger brother's eyes.

"She got clean when she was pregnant with you. I think she did try, yeah."

Trent said nothing, staring at the ground, his jaw set.

"I was only eleven when she died," Ryan said. "At the time, I thought she must not have cared about us at all to do the things she did. But now, you know, I guess she did the best she could."

"But not enough."

"No, not enough." Ryan couldn't sugarcoat the truth. "Losing her, and then losing you...it was pretty bad for me. I did a lot of stupid shit, but I've never touched drugs. Not once. Not after seeing what they did to her."

"I'm sorry," Trent said, his voice gone quiet. "It's not fair that you had to grow up in foster care. I had, like, a pretty average childhood. I mean, I thought it sucked plenty, but getting grounded for breaking curfew doesn't compare to what you went through."

"Life's not fair, Trent. I did okay, and things have turned out good for me. Not to be all mushy and shit, but I just want you to know how much it means to me having you here. Soon as I could after I turned eighteen and aged out of the system, I left Haven and moved around, looking for you. Hoped maybe you were somewhere nearby so that I could track you down."

"Really?" Trent turned to look at him.

"Yeah, man. Family's everything, right? Whatever happens, when you go back home or back to school or whatever, we're family now. You're never getting rid of me." He gave his brother a slap on the back.

A smile creased his brother's cheeks. "That's totally cool with me."

"Good. Maybe I'm hard on you sometimes because I don't want you to make the mistakes I did. Just punch me if I start to sound too annoying, okay?"

Trent laughed a little at that, shaking his head.

"You know they have those ancestry kits now. You send them a cheek swab or whatever, they test your DNA and tell you where you're from. If you really want to know."

"I never thought of that." Trent sounded thoughtful. "People tell me I look Korean, but I've always wondered."

By the time they had finished checking over the ropes course and noted all the repairs that needed to be made, Ryan felt really bonded with Trent for the first time.

* * *

Emma finished up at Off-the-Grid a little past four thirty. The guys were all out on the property doing who-knew-what, and her seasonal employees had already gone home so she went inside to wash up. She scrubbed up in the bathroom then went into the kitchen for a glass of water. Yeah, she was dawdling, hoping she might get to see Ryan again before she left.

Because...well, now that they'd started kissing, she couldn't seem to get enough. But she had no idea where he was, and she couldn't think of another reason to hang around so she headed for her car, trying not to feel disappointed.

"Hey," Ryan called to her from across the yard, waving as he stepped out of the woods.

She felt herself grinning like a fool and didn't even care. "Hey yourself."

"You heading out?" he asked as he walked toward her.

"Landscaping's all finished," she said.

He glanced over at the daisies and begonias she'd spent the afternoon planting. "Looks great. You have time to go for a ride?"

"Yes." She stepped in close, not quite touching him since they were in the parking lot where anyone could see, but close enough that her whole body sizzled with awareness. "What did you have in mind?"

A hot glint came into his brown eyes. "A whole lot more than I have time for. Unfortunately, I have to be back here in an hour or so for another appointment."

Her heart thumped against her ribs. "We could have a lot of fun in an hour."

With a wicked smile, he motioned for her to follow him to his bike. He unclipped both helmets and handed her the spare.

"You don't usually carry both, do you?" she asked as she settled it on her head.

He gave her another heated look. "Never let it be said that I don't plan ahead."

He'd been thinking about her when he left for work this morning. Her insides turned into a mushy mess as she melted for him all over again. Oh, this man... She watched while he got the bike started then she slid into place behind him. She wrapped her arms around him and hung on as he pulled out onto the road.

Today the Harley seemed to rumble beneath them with increased urgency, or maybe that was just the hum of anticipation burning in her blood because she and Ryan had officially agreed to become "friends with benefits" this morning, and she was going crazy thinking about all the possibilities.

He turned down a road that led out of town, winding up into the mountains. A few minutes later, he pulled off at a spot labeled as a SCENIC OVERLOOK. This particular pull-off was hidden from view of the road, and if she wasn't mistaken...

"Isn't this the place all the local teenagers come to make out?" she asked once he'd turned off the engine.

He turned his head, and the look on his face sent sparks pinging around inside her. "You ever been here?"

She shook her head. "But I bet you have."

"Actually, no." He extended a hand to help her off the bike. "Always wanted to bring a girl here, though, back in high school."

"So why didn't you?"

"No car."

Right. Of course he hadn't had a car, being in foster care. "I didn't have one either. Bought the world's most ancient

Toyota Celica after graduation, the kind with the headlights that flipped up and down when you turned them on and off."

"Mine was a Ford Escort, also ancient. Bought it when I was twenty and drove it straight out of town."

"I remember," she said softly. It had been only a few weeks after Derek's funeral. Ryan's departure had nearly crushed her, right after losing her brother.

Ryan brushed his lips against hers. "Never kissed a girl I had so much history with."

"Kind of weird, right?"

"Sometimes, yeah." His eyes crinkled with a smile. "But mostly... not nearly as weird as I thought it would be."

They walked to the barrier overlooking the mountains beyond, rolling hills that vanished into the misty clouds overhead. This place might be full of teenagers getting naughty in parked cars after dark, but right now, they had the place to themselves.

"It's beautiful," she murmured, her hand in his.

"It is, but that's not the view I came here to enjoy." He turned to face her and tugged her in close.

"I like the way you think," she whispered against his lips, and then she kissed him.

Their kiss was hungry and intense and *raw*. She clasped her hands behind his neck as his tongue thrust against hers, hot and thrilling. Her body was on fire, pulsing with need, completely consumed with this man who was gripping her ass, holding on to her like he couldn't get her close enough, like even a millimeter of space between their bodies was too much.

"Ryan," she moaned as he bent his head to nibble at a sensitive spot on her neck.

"You make me so hot," he rasped. His hands slid up under her shirt, deliciously rough against her bare skin.

"More," she whispered.

He let out a harsh laugh. "That's why I bought you here. Knew I couldn't control myself if I got you alone anywhere near a bedroom."

"No fair," she grumbled.

"When I get you naked for the first time, it won't be when I have to be back at work in less than an hour." Then he kissed her again, and she couldn't think of anything but the way his lips felt on hers, the hot thrill of his hands as they palmed her breasts, and his hard length straining against her belly.

They kissed until she was dizzy for air, drunk with lust, totally blinded with need. When he finally lifted his head, his pupils were so wide his eyes looked black. His chest heaved against hers.

She blew out a breath and smiled. "Then I think we need to make plans when neither of us has to work."

CHAPTER TEN

*E*mma had her third rock climbing lesson on Thursday. Two days since she and Ryan had gotten naughty in the back hall of The Music Factory. One day since they'd agreed to become friends with benefits. Zero seconds since she last thought about what that was going to be like and when it would happen.

Ryan stood below her, belay rope in hand, as she struggled up the rock face. She'd gotten some of the basic terminology down now—she knew about smears and edging techniques that let her put her feet on impossibly small ledges and indents in the rock that somehow her climbing shoes held on to. She'd gotten better at keeping her weight in her toes and using her arms for balance.

And today, she was aiming for the top.

"That's right. Move your left foot over...yeah," Ryan encouraged her from the ground.

"Dammit." She'd reached the area near the top that stymied

her every time. Wide and flat and impossibly smooth, she simply couldn't see a way to get past it.

"You're thinking about it too hard. Just feel the rock for your next move."

"That makes absolutely no sense, you know." If she sounded a little bit miffed, that's because she was. Learning to rock climb was one of the first goals she'd set for herself when she'd decided to shake things up, and so far she sucked at it.

"Reach with your right hand," Ryan said.

She did, and her fingers slid into a little crease she hadn't noticed. Aha! She shifted right, following the new direction he'd led her in and...

Off the rock she went, swinging out as the harness broke her fall. She groaned as he lowered her to the ground.

"Don't get frustrated," he said. "You're doing great for your third lesson. Learning out here on the rock is a lot harder than learning on an indoor wall."

She huffed out a sigh and grabbed the rock again. An hour—and four falls—later, she was ready to give up. This was the "bunny slope" of Off-the-Grid's rock climbs, and she couldn't even master it.

"Guess my time's up for today," she said, resting her hands on her knees as she glared up at the rock that had bested her.

"I don't have any other appointments this afternoon. You want to give it one more try?"

"I don't know..." She glanced up at the rock again. Her muscles shook with fatigue, and her temper was simmering straight toward red.

"Take a few deep breaths, and this time, I want you to focus on working *with* the rock instead of against it."

"Why do you sound like such a hippie all of a sudden?"

she asked as she gripped the rock, hauling herself up. By now, she knew the first few moves by heart.

Ryan laughed long and hard behind her. "First time I've ever been called a hippie. But seriously, the rock is not your enemy. Stop fighting with it."

"Whatever you say, Hippie." But she was smiling as she worked her way up to her trouble spot, looking for the secret handhold Ryan had guided her toward earlier. The place where she'd now fallen five times in a row.

She swung her foot and toed into an edge far enough out to the side that she knew she must be giving Ryan an eyeful from below. She'd give him hell for staring at her ass, but she couldn't breathe, couldn't move for fear of falling.

The top was just past her fingertips.

Sucking in a slow, shaky breath, she shifted her weight onto her right foot. It held. Muscles trembling from the strain, she swiveled her hips to bring her left foot in, seeking purchase on a nearly invisible smear on the rock beneath her knee.

"Atta girl," Ryan said from below, his voice seeming to filter in from a million miles away.

Cautiously, she straightened her legs, testing out her precarious new footholds. And…she was eye level with the top. Squelching the urge to celebrate prematurely, she slung her elbows over, grabbed on to the anchor securing her line, and scrambled over the edge in about as ungraceful a move as humanly possible. Her feet scuffled against the rock face until her left toe snagged on something, giving her the boost she needed.

Oomph. She landed in a heap on top of the rock. "Oh my God. I did it." She pushed up into a sitting position, her chest heaving, muscles shaking like Jell-O. "I really did it!"

"Don't move a muscle," Ryan said, his voice taut.

She froze, thinking for a moment she was in danger. But he unclipped his harness from the belay line, gripped the rock, and started climbing toward her with a speed and ease that made her feel like a total novice all over again.

It took him about two minutes to climb the rock face that had taken her at least fifteen, and he wasn't even wearing a harness. He hauled himself up beside her, pulled her into his lap, and covered her mouth with his.

Oh. She let out a gasp of surprise as heat spread like wild-fire inside her.

"I'm so fucking proud of you." His voice was low and gruff, thick with lust and pride, and it tickled all her sensitive nerve endings, turning her to jelly in his arms.

"Thanks." She leaned forward to kiss him back, her victory all but forgotten in the heat of his kiss, the scorching stroke of his tongue against hers, the delicious feel of his hands skimming down her sides to grip her butt, drawing her closer against him.

She shifted so that her knees dropped down on either side of his thighs, straddling him. He was hard, so hard, and the bulge in his jeans pressed into her right where she burned for him. She rocked her hips against his. The friction of his jeans through the thin cotton of her yoga pants was enough to make her lose her mind.

Ryan pressed her more firmly against his erection. "Watching you climb that rock is the biggest fucking turn-on."

Really? She must have looked ridiculous, flailing around as she scrambled for the top. "It would be really *bad* if you took me right here." She emphasized the word as fantasies of them having wild sex up here on top of the world exploded through her brain.

He groaned. "Bad in all the wrong ways. Bad in the

'bruises and scrapes where the sun don't shine' and potentially fall to your death in the throes of passion kind of way."

Well, when he put it that way...

He shifted her to a more ladylike position in his lap, then kissed her again. "But I couldn't go another moment without kissing you."

Something about the way he said it sent a warm tingle up her spine. He sounded possessive. Of her.

"Did you get a good look at the view?" he asked.

"I like the view." She smiled, staring straight into his eyes. She'd spent the better part of her life fantasizing about him looking at her the way he was right now, and yet the reality was still better than she'd imagined.

He dipped his head and kissed her again. "I mean the view around us. It's always better when you've scaled the rock to get here."

She turned her head, seeing the forest around her for the first time from her new vantage point, and yeah, it was pretty awesome. She slid out of his lap and crawled to the edge. Lying on her stomach, she looked down at where she'd started. "Wow. It looks even higher from up here."

"Not bad, huh?" He came to lay beside her. "I climb up here when I need to clear my head."

"I can see how this would do it." She lay there for several minutes, just staring out at the vista in front of her. "Thanks for pushing me to try again."

"Any time."

She listened to the birds chattering in the trees, then rolled to her back to watch the sunlight filtering through the canopy of leaves overhead. "I could stay here all day."

"Fine by me," Ryan said. "Hey, how's the memorial coming?"

And just like that, her peaceful mood was ruined. "I met with the Town Planning Committee this morning, actually. They rejected my design."

"What? Why?"

"They thought it was too trendy." Emma stared up at the trees overhead, avoiding Ryan's concerned gaze. Lucas and Mary had warned her this might happen, but it still hadn't prepared her for the enormous sting of the Planning Committee's rejection.

"I'm sorry, Em. That's lousy." He lay beside her, taking her hand in his. "But it's just a bump in the road. You'll come up with something else, something even better."

"I sure hope so." She turned her head to look at him. "What's next, Ryan?"

His brown eyes were alive with the dappled light of the forest around them. "I assume you don't mean right here, right now."

"No, apart from the fact that we're lying here on this rock we just climbed...what comes next with all the kissing and stuff?"

"Not quite sure myself." His lips curved in a wicked smile. "But if you have any wild fantasies in mind, I thought our trip to Charlotte this weekend might be a good time to fulfill them."

She gulped audibly, her throat gone dry as sandpaper. "Oh." Yes. Their trip to Charlotte to get her tattoo.

"So let me hear it, baby. What naughty fantasy do you want to indulge first?" His voice was delightfully rough, his eyes having taken on a slightly wicked gleam.

"Um." *Gah.* He'd rendered her speechless. "Surprise me."

"Oh, baby, that is a definite 'can do.'"

* * *

Ryan rolled the Harley into Emma's driveway just past noon on Saturday. He'd told her to pack a backpack with a change of clothes and something nice to wear later. Hopefully she knew how to travel light because taking the bike was going to set the mood for their whole trip.

She came out her front door wearing pale pink jeans that fit her like a second skin, knee-high black leather boots, and a fitted black jacket, her hair hanging in golden waves down her back, and *fuck*, he was hard as steel just looking at her. She carried a backpack slung over one arm, sunglasses in hand, her blue eyes bright with excitement.

He stood and pulled her into his arms. "You look... you're fucking stunning, Emma."

"Really?" She looked up at him with an amused smile. "I'm just wearing jeans."

"A woman dressed to ride is my weakness."

"I'll keep that in mind," she said, leaning in to kiss him.

He pressed a finger to her lips. "Better not. Can't ride with a hard-on, and you are turning me on big time right now."

She glanced down at the front of his jeans, a soft smile curving her lips. "I talked to your brother this morning. We were thinking about getting the group together over at Ethan and Gabby's place sometime soon for a game night. She's got a video game console, and I've got loads of board games."

"Okay," he said, confused by the shift in topic.

"Did it work?" she asked, gesturing toward his crotch.

Ah. Now he got it, and yes, her diversion had worked. "Like a charm. You ready?"

She nodded, shrugging the backpack over her shoulders. He handed her his spare helmet and mounted the bike. It roared to life beneath him, and Emma climbed on behind him, sliding into place like a pro. Her hands wrapped around his waist, locking into position.

He pulled out onto the road, invigorated by the slap of mountain air. He took his time winding down from the mountains, sticking to the twisting back roads that got his adrenaline pumping for as long as possible. A couple of hours later, as they neared Charlotte, he merged onto the highway for the remainder of the trip.

Emma's arms tightened around him.

Yeah, this felt a lot different from the mountain roads they'd left behind. The highway was flat, fast, and clogged with other vehicles. He settled in with the flow of traffic, watching as the Charlotte skyline unfurled before them. It had been almost a year since he'd left the city. It had held a certain appeal once. Now he found himself missing the winding roads and fresh air in Haven. Course, he'd brought one of the best parts of the mountains here with him this weekend.

They exited the highway on South Boulevard, headed for House of Ink, which he'd once managed. Emma had been e-mailing back and forth with its co-owner and Ryan's good buddy, Stephen Betts, to finalize the design for her tattoo.

Ryan rolled up to a stoplight, and Emma leaned in. "Is it just me or are some of these cars coming a bit too close for comfort?"

"Just feels that way because you're not used to riding in traffic. Don't worry, babe. I'll keep you safe."

"You'd better." He could hear the smile in her voice.

The light turned green, and he guided them through his old neighborhood until House of Ink came into view, a nondescript storefront lit with a neon sign.

Ryan rolled into a spot out front and cut the engine.

"Oh boy," Emma whispered behind him.

"Nervous?"

"A little."

"Don't be. You're in good hands with Stephen."

"Tell me the truth," she said, sliding to her feet. "How bad does it hurt?"

"Like a son of a bitch," he answered with a grin.

"Hmm." She propped her hands on her hips and eyed the front of the shop. "Okay, the truth is, I'm terrified right now."

"Not too late to change your mind," he said.

She lifted the helmet from her head and shook out her hair. "No way. Come on. Let's go inside before I lose my nerve."

He caught her hand and tugged her up against him. "Seriously. Be sure about this." And he wasn't just talking about the tattoo.

She pressed her lips against his. "I'm sure. This is something I've always wanted to do but never had the courage. You'll hold my hand if I need you to, right?"

"Right." And if he sounded a little gruff, it had nothing to do with the raw emotion stamped all over Emma's face right now. God, she was amazing.

He locked their helmets on the bike and followed her inside. The place hadn't changed since he'd last seen it, and the familiar surroundings hit him with a wave of nostalgia. He'd had a couple of good years here. He itched to pop into his old office, see how the new guy was doing.

"Ryan!" Stephen came out from the back and pulled him in for a hug and a clap on the back. "It's good to see you, man. How's it going?"

"Good. The new business is doing really well."

"And you must be Emma," Stephen said, extending a hand. "Stephen Betts."

"Nice to meet you." Emma was looking around the place, wide-eyed.

Ryan would bet she'd never stepped foot inside a tattoo parlor before. He sure as hell hoped she didn't regret this—regret *him*—after the whole thing was said and done.

"The pleasure is all mine." Stephen, for all his hulking size, shaved head, and heavily inked skin, was nothing short of a gentleman, one of many reasons Ryan had brought her to him. "Let me show you around the place before we get started."

"That sounds great," Emma said, curiosity gleaming in her eyes as she glanced around the lobby, eyeing the artwork on the walls. "Are all of these your designs?"

"Mine and my brother Sean's. He's not here today, and he was real disappointed to miss seeing you guys." Stephen led her down the hallway, where several tattoos were in progress in rooms on either side of the hall.

Emma gave Ryan a wide-eyed look. He squeezed her shoulder.

"I've got your design all ready to be transferred," Stephen said, indicating an unoccupied room on the left. "Restroom's all the way down on the right if you want to freshen up, and feel free to help yourself to a soda from the mini-fridge across the hall. I know y'all had a long ride."

"Thanks so much," Emma said with a grateful smile, heading down the hall.

"Looks like the mountains have been good for you," Stephen said, stepping into the room to get things ready.

"Sure have. Things going good here?"

"No complaints. Miss having you around." Stephen cracked a smile. "Been thinking about riding up sometime to try out that zip-line course of yours."

"Yeah? That'd be great, man. Any time."

"New business. New girl. You're puttin' down roots, huh?"

Ryan straightened. "I'm going to stick in Haven, yeah. But Emma and I—"

Stephen put a hand up. "Not my business. Just good to see you looking happy, that's all."

Emma walked into the room then, Diet Coke in hand. She cracked it open and looked from Ryan to Stephen. "Okay, let's do this."

Ryan went down the hall to grab himself a drink and ended up meeting the new manager after all. By the time he made it back to Emma's room, she was in the chair, fully reclined. Her skin-tight jeans were unzipped and pushed down far enough to reveal a flash of pink lace and enough creamy skin to knock the knees right out from under him. Stephen sat on his stool at her side, carefully transferring their design onto her hip.

Ryan leaned against the wall, one foot crossed over the other, hoping he looked nonchalant and not like the idiot who'd brought his girl here to have her skin inked before he'd gotten her naked, letting Stephen see parts of her Ryan himself hadn't seen yet. The next hour was going to be pure torture. He gulped from his Coke, trying not to stare at that scrap of pink lace and imagine what the rest of it looked like.

At least he'd brought her here, where he could be sure Stephen wasn't looking or touching inappropriately. The man was happily married and completely professional at all times. Nope, the only person in the room ogling Emma's exposed hip and having X-rated fantasies was Ryan.

After Stephen had transferred the design onto her skin and showed it to her, he got down to the real business at hand. At Ryan's suggestion, Emma had her ear buds in and was listening to music, eyes closed. She flinched when Stephen first touched the needle to her skin, and the room filled with the buzz of the tattoo machine.

Ryan watched for a few minutes to make sure she was okay. Her face scrunched up a few times, but she seemed to be handling the discomfort just fine. Emma's tattoo was fairly simple. Stephen inked the black parts first, weaving an anchor subtly into the stem of the flower just as she'd envisioned. Then the poppy began to take shape in brilliant hues of red.

Ryan thumbed through e-mails on his phone and snuck peeks as Stephen worked, still wondering how the hell he hadn't foreseen the problem with her bared skin and his filthy, sex-starved brain. But as soon as they got out of here? All bets were off. He ought to wine and dine her before he took her to bed, but *fuck*, he needed her in the worst way.

She'd said she wanted to be a little bit wild, but did she really mean it? He sure as hell hoped so because he didn't know how to be tame.

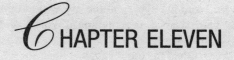

CHAPTER ELEVEN

*E*mma stood in front of the mirror of their hotel room, jeans unbuttoned and resting low on her hips, staring at her new reflection. Her tattoo was sealed beneath some kind of Saran Wrap-like bandage that wasn't exactly the sexiest thing ever, and the tattoo itself was red and sore, but...but she *loved* it.

It was perfect.

Absolutely perfect. Ryan's friend Stephen had taken her idea and turned it into something even more beautiful than she'd envisioned.

Ryan stood behind her, his expression heated. "Only one thing sexier than a woman dressed to ride."

"Oh yeah, what's that?"

"A woman with a tattoo." He slid her into his arms, his hands staying well clear of her freshly inked skin.

"Is that so?" She hadn't had much of an opinion on tattoos until recently, but yeah, she was a big fan now, too. Ryan's tats were definitely a turn-on.

"I lied," he said, tracing his fingers over the edges of her bandage. "There's one thing even sexier than a woman dressed to ride or a woman with a tattoo."

She looked into his eyes, and the expression on his face could only be described as scorching. "What?" she asked, sounding breathless.

"You." He crushed his mouth against hers.

Well, she had no idea what to say to that, but the way he was kissing her had rendered her speechless anyway. They were alone together in a hotel room, and her mind was about to overheat with all the possibilities. Ryan kissed her like kissing was an art form and not merely the precursor to sex. Although right now, sex was the only thing on her mind.

"A nice guy would take you to dinner first," he said, his voice a low growl in her ear.

She whimpered. "How many times do I have to tell you? I don't want nice. And the only thing I'm hungry for is you."

"Thank God." He yanked her up against him, his hips slamming into hers. His dick strained the front of his jeans, making her burn.

She gripped his shoulders and jumped, wrapping her legs around his hips, and *oh*...Her back slammed into the wall, and he was kissing her like a man possessed, his body pressed against hers. This kiss was different from its predecessor—this kiss said he had to have her or die trying, and God help her, she was about to come just from the feel of him pressed between her legs.

"Hurry," she whispered, rocking her hips against his.

"Never." His voice was a growl, his breath hot against her neck. He peeled her shirt over her head, baring her pink bra. A rough groan tore from his throat as he touched her breasts, then his hand slid down her belly, already exposed from where she'd been admiring her new tattoo. His fingers lingered at the edge of the clear bandage covering it. "This has been torturing me all fucking afternoon."

"My tattoo?" Her skin tingled beneath his touch.

"Your skin, the tattoo...all of it. Killing me that Stephen got to touch you here before I did." He was touching now, his fingers skimming the lacy trim of her panties.

Emma wanted to do some touching of her own. She gripped his T-shirt and tugged. He lifted his arms so that it slid over his head, and *oh my*, his chest. A dusting of dark hair covered his well-toned abs, thickening as it disappeared inside the waistband of his jeans. She ran her fingers through it and gave a light tug.

A rough sound tore from Ryan's throat. He spun them around, tossing her onto the bed. Before she could move, he gripped her jeans and tugged them off, leaving her in only her bra and panties.

"So fucking sexy," he whispered, nipping at her through the satin of her bra before he popped the clasp, freeing her breasts. He took them in his palms, bringing her nipples into aching peaks with his touch. "I've been about to lose my mind this past month, wanting to touch you."

"Me, too." She reached for him, sliding her hands over the smooth skin of his back.

"You're even sexier than I imagined," he murmured as his hands ventured lower, tugging at her panties. He palmed her ass and squeezed, making her gasp.

Her? Sexy? She'd been called cute. Athletic. Pretty. But Ryan was looking at her like she was a Victoria's Secret supermodel, and then her panties were off, and she forgot how to think. He stroked her sensitive flesh, and she saw stars.

"Hurry." She reached for the button of his jeans.

He hissed out a breath. "Really trying not to."

"I think I can change your mind." She lowered his zipper,

and he scrambled out of his jeans. His boxer briefs strained with his hard cock. She gripped him through the cotton, stroking up and down, drawing a rough sound of pleasure from his lips. He thrust his hips against her hand, and the ache inside her intensified. She slid his briefs down, and his cock sprang free. So thick. So hard. For her.

It was like she went outside her body for a moment, seeing herself and Ryan naked in bed together. *Finally.* She knew she was grinning like an idiot, but she couldn't help herself.

"What?" Ryan said, his voice all low and scratchy.

"It's just...you and me..." She gestured between them, and without warning, a giggle bubbled up out of her. She slapped a hand over her mouth.

Ryan froze, his expression gone wary. "You having second thoughts?"

"What? No!" Her giggles vanished. "No...it's more like, I can't believe this is finally happening."

"Yeah." He reached for her, pulling her up against him, and then they were frantic again, kissing, touching, groping. He slid one big muscular thigh between her legs, his cock pressed against her belly, their bodies rocking together as their tongues tangled. He groaned into her mouth, and she couldn't wait another moment.

She dove for her backpack where she'd put it down beside the bed, reached into the outer pocket where she'd dumped the contents of an entire box of condoms, and grabbed one of the foil packets.

Ryan watched her through heavy-lidded eyes, an amused smile on his face. "You came prepared."

"Once a Girl Scout, always a Girl Scout." She ripped the packet open, and he sat back, allowing her to do the honors. She rolled it onto him, feeling him thicken even more beneath her touch.

Ryan was breathing hard, his eyes glittering dark as coal in the dim light of the hotel room. As soon as the condom was in place, he pounced, pinning her to the bed. "Emma," he whispered, his voice shaking slightly.

"Ryan." She wrapped her legs around his hips, drawing him closer until the weight of his shaft pressed against her belly.

He stayed that way for several long seconds, while her body burned and his cock pulsed against her. Then he bent his head and kissed her. He reached between them, positioning the thick head of his cock against her entrance. She gasped, pulling him closer, urging him on.

With another rough kiss, he pushed inside. Pleasure surged inside her as he filled her. He stroked slowly in and out, building a delicious friction between them that was so good, so good...

"Christ, Emma," he rasped, "you feel so fucking good." He thrust harder, his hips pressing painfully into her freshly inked skin.

"Tattoo," she panted.

"Shit. Sorry." He shifted his weight, which somehow seemed to bring him even deeper inside her on his next stroke.

"Don't apologize...oh God...yes..."

Ryan cursed under his breath then claimed her mouth for another heady kiss. His tongue stroked hers while he thrust inside her, and *oh my God*, it was like magic.

"Harder," she whispered against his lips.

He paused for a moment and met her gaze, his eyes impossibly dark, and then he started to move again, thrusting harder, faster, until stars were dancing behind her eyes. He lifted her hips, adjusting the angle of their bodies, and *oh shit*.

"Yes," she gasped. "More."

He reached between them, stroking her with his fingers while he pounded into her, and she shattered.

"Open your eyes," he said roughly. "I want to see you when I come."

She opened her eyes as her orgasm crested. Their eyes met. Ryan thrust again, hard, then stiffened as he found his own release. They clutched at each other, panting, their bodies entwined as they rode out the waves of passion together.

He collapsed on the bed beside her, one arm thrown across his face. "Fuck. That was amazing."

Yeah, it really had been, but to hear it from Ryan's mouth? Even more amazing. Her body still tingled with pleasure. "It really was."

* * *

Ryan came out of the bathroom to find Emma standing beside the bed, dressed in a slinky black dress that clung to her body just right. She'd put the black boots back on, and they nearly reached the bottom of the dress, revealing just a hint of her pale, smooth legs. *Fuck*, she was gorgeous.

"You look amazing," he said.

"Thanks. I figured this wouldn't bother the tattoo." She patted her hip.

"Smart thinking." He crossed the room and pulled her into his arms. He lowered his mouth to hers and kissed her until they were both out of breath and his dick was straining the front of his pants. "We'd better go to dinner now before we wind up naked again."

She nodded, reaching for her purse, a happy glow on her face.

And he'd put it there. He felt a primitive urge to pound his chest and shout it to the world. Instead, he took her hand and walked with her out of the hotel and down the street to the Onyx Bar. The place wasn't trendy by any means, but the food was excellent and the décor was offbeat, with a bit of the edgy feel Emma seemed to be craving. There was even a club downstairs if she wanted to go dancing later.

"Wow," she said as they stepped through the front door. "This is great."

The dining room was decorated mostly in black, aside from the white-tiled floors. The music was loud, the lighting low. The perfect place to sit close and whisper in each other's ears. The hostess led them to a small table near the back. A candle flickered in its center, casting shadows across the dark tablecloth.

Emma leaned in so that candlelight danced across her face. "I love this place already."

"The food's good, too."

"Great, because I'm starved," she said.

Their waitress arrived, and Emma ordered a strawberry martini. Ryan got a beer. Truthfully, as hard as it had been not to stay in bed with Emma all evening, he was starving, too, and the chance to take her out here in Charlotte was something he couldn't pass up.

"I think this whole 'friends with benefits' thing is the best decision we ever made," Emma said with a wink, a wide smile on her face.

"Yeah." He still had a bad feeling it might backfire on them at some point, but right now? Right now he was loving every minute.

They both ordered steak, and three martinis later, Emma sighed dreamily into the candle at the center of their table. "This was fantastic."

"Want to go dancing?" he asked.

Her eyes sparkled. "That sounds fun."

So they went to the nightclub downstairs, and they danced. This time, there was no pretense between them, and he couldn't keep his hands off her. Emma danced with a kind of wild abandon that he couldn't get enough of. She flung her hands in the air and twirled, totally lost to the beat. With a sly smile, she backed up, grinding her ass against him. His dick turned to granite inside his jeans.

She spun to face him then leaned in to whisper in his ear, "I want to try something new tonight."

"What's that?"

She grinned, her hips bumping against his. "Surprise me."

All the blood in his body settled into a deep ache in his groin. "Are you saying what I think you're saying?"

She nodded, a wicked gleam in her eyes, still dancing. He, on the other hand, was so turned on he could barely move. *Surprise me.* Oh, he would, but in the meantime, she kept surprising the hell out of him.

She settled in his arms, her hips still moving to the music. He drew her close, letting the rhythm of the music guide them as her hips wiggled to the beat. "I need you in my bed," he growled in her ear. "Now."

She sucked in a breath, her eyes sparkling in the reflection of the disco ball overhead, and made a beeline for the door. He hooked an arm around her shoulders and hustled her back to their hotel, not stopping until they were inside their room with the door locked behind them. Emma stood in the middle of the room, cheeks flushed, watching him expectantly.

His entire body pulsed with barely leashed need. He reached for the thin, blue scarf that she'd discarded by the bed after they arrived. Emma followed his actions with her gaze, her chest heaving. He took the scarf and covered her eyes, tying it behind her head. She sucked in a breath, reaching for him.

"No rushing me this time, baby," he said, walking her

slowly backward until they'd reached the bed. He reached behind her for the zipper of her dress, finding nothing but fabric.

"No zipper," she said, her voice breathless. "It's stretchy. It just goes over my head."

Interesting. He could work with that. He fisted his hands in the clingy black fabric and slowly worked it up her thighs, baring the black lacy thong she wore beneath. He groaned, pausing to touch her. Emma gasped, her knees parting.

He went slowly over her hips, careful not to snag the edges of the bandage covering her tattoo. It would be time to take that off soon, but first things first. He slid the dress up her sides and over her head, leaving her in nothing but a black lacy bra and thong, leather boots, and the scarf still tied over her eyes.

He stood there for a moment, just drinking her in. *So fucking sexy.*

"Please," she whimpered.

"Please what?"

"Touch me."

He gave her a nudge with his hands, and she sat on the bed. "No, baby, I want you to touch yourself."

She sucked in a breath. "What?"

"You said you wanted to try something new." He unzipped her boots one at the time and tugged them off, then trailed his fingers up her legs and over her stomach.

She squirmed.

He popped the clasp and removed her bra then slid her thong down her legs. "Pretend I'm not here," he murmured. "Show me how you please yourself."

"Ryan..."

He lay on the bed beside her, his own body strung so tight that the lightest touch might make him snap yet completely caught up in the moment, watching as she lay back on the bed, her fingers trailing down her stomach to dip between her legs.

"That's right, baby," he said. "Show me how you like it."

She touched herself, cautiously at first, as though still self-conscious about the fact he was lying here beside her, but soon she gave herself over to her pleasure, moaning as she grew more aroused.

His cock strained within the confines of his jeans, growing harder with each stroke of her fingers between her legs. He'd never been so mad with lust yet so totally focused on her pleasure.

"Ryan," she whispered, rolling toward him, "I want you to finish."

"My pleasure," he murmured, at last allowing himself to reach out and touch her. He ran his hands over her body, taking time to touch and explore. Emma shifted restlessly on the bed, having already brought herself too close to the edge, but he wasn't rushing. Not this time. He kissed his way around the perimeter of her new tattoo—that flower was going to be his downfall. Dangerously sexy. Intoxicating. He couldn't wait until it had healed so that he could touch it.

Finally, he settled between her thighs. Emma whimpered. He stroked her, and *fuck*, she was so wet for him. His cock thickened, pressing painfully against his zipper. Ignoring it, he kissed his way up her thighs until he reached her center, and then he put his mouth on her.

Emma gasped, fisting her hands in the sheets. He took his time, pleasing her until she writhed beneath him, panting his name. And then, with a moan, she came against his tongue. Her hips bucked, and her body tensed, and then she collapsed against the sheets with a breathless, "Holy shit."

He kissed his way up her belly to her mouth. "You're spectacular when you come."

Her cheeks grew even pinker. Then she reached up and removed the scarf from her eyes. "My turn." She went up on her knees and tied the scarf over his eyes.

Immediately all his other senses were heightened. His body ached, waiting for her touch.

"First, let's get you out of these clothes." She lifted his shirt over his head. Then her hands were on his jeans, lowering the zipper that had been torturing him ever since they got back to the hotel. *Hallelujah.*

She stroked him through his boxer briefs, and he gritted his teeth. He shucked his jeans and briefs, then he sat there, blindfolded, his dick impossibly hard and desperate for her touch.

"You're so sexy," Emma murmured, her voice tantalizingly close. "I could just sit here all night and look at you."

"Please don't." He managed a harsh laugh.

"Don't worry." He could hear the smile in her voice. "I like touching you even more." She took him in her hand, stroking up and down his shaft.

Fuck, yeah. "Harder," he said gruffly.

Emma picked up the pace, stroking him with one hand while she cupped his balls in the other, and ah, *fuck.* So good. His whole world had reduced to the feel of her fingers on him and the need blazing inside him, growing more insistent with each stroke of her hand.

And then, her hands were gone. He groaned, his dick straining into the emptiness left behind. Torture. This was torture, and he was loving every second. Her warm breath whispered across his aching flesh. He sucked in a breath and held it, waiting in the darkness of the blindfold, and then the head of his dick slipped into the wet heat of her mouth. He swore as her tongue swirled over him, licking and sucking. She took him deeper, and *fuck*, he was a goner.

He struggled to hold back, not to thrust himself against her. She slid him in and out of her mouth while her tongue worked him into a frenzy. Already he felt his orgasm building, tightening in his balls, burning through him as the pressure built.

Sucking in a breath, he gripped her shoulders, pushing her back. "Emma, baby, I'm about to come, and I want to be inside you when I do."

She released him from her mouth, and he lay there, too painfully aroused to move. Next thing he knew, he felt a condom being rolled down his aching length. Emma straddled him, sinking down onto him. And ah, *fuck*. He was close. Too close. He gripped her waist, slowing down her pace. She grumbled in protest.

He reached between them and touched her where their bodies joined. He found her clit and stroked, hitting a rhythm with his fingers that made her pant. She rode him hard, and he held on for the ride, barely daring to breathe, desperate to hold himself back until she'd joined him.

She swiveled her hips with a gasp, and then her body clamped down on him, spasming around his dick as she came. With a growl, he thrust inside her once, twice, and then his own orgasm came, ripping through him so powerfully that he lost all control of himself, his hips bucking against hers as he rode out the waves of red-hot release.

Afterward, as he lay there, limp, spent, and still blindfolded, he felt as if his whole horizon had shifted. He never would have imagined he'd have some of the hottest sex in his life with Emma Rush. And now all he could think about was doing it again.

CHAPTER TWELVE

I have a detour for us on the way home," Ryan told Emma the next morning after they'd checked out of the hotel.

"Oh yeah?" She climbed onto the bike behind him, ready to go pretty much anywhere he wanted to take her. "Where are we going?"

"You'll see."

The engine roared to life beneath them, and she hung on for the ride. In the past month, she'd become just as addicted to motorcycle rides as she had to the man giving them. Ryan guided them out of the hotel's parking lot and down South Boulevard, past a string of storefronts including House of Ink. They merged onto the highway, the morning air crisp and refreshing as it whipped across her skin. After about ten minutes, they left the highway and meandered through a business park on the outskirts of Charlotte, all but deserted at this hour on a Sunday.

And Emma officially had no clue where Ryan's detour was taking them.

He guided the bike into a big, empty parking lot in front of a rather nondescript four-story office building. Her gaze caught on a sculpture in front. It was silver and made up of moving pieces, like the figure had been carved into dozens of horizontal slices that rotated back and forth. A fountain sprayed from the front of the sculpture into a large pool.

Ryan parked and turned off the bike. "Cool, right? It's called *Metalmorphosis*."

Emma stared at the moving sculpture, mesmerized. "I love it."

"When the pieces all line up, it's the shape of a man's head."

"Oh." She watched the pieces move. "Yeah, I see it now."

He held his left hand out, as he always did to help her off the bike. She gripped it and climbed off. Together, they walked over to the sculpture and stood watching it. The pieces were shiny, almost like mirrors, reflecting the water below.

"You were having trouble coming up with an idea for the memorial," Ryan said, sliding an arm around her shoulders. "So I thought we could ride around this morning and see some interesting structures. Maybe something will give you a nudge in the right direction."

Wow. Her heart squeezed, filling her up with warmth. "That's really sweet of you."

He gave her a comical look. "Whatever you do, please don't call me *sweet*."

She leaned in and kissed him. "Fine, but I really appreciate this." And it might be exactly what she needed. This sculpture was way too trendy for the Town Planning Committee's taste, but seeing the way the light played off the metal, reflecting the water, was definitely sparking something in her imagination.

After they left *Metalmorphosis*, Ryan took her to several more landmarks, everything from an old church to something called the *Reclining Bulls Statue*, which was as odd as its name suggested but oddly inspiring. By the time they rolled onto the highway headed for Haven, Emma's mind was buzzing with ideas, and she owed it all to Ryan.

Oh yeah, her crush was rapidly blooming into something bigger. Much bigger.

They got to her house just after one o'clock. Ryan had to hurry straight to Off-the-Grid for an afternoon of scheduled rock climbing lessons so Emma went inside to round up the girls and dish about her night in Charlotte. Except...she and Ryan hadn't discussed what would happen once they got home. Were they keeping things private or were they officially dating now?

Dating? Or just hooking up? Crap. She slapped a hand to her forehead. She was so bad at this, but whatever it was, it was *amazing*, and screw it, she needed to share with her friends.

Girls' night? she texted Gabby, Carly, and Mandy.

I'm in! When and where? Gabby replied almost immediately.

My place. I'm thinking Magic Mike XXL, pizza, and ice cream? Emma texted. She'd been out last night. Tonight, she just wanted to curl up on her couch and hang out with her friends.

Yessss, Mandy texted. I'll bring the ice cream.

Within minutes, they had the whole thing planned. Emma fist-pumped the air, then went to her room to freshen up and change into a stretchy cotton skirt. The tattoo had been sore ever since she put her skinny jeans back on to ride home from Charlotte. Overall, it wasn't bothering her too much, though. Ryan had only let her take a quick, lukewarm shower this morning, telling her to avoid hot water until it had healed, which was a bummer, but it would all be worth it in the end.

She stood in front of the mirror in her bedroom, letting the skirt sit low on her hips so that she could admire the little red poppy on her skin. She loved it even more than she'd thought she would, and the way Ryan had looked at it...

Phew.

They'd shared one of the most memorable nights of her life. Wherever their relationship went from here, she'd never regret a single moment they'd spent together.

With a happy sigh, Emma went into the living room, Smokey at her heels. She sat down on the couch with a notepad and pencil to start sketching out new ideas for the memorial, and...the next thing she knew, Smokey was meowing in her face. She blinked, glancing at the clock.

It was a few minutes past five, and apparently she'd just slept away the whole afternoon. Her neck protested as she got up, kinked from dozing in an awkward position on the couch. So perhaps she hadn't gotten much sleep last night...

Her phone showed three new text messages. Predictably, the first two were from her friends, still discussing details for tonight. The third was from Ryan. Her heart skittered in her chest at the sight of his name.

Tomorrow after work—your place or mine?

A warm thrill shot through her. Mine, she replied.

I'm there, he texted right back.

She couldn't wait. In the meantime...

She hurried to order pizzas to be delivered and rented *Magic Mike XXL* through her Apple TV. On cue, the doorbell rang. Smokey darted for the safety of the bedroom.

Emma went to open the door. Carly stood there, carrying a bottle of white wine.

"Hi." Emma motioned her in.

"So are we celebrating or commiserating?" Carly asked.

"I think I know the answer to that question," Gabby said, coming up the walkway. "I heard Ryan took the day off yesterday and went to Charlotte with you to get a tattoo."

"You got a tattoo?" Carly exclaimed.

"Yes, but—"

"More importantly," Gabby interrupted, "what *else* did you and Ryan do in Charlotte?"

Emma laughed, ushering them inside. "You ladies cut right to the chase, don't you? Shouldn't we wait for Mandy to get here before I tell all?"

"Yes, yes, you should," Mandy said from the doorway, two tubs of ice cream in her arms.

Emma took the ice cream from her and walked to the kitchen to put it in the freezer. Carly opened the bottle of wine and poured four glasses. Wineglasses in hand, they headed for the living room.

"So, I got a tattoo yesterday," Emma said.

"Cool! What is it?" Carly asked.

"And where?" Mandy added.

"It's a red poppy, on my hip." She pushed down the waistband of her skirt to show it to them.

"Oh, wow. I love it," Gabby said. The others agreed.

"Did it hurt a lot?" Carly asked. "I've been thinking of getting one, too."

"Not too bad. It was pretty quick, anyway, for such a small tattoo." Emma took a gulp of her wine. "And to answer Gabby's other question—yes, Ryan and I spent the night in Charlotte, and yes, it's exactly what you're thinking."

"Oh my God!" Gabby squealed, clapping her hands together in delight. "Tell us everything."

"Well"—Emma could feel herself blushing already—

"maybe not *everything*, but let's just say, the sex was everything I was hoping for and then some."

"Way to go." Mandy looked impressed. "It's about time you had a little excitement in your life."

"Yes, it was." Emma chewed her bottom lip. "You guys want to hear something funny?"

They all nodded, hanging on her every word.

"I've had a crush on Ryan since high school." There, she'd said it. She'd never told a soul about her crush on Ryan. As a teen, it had seemed ridiculous. He was so much older and cooler. And as an adult, she'd just felt silly still harboring feelings for her teenage crush. But now? Now she'd slept with him, and the idea of her and Ryan was definitely not farfetched.

"Really?" Gabby's eyes were wide. "Wow. I never would have guessed."

"This changes things," Mandy said, tapping her wineglass thoughtfully.

"How so?" Emma asked.

"Because now this is much more than a casual hookup between two people who happen to be friends," Mandy said.

"She's right," Carly said. "You've been fantasizing about him since high school? That's a long time. You're probably already halfway in love with him, aren't you?"

"What? No!" Somehow she managed to dump her glass of wine in her lap. "Crap."

They were all staring at her.

"Seriously, I am not in love with Ryan. Not even close." She stood to go change out of her wine-stained skirt just as the doorbell rang. "That's the pizza."

"I've got it," Mandy said, waving her off.

Emma hurried into her bedroom and closed the door behind her. Smokey lay curled in the middle of her bed, eyeing her cautiously, as if she feared Emma might invite these intruders into her inner sanctum. Emma walked to the closet and pulled out a jersey dress, tossing her wine-stained clothes into the laundry basket.

She wasn't in love with Ryan. She'd always been pretty honest with herself about her emotions. So she could admit—to herself at least—that she had real feelings for him, feelings that went far beyond a casual hookup, but it wasn't love. Not yet. It definitely could be, if she stayed with him for too long. So she'd have to be careful not to let that happen because she was pretty sure the whole point of "friends with benefits" was to keep messy feelings out of the equation. And if she got into the program at the University of Georgia, she'd be leaving Haven in a few months anyway.

She walked back out to find the girls gathered in the kitchen, filling plates with pizza.

"So you were telling us about how you're not in love with Ryan?" Mandy said with a grin.

"I'm really not. This is just a fling, an adventure before I leave town."

"Mm-hmm," Mandy said. "I have a feeling in a few months, we'll be saying, 'We told you so.'"

* * *

Ryan paced the aisles of the grocery store after work on Monday. This afternoon he'd remembered something Emma had said to him a few weeks ago at Off-the-Grid, about how she wanted to have the kind of sex she'd only read about in romance novels. He had no friggin' clue what kind of sex people had in those books, and he sure as hell couldn't ask anyone about it so he was just going to have to wing it. Because he wanted to be the man who gave Emma the kind of mind-blowing sex she'd only read about.

Yeah, he'd lost his mind.

And that was why he found himself at the grocery store after he'd left Off-the-Grid, shopping for "accessories" for his evening with Emma. If Ethan or Mark saw him now, he'd never hear the end of it. He paid for his purchases and left quickly, tucking the bag into one of the saddlebags on his bike before heading toward Emma's apartment.

He was feeling all sorts of things as he rode toward her building. Desire. Excitement. And a small amount of trepidation that things wouldn't be the same here on their own home turf. That he'd violated some kind of bro code by sleeping with his best friend's little sister, the same sister Derek had warned him to keep his hands off of.

All of that faded away when he pulled into her driveway and saw her standing there in the doorway, wearing a white tank top and a striped skirt that sat low enough on her hips to show off her new tattoo.

His. She was his, and she was perfect.

He walked to her and pulled her into his arms. "Hey."

"Hi." She twined her hands around his neck, smiling up at him. "What's in the bag?"

"A few, uh, things."

"I'm intrigued," she said, peeking down at the plastic grocery bag in his right hand.

He stepped her backward through her front door and closed it behind them. "That's better."

Then he set the bag down and flattened her against him as he lowered his mouth to hers. Her lips parted, inviting him inside, and damn, he was lost. He kissed her until all the chaos in his brain had stilled, replaced by the fire Emma had ignited inside him. *This woman.* Would he ever get enough?

"Okay, I'm curious," Emma said when they'd come up for air. She bent down to pick up the bag, poking through it with a big smile on her face. "Whipped cream. Chocolate syrup. And champagne. Well, well, what did you have in mind tonight, Hot Stuff?"

What he might have gained in intent, he definitely lost in presentation. Dropping a plastic shopping bag of sex foods in her foyer was *definitely* not how the guys in her romance novels did it. He scrubbed a hand over his eyes. "Um—"

"For the record," she said as she walked toward the kitchen with the bottle of champagne in her hands, "whatever it is, I am definitely interested."

He gave himself an internal high five. "That so?"

"Yes." She wrapped a hand towel around the neck of the champagne bottle and popped the cork. Then she went up on her tiptoes to take two champagne flutes out of a top cabinet and filled them. "To an evening of sugary experimentation," she said, holding one of the glasses out to him.

"Sounds a bit kinky," he said with a grin as he clinked his glass against hers.

"Indeed." She took a drink as a smile played about her lips. "You are always full of surprises, Ryan Blake."

"You bring it out in me."

They stared at each other for a moment. Then she walked into his arms. "What the hell are we standing around in the kitchen for?"

"Good question." He picked up their champagne flutes and waited for her to lead the way to her bedroom. She paused in the hallway to pick up the bag of goodies he'd brought. He followed her through the doorway into a very girly bedroom with a flowery bedspread, lacy curtains, and a pissed-off-looking gray cat sprawled in the middle of the bed, regarding him through icy blue eyes.

"Get lost, Smokey," she said, shooing the cat with her hands. It glared at her and slunk off into her closet. Emma pulled the bottle of chocolate syrup out of the bag, squirted some onto her finger, and sucked it into her mouth.

His dick surged against his zipper. "Strip."

Her eyes widened. She set the bottle on the table beside her bed then reached down and hooked her thumbs into the waistband of her skirt. With a little smile, she eased it down over her hips, revealing white, lacy panties. It was all he could do not to put his hands on her, but watching her undress herself was its own form of foreplay.

She dropped her skirt to the floor then slowly lifted her top over her head, leaving her in nothing but panties, and, *fuck*, she was stunning. That tattoo...

She wiggled out of her panties, and then, completely naked, she sat on the edge of her bed, crossing one leg over the other. "Your turn." She pointed a finger at him. "Strip."

He shucked his clothes in record time, his dick growing even harder beneath her heated gaze. As he watched, she pushed the comforter off the end of the bed and beckoned for him to join her. He slid onto the bed beside her, his thigh skimming hers, and that contact alone was enough to make his pulse pound.

Emma reached for the bottle of chocolate syrup, a wicked smile on her face. She pushed him down flat on the bed and drizzled sauce across his chest, stopping just short of his dick.

He sucked in a harsh breath. "Fuck. Maybe we should have warmed it up first."

Her mouth formed a sexy little O. "Cold?"

Yes, but indescribably hot at the same time. "Not anymore."

"I'll warm you up," she said, and bent her head. Her tongue swirled across his chest, licking at the sauce. *Holy fucking shit.* He fisted his hands in the sheets and squeezed his eyes shut. By the time she'd reached his belly button, he was done for.

He sat up, flipping the tables before she took him past the point of no return.

"My turn." He reached for the bottle.

Emma lay back, her cheeks already flushed, her breathing rapid. He trailed syrup over her breasts and stomach, making her squirm. "Okay, you're right. It's cold."

He kissed her breast, then tugged her nipple between his teeth and gave it a slight nip. Emma lurched beneath him, her hips arching up to meet his. He took his time sucking all the chocolate from her breasts. At some point, he dipped his hand between her legs, stroking her as he followed the chocolate trail across her body.

Emma writhed beneath him, her hips pushing against his hand. He gave her the pressure that she needed, sliding two fingers inside her as he went.

He kissed his way down her belly, and she arched up off the bed. "Ryan—"

"Go ahead, baby," he murmured. "Come for me."

And she did. Her hips bucked against his hand, and the expression on her face as she came was so fucking gorgeous. He pressed himself against her, letting her pleasure fuel the need already pounding in his dick.

"Wow," she whispered.

"That was hot."

She rolled over, squirted chocolate syrup onto her palms, and wrapped her hands around his dick. "You know? I think I'm a fan of chocolate sauce."

He groaned. "Me, too, baby. Me, too."

* * *

Emma lay in bed, a little bit chocolatey and a whole lot satisfied. "That was amazing."

"As good as what you read about in romance novels?" Ryan asked, an oddly serious look on his face.

"What?" Where in the world did that question come from?

"You told me that day at Off-the-Grid," he said. "You wanted the kind of sex you'd read about in romance novels."

Ooh. Yes, she did remember saying that. At the time, she'd mainly been trying to push his buttons, but it was true, too. She'd wanted the kind of toe-curling, mind-blowing sex she'd read about and hadn't been sure was possible in real life. Was this why he'd shown up with champagne and gooey accessories? If so, that was...well, it was adorable. And also maybe the most romantic and thoughtful thing a man had ever done for her. *Oh, her heart*..."Actually, I think we crossed that one off in Charlotte. You've got nothing to worry about in that department."

He smiled, his expression softening. "Good to know. Shower?"

"That's a definite yes." She was a sticky mess, and he probably was, too. She slid out of bed and led the way into the bathroom. "How long do I have to take these quickie, lukewarm showers?"

"Another week or so," he said. "So as much as I'd like to utilize this shower for a different kind of quickie, better not."

She pouted. "That's a tragedy."

"Indeed." He was smiling, but his cock was already hard again, jutting toward her in silent invitation.

"Maybe we should wash each other? You know, to be speedy." She hopped in, crooking a finger in his direction.

"I like the way you think." He stepped in behind her and grabbed the bar of soap.

She gasped as his hands slid up her sides to cup her breasts. The lukewarm water was a definite turnoff, but his hands were hot enough to make up for it. She helped herself to some suds and took him in her hands.

He was rock hard beneath her touch, but equally intent on keeping his word to get them in and out of the shower quickly. So they lathered up—while working themselves into a lather—rinsed off, and dashed back to her bed, where Ryan took her right outside herself with pleasure all over again.

"That was amazing," she murmured against his neck as they lay tangled in each other's arms.

"It's the craziest thing," he said, stroking her hair. "You and me, together like this."

"Maybe that's part of what makes it so great. We've known each other so long, there's none of that awkward getting to know you stuff."

"Maybe." He sounded thoughtful. "I've never slept with a friend before. Hell, you're my only female friend, Em. I guess we just proved that saying about men and women not being able to be friends without wanting to sleep together."

"Yes." She giggled. "Although, I have to admit, I've never had sexy thoughts about Ethan or Mark."

His arm tightened around her. "Good."

They were quiet for a minute, just lying in each other's arms.

"We're kind of alike, I guess," he said finally. "No real family to call our own. Just our own little makeshift family of fellow misfits."

"Yeah." Her throat felt tight. She'd been lucky; she hadn't ended up in foster care, but she'd always felt out of place in the Mackenzies' home. They'd been wonderful, but they weren't family. Ryan understood. "The misfits of Haven. That's us."

"It made it bearable . . . having you guys," he said.

"Even if you treated me like I was a pesky little gnat?" She nudged him playfully.

"You were a pesky little gnat in high school." There was humor in his voice. "But you turned out okay."

"That's good to know." She giggled, glad they could find humor in such a serious topic. Then she sobered. "Do you think about your mom a lot?"

He was silent for a few seconds. "Yeah. You?"

She nodded, as tears burned in her eyes. "Every day. I could have used her advice a time or three when you were making me crazy last month, trying to keep us in the friend zone."

Ryan frowned. "I think she'd have told you I was right."

"In high school? Yes. But not now." No, she had a feeling her mom would approve of Emma dating modern-day Ryan very much.

"She'd have kicked my ass if she didn't approve," he said with a smile.

"This is true." Her mom had been feisty, and opinionated, and fiercely protective of Emma and Derek.

"You know, there weren't many parents who liked me back then, and let's face it, they weren't wrong. I was bad news. But your mom . . . she was all right. She wasn't crazy about Derek hanging out with me, but she didn't write me off either. In fact, she had my back a few times, tried to point me in the right direction. I'll never forget that."

"Really?" Hot tears splashed over her cheeks. "She never told me."

"She was one of the good ones," Ryan said softly, reaching up to wipe her tears away.

"Yeah, she was. Not many people know what it feels like, losing your mom when you're still a kid." She'd been fifteen. Ryan had been eleven. Maybe the hardest time to lose a parent, in that delicate age between childhood and adolescence.

"Hell of a thing to have in common, but there it is." He tugged her in closer.

"Well, it's nice somehow…to be able to talk about it with someone who understands. I don't know, that doesn't really make any sense, does it?"

"Makes perfect sense to me," he said.

"I'm glad," she whispered, holding on to him. She smiled against his chest. "Another advantage of this 'friends with benefits' thing…deep conversations we'd never have with someone we'd only been dating a few days."

"Yeah."

They lay there for a while, naked and entwined, talking about everything from her brother to his future plans at Off-the-Grid. It was nice, and comfortable, and…intimate.

"Hungry?" he asked as the sky outside her bedroom window glowed with the golden tones of sunset.

"Starved. Want to go to Rowdy's?"

"Yeah." Something in his expression loosened, as if it were a relief for him, too, that they could maintain the casual aspects of their friendship even while they were burning up the sheets together.

They dressed, and she tamed her sex-rumpled hair before they walked outside. "Um." She eyed his bike, then looked down at her skirt. "How about I drive this time?"

"Deal," he agreed. They chatted easily on the short drive into town, and she parked in the public lot beside the Town Square. "Any new ideas for the memorial?" he asked as they walked past its future site.

"I'm working on a new design that I'm kind of excited

about." *Really* excited about, if she were being perfectly honest with herself, which made her doubly nervous to show it to the Town Planning Committee.

"That's great," Ryan said, giving her hand a squeeze.

"Your little detour yesterday really worked. Thank you."

"Any time." They walked hand-in-hand through the door into Rowdy's, passing Ethan on his way out, carrying a to-go box.

He broke into a wide grin, his gaze passing between them. "So the rumors are true then."

"Fuck you," Ryan said, flipping him off.

"Nah. I'll stick with Gabby. You two lovebirds enjoy yourselves." With a wave, he was gone.

Emma shook her head with a smile as the hostess showed them to a table. Not their group's usual table, but a smaller one, near the back. It felt...odd. Like this table for two made the shift in their relationship real in a way all the sex somehow hadn't.

Ryan looked shaken by it, too. "Huh," he said as he sat across from her.

Okay, so there was definitely going to be an adjustment phase for them. "At least we know each other well enough to just say, hey, it's weird sitting at a different table?" She tilted her head with a smile.

"Yeah." He looked relieved. "That is good."

"And you don't have to ask me what I want, because you already know I want to share a platter of wings. And I don't have to worry about getting wing sauce on my face and looking like a slob in front of my date because, well...you're *you*." She winked at him.

"Good to know."

Their waitress approached, a girl named Tina, who often served them. She glanced between them, one eyebrow raised, as she took their order. Small town like this, they were certain to get plenty of raised eyebrows, but Emma didn't mind.

"How's Trent?" she asked once Tina had left. "I haven't seen him around much lately."

Ryan frowned. "He's spending too much time at that damn club, if you ask me."

"It's not the best use of his free time, but really, there are so many worse things he could be doing."

"Believe me, I know. I guess I just want him to be more mature than I was at his age. I want him to realize he's making a dumb-ass mistake by not sticking with college."

"College isn't everything."

Ryan looked down at his hands. "Hell, I know that. I never went, and I turned out okay. But Trent had a four-year education at a great school just dumped in his lap, and he's throwing it away."

"I know." She knew because, at Trent's age, she would have given anything for the opportunity to attend college. "I get it. But he has to decide for himself, and if you push too hard, it's going to backfire on you."

Ryan scrubbed a hand over his jaw. "Know that, too."

She laid her palm over his. "You love him. You want what's best for him. But you guys just found each other. Try to enjoy having him here and let his parents worry about kicking his butt when he's stupid, okay?"

CHAPTER THIRTEEN

By the time Emma and Ryan had finished their meal, they'd bumped into no fewer than three people they knew. This was par for the course in a town like Haven, but it also meant word of their relationship was going to spread far and fast. She didn't necessarily mind, but how did Ryan feel about it?

"You want to swing by the bakery for something sweet?" he asked after he'd paid the check (and no, she wasn't used to that yet either).

"The answer to that question will always be yes," she answered with a smile.

"Thought so, but I know better than to make assumptions where women are concerned."

She stood and shrugged into her denim jacket. It had been in the eighties earlier today, but here in the mountains, the temperature always dropped after dark. Ryan slid his hand into hers, and together they strolled down the sidewalk from Rowdy's to A Piece of Cake.

Inside the bakery, Carly greeted them with a friendly wave.

"You're here late tonight," Emma commented. Usually her friend opened the store, arriving at some ungodly hour to bake then went home by midafternoon.

"I'm short-staffed this week," Carly said. "But I'll make up for it later this month when I'm in LA with Sam."

Emma gazed at the contents of the dessert counter, her mouth watering. "What's good?"

"All of it, of course," Carly said with a smile. "But these lemon buttercream cupcakes are pretty delicious, if I do say so. I'm also partial to the carrot cake with cream cheese frosting."

In the end, Emma and Ryan each got a lemon buttercream cupcake to go so that they could take them outside to sit in the square. The need for fresh air was in her blood. His, too, if his lifestyle was any indication. Carly gave her a not-so-subtle wink and a thumbs-up as they headed out with their goodies.

"I take it you already told your friends about us," Ryan said drily as they walked toward an empty bench.

"I did. You don't mind, right?"

"Nah." He sat on the bench, looking at his cupcake as if he had no idea how to eat it. "Cupcakes didn't have this much frosting when we were kids."

"I usually eat the icing first and then the cake," she said, licking at the lemon buttercream. *Mm.* It was delicious. The perfect blend of sweet and tart.

"That sounds sacrilegious somehow." He peeled back the paper and took a big bite of his cupcake, icing and all.

"Sometimes I like to enjoy the best part first." She licked more icing.

"Aren't you supposed to save the best for last?" he asked, his eyes tracking to her tongue.

"I think that's a silly saying. What if you never get the

chance to enjoy the best part because you waited too long?" She'd lost enough people in her life to know that time was not something to be taken for granted.

"Never thought of it that way." He kept shoveling his cupcake into his mouth.

She finished eating her icing, then started in on the cake.

"The memorial's going to look great over there," Ryan said, staring over at the grassy area she'd soon be transforming into Haven's memorial garden. "I'm proud of you, you know? You've really made something of yourself here."

"Thanks." Her heart squeezed. "I have Mary and Lucas to thank for that. When they gave me my first job back in high school, I never imagined that I'd still be working at Artful Blooms ten years later. I thought I wanted to be a teacher. Did I ever tell you that?"

"No. You'd have made a good teacher, though, I think."

"I took the job at Artful Blooms thinking I'd save up for a few years then get my teaching degree. I never planned to stay, but I'm so glad I did. I can't imagine doing anything else."

"Generally the best things in life have always taken me completely by surprise," Ryan said, staring out across the square.

"And the worst."

His brow furrowed. "Definitely the worst."

"So what you're saying is, the things we plan for end up being the mediocre parts of life?" She smiled as she popped the last bite of cupcake into her mouth.

"Guess so. That's not so romantic, is it?"

"Maybe not, but I think you're right."

"I like being taken by surprise. You, Emma Rush, definitely caught me by surprise this year. This"—he leaned in and kissed her—"totally blindsided me. And now I can't fucking get enough."

* * *

Ryan spent the next week working his ass off at Off-the-Grid and spending every free moment with Emma. And not just screwing her brains out—although they did plenty of that—but rock climbing together, sharing meals and laughs, and enduring plenty of amused looks from the rest of the group in the process.

Wednesday night saw them all gathering at Ethan and Gabby's place for game night. The women seemed pretty excited about it. Ryan would have rather had Emma all to himself that night, but this could be fun, too. As long as he got to take her home afterward.

Gabby and Emma had set up a pretty impressive spread of food in the kitchen. There were all kinds of chips, dips, wings, cookies, and a cooler full of beer. He filled a plate, cracked open a beer, and ambled into the living room. Ethan was jumping around in front of the TV, playing some kind of interactive video game. Trent sat on the couch, engrossed in his cell phone.

"Where's Mark?" Gabby asked, propping her hands on her hips as she surveyed the room.

"He told me to make an excuse for him," Ryan said.

"Nice excuse," Emma said with a giggle.

Ryan shrugged. "He's not so much into games."

"Ethan told me he's big into video games," Gabby said, looking miffed. She whipped out her cell phone, presumably to call Mark.

"He is," Ethan agreed, jumping into the air. His character on the TV screen did the same, leaping over an obstacle in his way. "And the designer of his favorite video game happens to be my fiancée, although..." He dodged to the left, and his character took a hit to the nuts, knocking him off his platform into the water below. "Fuck. I can't remember if I ever told Mark that Gabby helped write *King of the Desert*."

Ryan took a drink from his beer. "I can't remember if I mentioned video games when I told him about tonight either. Might have just said games."

Emma rolled her eyes. "Men suck at communication. Who wants to play Cards Against Humanity?"

"Me!" Gabby gave an enthusiastic thumbs-up, phone pressed to her ear. "Mark, you better get your butt over here. We've got food, beer, and video games. Everyone else is here, and you should be, too." She ended the call. "Voice mail, dammit."

"I'll make sure he comes next time," Ethan said, again jumping through his virtual obstacle course. "He needs to get out more."

"Is it because of the war?" Gabby asked cautiously. "Does he have PTSD?"

Ethan stopped, causing his character to get whacked and fall into the water again. "Not sure I'd go as far as PTSD, but he's definitely got some issues."

"Has he talked to someone?" Gabby asked.

"I think he talked to a shrink at Fort Dix when he was stationed there after he got back stateside," Ryan said. "He's doing good, all things considered."

"I never asked what happened," Gabby said. "You know, his scar and everything..."

"He's never told us the details," Ethan said. "But I think it was pretty bad. It's not just the scar on his face. His leg is messed up and there were other injuries, too. He had to leave the Special Forces so when it was time for him to reenlist, it wasn't too hard for me to convince him to come out here and join us at Off-the-Grid."

"For what it's worth," Emma said, "and not to downplay

what he went through in the war at all, but he was kind of a loner in high school, too. I think it's just his nature."

"That's true," Ryan agreed. The only time he'd ever seen Mark come out of his shell had been with Jessica Flynn, his high school sweetheart. Then he'd pushed her away, too, when he enlisted.

Gabby sat on the couch, rubbing her hands over the front of her skirt. "Well, I hope he comes. He should be here with us."

"I agree." Ethan went back to jumping through obstacles.

Emma sat on the floor beside the coffee table and dumped out the contents of the Cards Against Humanity box. "Has everyone played?"

"Nope." Ryan sat beside her.

Gabby looked from him to Emma, and she might as well have had those cartoon hearts in her eyes. Ryan stiffened. He didn't mind that she knew, that everyone in the damn room knew he and Emma were hooking up, but okay...sometimes it was a little weird.

"I've played," Trent said, putting his cell phone down for the first time all evening. "It's pretty cool."

"That's high praise coming from you," Emma said with a giggle. She ran through a quick overview of the rules as she passed out cards.

Ethan grumbled as he turned off the video game and came to join them at the coffee table.

"You'll have fun," Gabby told him. "It's not a board game, and you're welcome to get as raunchy as you like."

He grinned. "Well, in that case..."

They played a few rounds—and the game indeed got raunchy. By the time Gabby won the third hand by playing her "An erection that lasts longer than 4 hours" card on Ethan's "A romantic candlelit dinner would be incomplete without _____," Trent was redder than a tomato, and

Emma had tears rolling down her cheeks she was laughing so hard.

There was a knock at the door, and Mark came in, looking sheepish.

"He knew better than to risk pissing you off," Ethan said with a laugh, pointing at Gabby.

She smiled smugly. "Get some food and a beer, Mark, and then I'll take you on in *King of the Desert*."

Mark's eyebrows went up.

"Fair warning," Ethan said. "She wrote the damn game."

"No shit?" Mark was actually smiling now.

"Yep," Gabby said. "Go on. I'll get it loaded up."

Emma scooted closer to Ryan. "This is fun."

"Yeah." He turned and looked at her, and the happy expression on her face made his chest feel all weird, like his ribs had just gotten too tight.

"I have news," she said, leaning in and dropping her voice.

"Yeah?"

"I met with the Town Planning Committee this morning, and they approved my new design for the memorial." She sucked her bottom lip between her teeth but couldn't quite hide the grin creeping over her face.

"That's fantastic." Before he'd even realized what he was doing, he had pulled her in and kissed her, right in front of the whole damn room.

"Aww, look at the lovebirds," Ethan announced, in case anyone had missed it.

All eyes turned to Ryan and Emma. Her cheeks turned pink, but she was still smiling.

"Yo, watch yourself." Ryan pointed his beer in his buddy's direction.

Ethan kept on laughing.

Ryan polished off his beer. It ought to make him fucking nuts to know that everyone in the room knew he was sleeping with Emma. Hell, it had only been a week and a half since he first had her in his bed. The whole thing was fucking insane.

But it wasn't. Because she was still Emma, and she was chatting happily with Trent while she boxed up Cards Against Humanity, and somehow this crazy group had become his family.

And he must be the luckiest son of a bitch in the world. No matter what, he had to make sure he didn't fuck it up when he and Emma went back to being just friends. He couldn't lose her—couldn't lose anyone in this room—but especially not Emma.

* * *

"Rowdy's after work tonight," Ethan said, popping his head into Ryan's office.

He nodded, his attention still on the spreadsheet in front of him. So far, their spring numbers weren't as high as they'd projected, and he needed to pinpoint where they were falling short. The zip-line was booked solid. Rock climbing lessons were still slow but ahead of their projections.

That only left Mark's survival skills classes. Ryan ran through their online ledger. Mark had booked one session last week, and none the week before. He'd been so busy helping Ethan with zip-line tours that none of them had noticed. *Dammit.*

This left them with a twofold problem: how to attract more interest in Mark's survival skills classes and how to free up Mark's time so that he actually had time to teach them. Maybe it was time to add another part-time staffer to help Ethan on the zip-line. Another salary might erode their meager profits, but summer vacation was fast approaching, and there ought to be a bounty of local college kids eager and willing to work on a zip-line all day. He'd spend some more time crunching numbers and scenarios and run it past the guys in their monthly meeting on Monday.

Several hours later, Ethan rapped on his door again. "Closing time. Let's go."

Ryan exited their accounting software and shut down his computer. By the time he made it to the lobby, Ethan and Mark were already there waiting.

"Trent took off a little while ago," Ethan said. "Got the feeling he had a hot date tonight."

"A date?" Ryan shrugged into his jacket. "With who?"

Ethan shrugged. "Beats me. Maybe that chick from the club."

"She's four years older than he is."

"So? They're both adults."

Yeah, but twenty-two still seemed a hell of a lot older than eighteen. Ryan followed them outside, where they each got into (or onto) their respective vehicles and headed for town. His thoughts strayed to Emma. What was she up to tonight? He pictured her as he'd left her last night, naked and satisfied.

Desire stirred in his belly. When would this crazy attraction start to fade?

He followed Mark's SUV into the lot in front of their condo building. Easier to park at home and walk the block and a half to Rowdy's.

"So, you and Emma, huh?" Mark said, sliding him a look as they waited for Ethan to park.

He nodded, grateful for once that Mark was a man of few words.

Ethan joined them, and they walked down Main Street and into Rowdy's, where the hostess showed them to their usual table. He glanced at the table in back where he'd sat with Emma last week.

Weird. This whole thing was still messing with his head.

Not that he regretted a single moment. Nope. This thing with Emma, whatever it was, it was one of the hottest relationships he'd ever had.

"You and Emma sure looked cozy last night," Ethan said once they had a pitcher of beer in front of them. "I hear you two lovebirds have been spending a lot of time together."

"Yo, since when do we discuss our love lives with each other?"

"Since my fiancée started knowing more about your love life than I do," Ethan said.

Ryan choked on a mouthful of beer. "Gabby knows— never mind, I don't want to know."

"Chicks share everything, you know that," Ethan said with a grin.

Which was why he didn't date girls. He just slept with them. *Hell.* "That's great, man. I guess you can just ask Gabby about it then."

Now it was Mark's turn to choke on his beer. When Ryan turned to glare at him, he looked an awful lot like he was trying to swallow a laugh.

"This is going to come back to bite me in the ass, isn't it?" Ryan said.

"Listen, I don't know what kind of kinky shit you two are into, but if it involves ass-biting..." Ethan broke off, laughing himself silly.

"You know what I mean, asshole."

"It probably is, yes," Mark said, his expression suddenly serious.

"It doesn't have to," Ethan said. "Just keep it casual if you don't want it to go anywhere. Usually these things fizzle after a month or two. If I were you, I'd try to let it take its natural course so that there are no hard feelings when you break up. I mean, this is Emma we're talking about. She's one of us. There's no cutting her out of the group just because you were an ass and fucked things up."

"That's exactly what I'm afraid of," Ryan muttered.

"So just play it cool, man. Maybe let her be the one to pull the plug. You're helping her sow her wild oats, right? So once she gets it out of her system..."

Mark looked between them. "What's this?"

"I heard the girls put her up to it, gave her a dare or some such shit," Ethan told him. "Emma said she wanted a hot fling, and Ryan was the lucky stud who wiped ketchup off her cheek."

"Christ. Gabby even told you about the ketchup thing?" Ryan polished off his beer and reached for the pitcher to pour himself another.

"I'm telling you. Chicks love to gossip."

"And I think you're turning into one." Ryan delivered the jab without any heat behind it because truly, the only one he was pissed at was himself. Emma had told him about the dare and the ketchup thing. He knew she was trying to live it up this year and try new things. But to hear Ethan say she was sowing her wild oats with him? That fucking stung. Because now that he thought about it, it was true. So she'd have her fun, get Ryan out of her system, and then find herself a respectable guy to settle down with.

That actually should have suited him perfectly because it would preserve their friendship when all was said and done. But it didn't. It burned in his gut like blistering hot coals.

CHAPTER FOURTEEN

*E*mma stopped at the Haven Deli after work on Thursday. Something she used to do about once a week: order takeout for dinner on her way home. But today, the prospect felt lonely. How had Ryan become such a big part of her life in such a short time? Doing her best to shake off the unsettled feeling, she made her way to the counter and placed her order for a hot pastrami sandwich to go.

"Emma?"

She turned, cringing inwardly because she recognized that voice, and yep...

Tristan Farrell, the world's most boring man—the man who'd dumped *her* for being boring—stood behind her in line, wearing a green button-down shirt and khaki slacks, a wide smile on his face. "Fancy seeing you here."

Emma mustered a smile of her own. "Small town."

"You look really great," he said, gesturing to her dress.

"Oh, um, thanks."

"So how have you been?" he asked.

"Good." *Great*, if she were being perfectly honest with herself. Her smile widened. "And you?"

"Never better." And he launched into a ten-minute update on his life while she prayed for her order to hurry up and get there. After he'd finished telling her about his mom's recent diabetes diagnosis, he paused. "Hey, you want to get together sometime?"

"What?" She drew back. Was he talking about a date? Because that ship had already sailed clear out of the harbor and halfway across the ocean...

"It's just"—he shifted from one foot to the other—"seeing you again made me realize I still have feelings for you. I just wondered if maybe you feel the same way."

"Sorry, but no, I don't." Maybe she shouldn't have been so blunt, but there it was. Seeing Tristan again had only reaffirmed for her how glad she was they weren't still together.

He scowled. "I've seen you around town with Ryan Blake."

She nodded. "Yes. Sorry, but I've moved on."

His scowl deepened. "Look, I don't get the obsession you chicks have with dating a dude with tattoos and a nice ride, but you know he's never going to be the guy you settle down with, right?"

Oh, he was starting to piss her off big time now. "Maybe not, but neither are you."

"I could be." He puffed his chest out with the words.

"With someone else, but not me."

His gaze traveled slowly over the clingy blue knit dress she wore, lingering on her red-painted toes. "I really like your new look."

"Is that what this is all about? You found me boring dressed as a tomboy, but if I sex things up a little, you want me back?"

"What? No, of course not..." But his sheepish expression told her everything she needed to know.

"We're finished, Tristan. With this conversation and everything else." Luckily, her sandwich arrived at just the right moment. She grabbed it and stormed past him out the door. For some ridiculous reason, she felt tears pushing at the backs of her eyes. Not because of Tristan, not exactly. But... well, because deep down she knew that what he'd said was true. Ryan wasn't the kind of guy who'd settle down with her. He hadn't been attracted to her at all until she'd changed her appearance to tempt him, and what did that say about her now?

She didn't want to look too hard at the answer to that question.

Instead, she drove home, changed into yoga pants and an old T-shirt, and settled in on the couch with her sandwich and a glass of wine to catch up on the latest episode of *Outlander*. Hey, if she didn't have her own man to keep her company tonight, she'd settle for her favorite fictional boyfriend, Jamie Fraser.

Still feeling lonely and unsettled, she polished off her second glass of wine. And her third. And then she apparently dozed off on the couch because, the next thing she knew, someone was knocking on her door, and Smokey's claws were embedded in her thigh. The disgruntled cat launched herself off the couch and hightailed it for the safety of the bedroom.

Still smarting from her run-in with Tristan earlier, Emma debated following her. Instead, she walked to the door and peeked through the peephole. Ryan stood on the other side looking devastatingly handsome, all sexy and windblown from his bike.

She yanked the door open. "Hi."

He gave her a funny smile. "You look all rumpled. Did I wake you?"

"Oh, um . . . I dozed off on the couch. What time is it?"

"Nine thirty." He was grinning now.

She scrunched her nose. "In related news, I'm officially an old lady."

"Or a woman who was up most of last night having her pretty brains screwed out?" He reached out and tugged her into his arms.

"I like that option better." She sighed as his arms closed around her. He smelled like leather and . . . beer. "Did you go out?"

"With Ethan and Mark," he said.

Then they were kissing, and she had a feeling she was going to continue to be sleep-deprived because she and Ryan just couldn't seem to keep their hands off each other. *I missed you.* It was all she could do to hold back the words. Because when she was in his arms, everything just felt so . . . right.

And she was so screwed because this was no casual fling for her. Ryan was one of her best friends, and now he'd given her the best sex of her life, made her feel alive in a way she never had before. And in this case, two plus two equaled . . . well, *love*. Or at least something headed very quickly toward love. Maybe a little part of her had always loved him, ever since she'd been the shy, dorky teenager that he'd seen only as a pest.

Later that night, as she lay naked and entwined with him in bed, she couldn't imagine ever doing this with anyone else. Which meant she needed to try to restore some sanity, pronto.

"Mind if I stay?" he asked.

"What?" Her mind was still in the future, imagining herself with Ryan, and he wanted to stay?

"Tonight," he said, his arm tightening around her. "You have another climbing lesson in the morning so we could just get ready together here."

"Oh. Yes, stay."

So he did. And when they woke up the next morning, they made love in the soft morning light, and it was gentler, sweeter, than it had ever been between them before. And she imagined starting every morning this way.

Oh yeah. She was in trouble. Big time.

After they showered, she dried her hair and pulled it back in a ponytail. It was only sensible to go rock climbing. But also . . . Tristan's words were still ringing uncomfortably in her ears, and she couldn't stand thinking that Ryan was only with her because she'd changed her appearance. She liked her new look. Loved it, actually. But maybe she'd go back to "traditional Emma," at least part time, to see what happened.

If he lost interest as soon as she reverted to yoga pants and ponytails, then it was all for the best. Because he was Ryan after all. He'd never had a real relationship that she knew of. He just had random hookups when the mood struck so it was ridiculous for her to expect him to want more than that with her.

They'd promised they wouldn't let this ruin their friendship when it was all over, and she meant it. She'd been his friend for years without him ever knowing about her feelings. And she could keep doing it, because Ryan was too important to lose.

* * *

Ryan watched as Emma disappeared over the top of the rock above him. "Way to go, Em. You nailed it."

Her face reappeared, peering down at him. She was grinning from ear to ear. "I can't believe I did that!"

This morning, he'd brought her to a different rock face on the property. This one was lower and less technically challenging, and so, with a little know-how in her skill set, she'd free climbed to the top.

No ropes. No harness.

It was a pretty kick-ass feeling. He knew. It still took his breath away every time he reached a summit, no matter how small. He boosted himself over the top, and they sat side by side, their legs dangling over the edge. "Nothing beats this feeling. Am I right?"

She nodded, staring out over the hill they'd just hiked. "It's pretty sweet. I never thought I could climb something like this."

"I knew you could. It's not that hard once you know how, and you've never shied away from a little hard work."

She turned to give him a sweet smile. "We have that in common."

"Comes from being on our own, I guess."

"Do you think you'll ever have a family of your own?" she asked, again looking out at the landscape before them.

He'd asked himself this question before, and more often recently. "Maybe," he answered honestly. Sometimes he wanted it more than anything. But he also knew the chances were high he'd screw it up. "You?"

"Yes," she answered without hesitation, and the wistful note in her tone tugged uncomfortably at his chest. "I want a family. I'm tired of being alone."

Alone. It was hard to think of her that way. Emma was always surrounded by friends. But friends weren't the same as family, no matter how much you loved them. He knew that as well as she did. Already the bond he shared with Trent was different from anything he'd ever experienced.

Family was a pretty awesome thing, maybe something he wanted more of. He was quiet while he let that thought sink in.

Emma looked over at him, her peaceful expression replaced now with a scowl. "You don't have to get all broody on me. I wasn't trying to sneak in a request for a commitment from you."

"What?" Somehow she'd gotten pissed off, and he had no idea how.

"I want a family *someday*, Ryan."

"And I hope you have one." It was true, even if right now the thought of her with any other man made him see red as a fucking lunatic.

She let it drop then, and they sat there on top of the rock for a few minutes in silence.

"So tell me about the memorial," he said, partly to fill the silence but also out of genuine curiosity. He'd been eager to hear more since she'd told him about it the other night at Gabby's house.

Her expression brightened. "It's going to be a semicircular cut of granite with all the servicemen and -women's names carved into it, facing a reflecting pool. I'm still fleshing out the gardens around it, but I see a lot of brightly colored flowers . . . and flags. Flags for all the divisions of the military."

"Sounds perfect."

"You inspired me that morning in Charlotte." She slipped her hand into his. "I loved the way *Metalmorphosis* reflected in the water, and it got me thinking about seeing the names on the memorial reflected like that, surrounded by flowers.

And the bottom of the memorial will appear as if it continues into the ground, like the cow statues you showed me. It kind of symbolizes how we all return to the earth after we die. Traditional but unique; that's what Lucas and Mary told me the Planning Committee wanted."

"I'd say you nailed it." He wasn't much for architecture, but he really liked what she'd described. And now he couldn't wait to see the finished product. It was going to be fucking fantastic.

They sat together on top of the rock until it was time for him to head back to Off-the-Grid to get ready for afternoon appointments. He started down first so that he could coach her if she got stuck, but she handled her descent like a pro.

"Thanks for bringing me out here," she said when they'd reached the bottom.

"You bet. So what's next?" he asked.

"Next?"

"You know, on your list of conquests. You've ridden on my bike, bested the rock, gotten your tattoo…"

"Oh." She nibbled her bottom lip. "I don't know. What do you think I should try next?"

"I'll give it some thought because I do love seeing you all shook up." He said it with a wink, and she laughed, but there was a bit of an edge in her tone, and he had a feeling she was still pissed about that moment up there on the rock, talking about families.

Had she been fishing for a commitment from him? Christ, he hoped not. He liked Emma, liked her a hell of a lot. Liked her way too fucking much to tie her down with his sorry ass.

"Moving to Georgia, I guess." She dropped that little bombshell with a casual shrug.

He stopped in his tracks, turning to face her. "Say what now?"

"I applied to the landscape architecture program at the University of Georgia. If I get in, I'll move there. There are more job opportunities for me to open my own business after I graduate."

"You're leaving Haven." He stared into her blue eyes, feeling like the ground had just fallen out from beneath his feet.

"If I get in."

"Well, of course you'll get in." He'd seen her work, and he didn't know shit about flowers, but he knew the gardens she designed were beautiful. She had talent and drive. She could do anything she put her mind to.

She shrugged. "We'll see. It's pretty competitive. And I'm not some kid fresh out of high school with shiny new SAT scores."

"No, you're a talented, ambitious landscape designer with ten years work experience."

"My grades sucked in high school," she said.

"So did mine. And we're both old enough now to realize that doesn't mean anything in the real world."

"Yeah, but to colleges it does. So we'll see. It's always been my dream to go through this program, get my degree, and open a landscape design company of my own."

"Well, I have to hand it to you. When you decide to shake things up, you go big. But this is awesome. I'm proud of you. And I have total faith that you're going to get in." Even if it might just break his heart a little bit when he had to let her go.

She was one of his best friends, after all. What would life in Haven be like without her?

"You want to do something tonight?" she asked after they'd hiked a few minutes in silence.

"Can't. I'm bartending from six until closing."

"Oh. Bummer."

Yeah, it was.

She looked over at him, a sexy smile curving her lips. "Maybe I'll stop by for a beer."

Now he was remembering that night not so long ago when she'd sat at the bar and driven him crazy in that form-fitting red top and jeans. The night he'd first felt this crazy pull of attraction between them. It just kept getting stronger every day. Didn't seem to matter that he'd had her in his bed. He still wanted her something fierce. "I'd like that."

"It's a date." She leaned in to give him a quick kiss.

They kept hiking, and soon the main building came into view. "So I'll see you later then?"

She nodded. "Thanks for the climb this morning. I never thought I'd do something like that, certainly not a few weeks after my first lesson."

"I have a feeling you can do anything you put your mind to."

She stopped and gave him a funny look. "Not *anything*, but you've got me thinking about the bluffs again. I want to do that with you this summer."

He stopped in his tracks. "The bluffs?"

"Yeah. I mean, nothing crazy like you and my brother used to do, but if there's an easy climb there I could do, I want to. And if not, I'll hike up. But I want to jump."

Yeah, she'd mentioned that when he brought her out there last month, but he hadn't thought about it since and didn't like it one damn bit. "Not a good idea."

"That's not what I asked," she said with a smile. "I'm jumping, and I want to jump with you. And I'd really like to do a little climb while I'm up there, if you know a place that's safe enough for a noob like me."

"Yeah, I know a spot." He did, and even though he still didn't like it, he'd keep her safe.

"Great." She pointed a finger at him. "So this is your warning. I'm doing it. You better teach me whatever I need to know in the meantime."

He could teach her how to climb and keep her safe from a fall from the rock. But how did he keep them from falling for each other? Because Emma was headed for bigger and better things soon, and he'd never, ever be the guy that held her back from chasing her dreams.

* * *

Ryan was halfway home when he noticed Emma's silver RAV4 on the road behind him. He'd been thinking about her all afternoon, about how sexy she'd looked as she climbed that rock this morning and the fire in her eyes when she'd decided to tackle the bluffs. The truth was, they had a lot of fun together, more fun than he'd ever had with a woman.

And she was leaving. He was having trouble wrapping his head around that fact.

When they passed the turnoff to her apartment, he realized she was following him. He couldn't take his eyes off the road to check his watch, but if memory served, it was only a few minutes after five, and he didn't have to clock in at The Drunken Bear until six. Which meant he had at least thirty minutes to spend with her.

He wanted to fuck her senseless, but really, any thirty minutes with her would do. A half hour talking about the weather or the stock market sounded good if it meant he got to be with Emma.

He pulled up in front of his condo and cut the engine. Emma's SUV pulled in beside his bike.

"You're working at six, right?" she said as she stepped out. She'd obviously been home since he saw her that morning because now she was wearing a white top and a long, blue skirt.

"That's right."

"Then we'd better hurry," she said with a wink as she walked toward his front door, already tugging at the top button on her blouse.

Fuck. What did he ever do to deserve her?

"I like the way you're thinking." He unlocked the door, and they tumbled inside in a tangle of groping hands and frantic lips. He pressed her against the wall, her legs wrapped around his hips, his cock pressed into her soft body, and he was lost.

Emma whimpered, rocking her hips against his. "Now," she whispered. "Right here."

"Now?" He could hardly hear past the blood thumping in his veins. His pulse throbbed, pounded, for her. For Emma.

She reached between them and unbuttoned his jeans. "Yes."

He slid his hands up her skirt. Her panties were the kind held together by just a string at her hips, a style he found particularly sexy and would usually take the time to enjoy, but today he hooked his finger underneath that string and yanked, ripping them right off her.

Emma let out a little gasp, then she wiggled her hips against him with a moan of pleasure. *Fuck.* He fumbled in his back pocket for his wallet and pulled out a condom, letting the wallet fall to the floor with a muffled thump.

He freed himself from his jeans, rolled on the condom, and pushed inside her.

"Yes," Emma whimpered. Her big, blue eyes met his. They stayed like that for a moment, bodies joined, him buried balls-deep inside her. Then she wrapped her arms around his neck, clinging to him as he pumped his hips, trying to hold back the frantic need that had overtaken him.

"More," she whispered. "Harder."

"Fuck, Emma," he said through gritted teeth.

"That's the idea," she said with a laugh that turned into a moan.

He thrust into her so hard his forehead smacked into hers. "Shit. Sorry."

"This never happens in the movies," she said with a giggle as she rested her head on his shoulder. "Do it again."

Christ. His forehead stung, but his cock was so hard it barely registered. He thrust into her again, harder, faster, and Emma hung on for the ride, urging him on with her whimpers and the way her heels dug into his ass. It felt so fucking good. His control snapped, and he pumped his hips so hard and fast he felt almost frantic.

She bounced in his arms to the rhythm he'd set, and then she tensed. Her body clamped down on him, and she screamed with pleasure. "Ryan! Oh..."

Boom. He came like a freight train going off the rails. A primal sound tore from his throat as pleasure slammed through him. His knees buckled, and he lowered them to the floor, his face buried in her hair, breathing in her fresh floral scent as his body trembled with aftershocks.

"Wow," she breathed against his neck.

"Yeah."

"We should do that again." There was laughter in her voice, but also awe.

"Fuck, yes." They stayed like that, not moving, until he'd recovered his wits enough to remember he had to get to work. He straightened, and Emma climbed off his lap, smoothing out her clothes. She grinned as she picked up the panties he'd ripped off her.

"A worthy sacrifice," she said as she walked into his bathroom to throw them away.

He stood, zipped his pants, and followed her into the bathroom to get rid of the condom. "Wish I didn't, babe, but I've got to run."

"Wham, bam, thank you, ma'am," she said with a smile. "I got what I came for."

"You are something else, Emma Rush." She just kept shocking the hell out of him. He stepped into his bedroom to clean up and change into fresh clothes then grabbed a super-sized candy bar and a can of Coke from the kitchen.

Emma stood by the front door. Her hair was rumpled, her cheeks flushed, her skirt still slightly askew. She looked thoroughly fucked, and it was all he could do not to take her to his bed and do it again.

Instead, he pulled open his front door. "So you'll stop by the bar later?"

She nodded then leaned in to whisper in his ear, "And you can wonder whether or not I'm still pantiless."

He yanked her into his arms and had just started to kiss her when he heard someone clearing their throat behind him. He looked past Emma to see Trent standing at the bottom of the stairs that led to the upstairs condos, a middle-aged couple behind him. The kid was staring at his feet, looking mortified.

Ryan stepped back from Emma. "Hey, Trent. I didn't see you there."

Trent shrugged. "So, um, my folks are here for a visit, and I wanted to introduce you."

Ryan looked again at the older couple standing behind Trent, the couple staring at him with an all-too-familiar air of condescension. Yeah, they probably knew exactly what he and Emma had just done. Way to make a great first impression. *Dammit to hell.*

CHAPTER FIFTEEN

*E*mma plastered a big, cheerful smile on her face as Trent introduced her and Ryan to his parents, Kate and Gary Lamar. "It's such a pleasure to meet you," she said.

"Yes, indeed," Kate replied, looking anything but pleased.

"I can't tell you how glad we all are to have Trent here with us for a little while," Emma said, giving Ryan's hand a squeeze.

"So you're Ryan's . . . girlfriend?" Kate paused before that last word, like it didn't quite fit.

Because it didn't. Even Emma knew that. She and Ryan were just . . . friends with benefits. Hooking up. *Having wild sex against the wall right below your feet.* She felt exposed, as if they somehow knew she wasn't wearing panties, that Ryan had ripped them off her just minutes earlier. But no. They didn't know that, not any of it, and it was none of their business. "Yes, I'm Ryan's girlfriend."

Ryan had gone oddly quiet, his brown eyes carefully blank. The tension in the air was thick enough to taste. She remembered Ryan telling her that Trent's adoptive parents had kept the two brothers apart, thinking Ryan was a bad influence. That was why they'd grown up not knowing each other, and that sucked, as far as she was concerned.

"How long are you guys in town?" Ryan asked, his tone even and polite.

"Through the weekend. We weren't expecting Trent to stay here in Haven this long." Another little barb lobbed in Ryan's direction by Kate Lamar. "We came to try to talk some sense into him."

"I like it here," Trent said.

"I'm glad you'll be here a few days because I'd really like to talk," Ryan said, "but right now, I'm afraid I'm running late for work."

"I thought you worked at that zip-line place Trent's been telling us about?" Gary Lamar said.

"I do, sir. I also bartend at the local pub a few nights a week."

"Oh." Kate's face scrunched into an expression of distaste.

"We'd love for you come out to Off-the-Grid tomorrow. Trent can show you around the place. He's been working hard," Ryan said.

Kate nodded. "Yes, I would like to see it."

"Great. I look forward to seeing you there." Ryan turned to give Emma a quick peck on the lips, then climbed onto his bike and cranked the engine.

Trent's parents recoiled, and Emma cringed. They'd spent Trent's whole life keeping him away from his brother, convinced he'd be a bad influence. And now that they'd come here to Haven, they'd stumbled on him making out with Emma, the two of them clearly looking like they'd just had an afternoon quickie. He was tattooed, and he rode a motorcycle, and he worked in a bar, but he was also one of the most honorable men she knew.

Trent was lucky to call Ryan his brother, and Emma would do everything in her power to make sure his parents knew that. But she wasn't going to cause a scene in front of Trent.

Instead, she drove home from Ryan's condo, fixed herself a sandwich, and sat down in the living room with her laptop to work on the final digital renderings for the Haven Memorial. The memorial itself would arrive next month, and then she could begin work on the reflecting pool and gardens that would go around it. She'd done four separate designs—one for each season. In the spring, she would accent the memorial with brightly colored tulips and dahlias. In the fall, she would plant a bed of mums. But her favorite was summer, when she would surround the memorial with brilliant, red poppies.

As the memorial would be completed in June, she'd be planting the poppies first, and she could hardly wait. The mayor was organizing a grand opening event on July first, with live music, food, and games for the kids. She was a bundle of nerves about it but also crazy excited. Chewing her bottom lip, she made one last tweak to the summer design then saved them all and sent them to Lucas and Mary for their input and approval.

And oh, *holy crap*, there was an e-mail from the University of Georgia in her in-box. Her heart almost burst out of her chest before she realized it was a request for additional information. They wanted to see her portfolio. Was that unusual? Most applicants to this program were fresh out of high school and didn't even have a portfolio yet.

Did it mean they were trying to look past her unimpressive GPA and SAT scores to let her work experience speak for itself? As she drafted a reply, attaching a link to the on-line portfolio she'd created when she found out Lucas and Mary were retiring, nerves swam in her belly.

She hadn't realized until this moment how much she wanted, *needed* to get into this program. It was her fresh start, the chance to learn everything she needed to know to be able to open her own landscape design business someday. She gulped a deep breath and pressed Send.

Please, please, please let this be a good sign.

She glanced at the clock. It was just past eight. Time to go see Ryan. First, she went into her bedroom to change. Her tattoo had finally healed enough that she could wear jeans again, but tonight she felt like dressing up. She slipped into a green wrap dress and bronze ballet flats and freshened up her makeup.

Why not? It was Friday night, and she wanted to look nice.

The look on Ryan's face when he caught sight of her made it all worthwhile. He turned his head and nearly dropped the glass of beer he held in his right hand. She smiled at him as she slid onto an empty barstool. "Hey."

"Untapped amber ale?" he asked, his eyes burning like cocoa under the track lighting above the bar.

"Yes, please." She crossed one leg over the other and watched him work.

Ryan projected a kind of laidback confidence in every area of his life, but here behind the bar, he seemed especially at home. He held a glass beneath the tap and filled her beer, then set it in front of her. He leaned in, his mouth brushing her ear. "Please tell me you're still not wearing any panties."

She winked. "Wouldn't you like to know."

He straightened, a new glint in his eyes. "I'll get it out of you by the end of the night."

"You're welcome to try." The truth was, she was wearing panties. Not even newly adventurous Emma was reckless enough to leave the house commando in a knee-length dress.

"I like a good challenge," he said, turning to wipe a water ring off the bar to her left. "Be right back." He headed over to check on some of the other customers. The bar was fairly busy tonight. In fact, Emma didn't see an empty stool in the place.

As she scanned the bar, her gaze settled on a familiar figure standing just inside the door. Jessica Flynn owned the Haven Spa, just up the road from Off-the-Grid Adventures. She'd been a year ahead of Emma in high school, but they'd had a few classes together and remained casual friends over the years. Emma waved, and Jessica headed her way.

"Hey, Jess. You here by yourself?" Emma asked.

Jessica shook her head, running a hand over her dark hair. "Actually, I'm meeting someone." She scrunched her nose slightly. "A blind date...or whatever you call it when you meet someone from one of those online dating sites."

"Oh, cool," Emma said with a smile. "I tried that a few weeks ago, too. Either there are a lot more cute, single guys in Haven than I knew about or some of them are using jazzed-up profile pictures."

"I hope for option A but fear option B," Jessica said. "So have you been on many dates?"

"Actually, no..." She slid a glance over at Ryan, who was busy mixing drinks for a group of middle-aged women at the end of the bar.

"You and Ryan Blake?" Jessica's eyebrows went up.

"Yep."

"Wow, I would not have pictured you two together." Jessica looked from Emma to Ryan and back. "But I think I like it. He's a good guy, you know. I knew him pretty well back in high school."

"Well, it's just casual," Emma said with a shrug, "but we're definitely having fun. So who's your date?"

"His name's Ruben Callihan. We've been e-mailing for a week or so. He seems nice. We'll see."

"Want me to be your safety? You know, you text me an SOS, and I'll come break up your date?"

Jessica blew out a breath. "Actually, after some of the online dating horror stories I've heard, that sounds like a brilliant idea."

"Awesome. You've got my number, right?"

Jessica thumbed through the contacts in her phone. "Yep, you're in here." She glanced over at the door. A tall, thin man had just entered The Drunken Bear, looking around nervously. "I think this is him. Wish me luck."

"Good luck," Emma said. "Send me an SOS if you need me."

"Will do, and thanks." With a wave, Jessica headed across the room toward her date.

Emma turned back to the bar and took a drink from her beer.

"How's Jessica?" Ryan asked, making his way back over to her. "I hardly ever see her around."

"I don't imagine she comes by Off-the-Grid much." Emma shook her head with a smile. Mark and Jessica had been hot and heavy for a while in high school, and their breakup had been messy, so messy that Jessica still wouldn't give him the time of day.

"This is true," Ryan said. "She pretty much still hates Mark's guts."

"Well, I don't see her all that much either, but she's doing good from what I know. The spa rocks, and it always seems busy when I'm there."

"You like those mud masks or whatever?" he asked, looking amused.

"I've tried them, and I like them, but my favorite is soaking in the natural hot springs."

Ryan's eyes heated. "The stuff of legends. I've never tried them."

"You're missing out. They're fantastic."

"I'll take your word for it," he said, "because I'm never setting foot in a spa."

She grinned. "Whatever, tough guy."

They were leaning in close now, so close she could see the honeyed flecks in his chocolate eyes, so close that the rest of the bar had melted away from her awareness. "Stand up," he said, his voice gone low and husky.

"Why?"

"I need to get a better look at that dress. Still trying to figure out what you've got on underneath it." His gaze dipped lower.

She stood, smoothing the front of her green dress, and did a little twirl for him before sliding back onto her stool. "So what's your guess?"

He leaned on his elbows, his voice low enough that only she could hear. "Yes, you're wearing panties, but I bet they're something really sexy."

She frowned at him. "How in the world can you tell that? Do you have x-ray vision?"

He grinned widely. "No, but that skirt doesn't even hit your knees, and it twirls a lot. No way the Emma I know would risk flashing this whole joint."

"You win." She leaned forward. "But if you'd like me to wear it for you somewhere more private, I'd be happy to."

"Definitely taking you up on that another time when I'm not working. Hang on a sec." He sauntered off down the bar, checking on the other patrons.

She watched as he turned his flirty bartender smile on every woman at the bar. Funny, tonight it didn't bother her a bit because now she could tell the difference. That was his professional smile, flirtatious but without any heat or intent behind it. Nothing like the way he looked at her, like it was all he could do not to get her naked every time he laid eyes on her.

While Ryan chatted up another couple, Emma glanced over her shoulder to check on Jessica. She spotted Jess and her date at a table against the back wall. They had beers in front of them and some kind of appetizer—wings, maybe?—on the table between them. Things looked like they were going well. They appeared to be deep in conversation, and Jessica was smiling.

Ruben's knee bounced rapidly beneath the table, but it was kind of sweet that he was nervous. He wasn't hot in a Ryan Blake kind of way, but he wasn't bad looking by any means. And let's face it, Ryan had heartbreak written all over him, while Ruben looked like the kind of solid guy who wouldn't bolt at the first mention of the L word.

Emma took another swallow of her beer and watched Ryan as he poured drinks. He mixed a margarita, served a couple of beers, and laughed at several jokes that probably weren't nearly as funny as his reaction. But it worked. She saw the tips people were leaving for him. The women all wanted to do him, and the men wanted to be him. He had a win-win going on with the customers.

"Bet you'll miss this when Off-the-Grid really gets on its feet," she said when he'd finally made his way back over to her.

"Hadn't bartended in years. Forgot how much I enjoy it."

"You're good at it." She swirled her beer and took another swallow.

"But to answer your question, nah, I won't miss it when the time comes to quit."

"No?"

He wiped down the counter as he talked. "No. Off-the-Grid's where it's at for me now. The potential to grow is endless, and I get to work with Ethan and Mark."

"You three really are close," she said.

"Like brothers."

She envied him that a little bit. She had lots of friends, but none as close as he, Ethan, and Mark were. "You guys are really lucky to have each other."

"Don't I know it." His eyes narrowed. "What about you? You still keep in touch with the Mackenzies?"

"Yes, but it's more like saying hello when I bump into them places and sending a card at Christmas." Emma had lived with the Mackenzies for three years, but they'd made no real effort to keep in touch after she turned eighteen. They'd never treated her like family. So Emma hid behind her smile and let them slip quietly from her life.

Actually, she'd done that a lot since losing her mom and Derek. She had plenty of friends, but no *best* friend...not until Gabby came along anyway. She was always surrounded by people, and yet somehow she still felt incredibly lonely.

"What about their daughter?" Ryan asked. "You guys used to be close. What was her name?"

"Clara. We grew apart, I guess. We're still friendly, but we don't really hang out." And a big part of that had been when Clara hooked up with Ryan right after graduation.

Right after Derek died.

Emma had never told Clara about her crush, but she knew Clara had suspected the truth. And so, when Clara slept with him, it had felt like the ultimate betrayal, when Emma's world was falling apart and Ryan still looked at her like she was a little kid.

"That's too bad," he said.

She shrugged. "Gabby and I have gotten really close, though."

"Yeah, you two definitely seemed to hit it off."

On the bar in front of her, Emma's phone lit with an incoming text message. SOS.

"Uh-oh," she said.

Ryan glanced down at her phone. "Someone in trouble?"

"Yeah, Jessica. She needs me to rescue her from her date." Emma glanced over at her friend's table, where Jess was still smiling and nodding along to whatever Ruben was saying. Emma tapped her fingers against the bar for a few seconds, formulating her plan. "Could you help me sneak out the back?"

"Sure," Ryan said. "Why?"

"I think I need to walk in through the front door like I just got here. I'm going to pretend to be her sister."

Ryan's brow furrowed. "But you look nothing like Nicole."

"Her date doesn't know that."

"How about you go over to her table as yourself, but pretend you're shitfaced, and your date ditched you, and you need a ride home?"

Emma scrunched her nose. "I suppose I could do that."

He leaned back with a smile. "Show us your chops."

She stood, wavering in her stupid ballet flats. Why hadn't she worn heels? They'd have made her job so much easier. "Wish me luck."

"You got this."

She gulped several deep breaths until the oxygen rush made her dizzy then she staggered toward Jessica's table in the back.

Jessica looked up, her eyes wide. "Emma? Are you okay?"

"Oh my God, Jess…I'm so glad you're here! I, um…" She swayed to the side, righting herself just before she fell flat on her face.

Jessica glanced over at her date, who was staring at Emma like she was some sort of freak show attraction. "Can you excuse me for a moment, Ruben?"

"Uh, sure," he said.

Jessica stood, hooked her arm through Emma's, and practically dragged her into the ladies' room. "Are you really drunk?"

Emma shook her head with a giggle. "Not even tipsy. But you can tell Ruben that I've had a few too many after my boyfriend ditched me, and I need a ride home."

Jessica grinned. "You really do rock."

"So what went wrong with Ruben?"

Jessica rolled her eyes. "The man's been talking about his ex-wife ever since we sat down. He's clearly still hung up on her. I thought he was going to burst into tears when he was telling me about their storybook wedding in Hawaii."

"Ew."

"Yeah. And he will *not* take no for an answer about us driving out to this place he knows about after we leave here to look at the stars. I am not going anywhere with this dude to look at the stars…or anything else."

"Definitely not."

"Okay then, let's do this."

Arm in arm, they headed back toward Jessica's table.

* * *

Ryan spent Saturday morning teaching back-to-back rock climbing lessons to a group of tourists. All novices, but athletic and eager to learn. They'd all done well, and one of them had even made it to the top.

Not bad for their first climb.

Afterward, he headed to the main building for a quick lunch before he spent the afternoon out on the zip-line course with Ethan and Mark. Emma and Gabby had volunteered to stop by with sandwiches from the deli, something they often did on the weekend when things were busy, but now it felt different somehow. Because Gabby was Ethan's fiancée and Emma was...well, he wasn't sure what she was anymore. They'd tossed around the terms "boyfriend" and "girlfriend" a couple of times to get out of otherwise sticky situations, but he wasn't quite comfortable with it.

He'd honestly never had a girlfriend. He had dates. Hookups. Already this thing with Emma was so much more than that. If he screwed this up and ruined their friendship, he'd never forgive himself.

When the house came into view, he saw Emma's SUV parked out front, but Trent was standing in the side yard with his parents, pointing and talking. They were here to see the place, and this was Ryan's chance to make a better impression than he had yesterday.

"Mr. and Mrs. Lamar," he said as he walked toward them, "I'm so glad you guys made it. Has Trent already given you a tour?"

Kate shook her head. "We just got here. Trent was telling us about the rock climbing you do. I used to climb when I was in college."

"No kidding?" He cracked a smile. Finally, a sliver of

common ground to share. "Climbing is kind of my specialty out here. You ever want to go up, you just let me know."

She returned his smile with a dismissive shake of her head. "Oh, goodness no. I haven't climbed in almost twenty years."

"You might be a little rusty, but I bet you haven't forgotten," he said. "They say it's like riding a bike."

"Looks pretty busy out here today," Gary said, glancing around. Ethan and Mark had just led a group onto the zip-line course and were going over safety information before they climbed to the first platform.

"Our weekends are booked solid now that warmer weather's arrived. I'm not needed on the course until one, though, and I'd love to show you guys around in the meantime."

"We'd like that, too," Kate said.

Ryan's stomach grumbled in protest, but it was worth missing lunch for the chance to try to smooth things out with the Lamars. Trent was his brother, and like it or not, these were his parents. It benefited everyone if they could all get along.

"So the business is profitable?" Gary asked, shoving his hands into the front pockets of his slacks as he watched Ethan get the group of tourists ready for their zip-line ride.

"Yes, sir. Right now, we're slightly exceeding projected earnings. I'm very pleased with how things are going so far, considering we've only been in business about eight months."

"Oh, I didn't realize Off-the-Grid was such a new venture," Kate said. "How did you decide to open a place like this?"

"It was my buddy Ethan's idea, to tell the truth, but it's pretty much a dream come true for all of us."

"Statistically, you know the majority of start-ups fail," Gary said.

Ryan nodded. "That's true, sir. I believe wholeheartedly that Off-the-Grid will be in the minority that succeeds, but if I'm wrong, we'll dust ourselves off and try something new."

"Well, we certainly hope you succeed," Kate said with a slightly pinched smile.

"Thank you. I appreciate that."

"The zip-line is totally sick," Trent said, brushing a lock of hair out of his eyes. The kid insisted on wearing his hair in this ridiculous style with long bangs in the front that were always hanging in his eyes. It was probably cool by club standards but totally unsuited for outdoor work like he did here at Off-the-Grid.

"Trent helps us take clients up on the course now," Ryan told them. "In fact, he'll be going out with me with the group at one o'clock."

"Oh?" Kate looked surprised. "I didn't realize Trent was helping with the customers."

Trent rolled his eyes. "Yeah, it's like they treat me like an actual adult or something."

Gary gave him a sharp look. "Watch your tone when you're speaking to your mother."

"Sorry," Trent mumbled, kicking at a stone on their path. "I didn't know you used to go climbing, Mom."

She nodded, saying nothing.

The Lamars seemed like decent people. Surely Ryan could convince them the same about himself before this trip was over. "Climbing's always been my escape," he said. "There's no room for anything else in your mind while you're out there. Just you and the rock."

"It's true," Kate murmured.

Ryan offered her his most persuasive smile. "You've got

to try it out before you leave town, Mrs. Lamar. Maybe once he's seen you reach the top, I can even convince your son to give it a try."

"Hey," Trent complained with a grin.

"Kate," she said. "Please call me Kate."

Ryan kept his smile firmly in place. "I'd love to take you for a climb while you're in town, Kate. What do you say?"

* * *

It was almost nine by the time Ryan got home from Off-the-Grid, and his belly grumbled painfully. He'd missed lunch to take the Lamars on a tour of the property, and the candy bar he'd shoved in his mouth midafternoon wasn't cutting it. It had been a worthwhile sacrifice, but he needed some real grub pronto.

He stowed the helmet on his bike and strode toward his front door, pondering whether to call Emma and see if she wanted to grab a bite. No doubt she'd eaten already, but . . . he missed her. He hadn't gotten to see her when she'd stopped by Off-the-Grid today, hadn't seen her since she'd rushed out of The Drunken Bear with Jessica last night.

"Ryan, could we have a word?"

He turned at the unexpected female voice to find the Lamars walking toward him down the sidewalk.

"Sorry to ambush you, but we saw you on your bike," Kate said, "and we had been hoping for a chance to speak to you privately."

"Yes, of course. Come in." He flicked on the light in the entrance hall then motioned them into his condo ahead of him. "How are you enjoying Haven so far?"

"It's a lovely town," Kate said, "and Off-the-Grid Adventures seems to be doing well. You should be proud."

"Thank you. I am." Something clenched deep in his chest at this unexpected praise from the people who'd hurt him so badly when he was a child.

"But we don't want Trent to stay here," Gary said, his expression sour and unfriendly, as usual.

Ryan kept his face impassive. "I understand that. His home is in Missouri with you."

"But you've given him a job and an apartment here," Kate said.

Ryan shrugged. "He wanted to stay awhile. He wanted to get to know me, and you may not realize this, but there is nothing I've wanted more in my life than to get to know my brother."

"You're not good for him. You weren't then, and you still aren't." Gary somehow managed to look down at him even though Ryan had several inches on the man.

Ryan met his gaze dead-on. "Maybe I wasn't much of a role model back then, but you never gave me a chance. I was only eleven." *Maybe you could have opened your home to me, too, or at least mentored me, instead of turning your back on me when I was just a troubled kid.*

"It was easy to see you were one of those boys who…" Kate drifted off, studying the hardwood floor beneath her loafers.

Ryan clenched his fists at his side. "Was a lost cause?"

"It was too late to save you, Ryan, but it wasn't too late for Trent." She had the good grace to look apologetic. "It was best for everyone that we gave Trent a fresh start."

"That's bullshit." The words burst from his throat before he could contain them. "Maybe it was easier for you to pretend that I didn't exist, but it sure as hell wasn't best for me. Trent was all I had left in the world, and you took him from me."

His words hung in the air, harsh and bitter.

Gary and Kate both took a step backward, eyeing the door.

Fuck. He'd wanted to mend his relationship with the Lamars, but this... this he couldn't take. He was so goddamn tired of not being good enough for them.

Kate lifted her chin. "What's done is done. We did the best we could for our son, and now we want him to return to Missouri with us."

"He's eighteen. He can stay here if he damn well wants to." Ryan heard the anger in his voice. This wasn't what he'd wanted, not at all.

"We know that," Gary said, "but we need you to stop filling his head full of whatever rubbish you've been feeding him since he got here. We want him to re-enroll in Missouri College for the fall semester. He belongs back home with us, not clubbing and riding zip-lines here with you."

"I can't make him re-enroll any more than you can." Ryan drew a deep breath, trying to rein in his temper. "Trent's an adult, and as you well know, he is *working* for me at Off-the-Grid, not playing around on the zip-lines. It took some doing, but I got him off his cell phone and putting in some good, hard work out there, and I won't apologize for it."

Kate's chin lifted. "Trent's held jobs in the past. He's not an irresponsible kid."

"Frankly, he'd still be in college if he hadn't been so set on coming out here to find *you*," Gary said.

Ryan's pulse roared in his ears as his control snapped. "He dropped out of college because he wants to become a DJ. And it is fucking insulting—pardon my French—that you two continue to judge me by the way I acted when I was eleven. I was a kid! I'd just lost my mother. Yeah, she was a junkie, but she was all I had, besides the baby brother you were so hell-bent on keeping me away from. And you know what? Despite all that, I think I turned out pretty damn well. So you can take your sanctimonious act and shove it because I'm done listening."

"How dare you speak to us that way!" Gary roared, his face as red as a lobster fresh from the pot.

Ryan turned away, disgusted. "You expect me to keep being polite when you've done nothing but insult me in return? I've had enough. You want Trent to come home with you, you're going to have to convince him yourselves."

CHAPTER SIXTEEN

*E*mma heard the motorcycle coming long before it reached her apartment. Hoping it might be Ryan, she climbed out of bed and tiptoed toward the front door. His familiar form came riding out of the darkness and pulled into the driveway. He parked, killed the engine, and then just sat there in the dark, head down, shoulders hunched.

She opened the door and went to him. The cool nighttime mountain air slithered across her bare skin, raising goosebumps over her flesh. She walked toward him, the cold pavement stinging against her bare feet.

"I don't know why I'm here," he said, his voice low. "It's late. I didn't want to wake you."

"I was awake. I'm glad you're here." She touched the sleeve of his jacket. "You okay?"

His silence spoke for him.

"Want to take me for a ride?" she asked, since he didn't seem eager to talk.

His hungry gaze settled on her pink nightgown, making her sizzle beneath it.

"I'll be right back." She dashed inside, yanked her gown over her head, and pulled on a blue top and her skinny jeans. She zipped up her boots and her jacket and went back outside.

Ryan hadn't moved. Something was definitely up with him.

She put on her helmet and climbed onto the bike behind him, sliding her arms firmly into place around his waist.

He revved the engine and guided the bike back onto the road, roaring over the deserted mountain roads outside Haven with the moon as their guide, the night as their witness. It was just as magical as that first night when he'd given her a ride home after work.

Beneath her palms, Ryan vibrated with tension, his body wound as tight as the machine below them. She'd seen him with Trent's parents at Off-the-Grid this afternoon, and she hoped like hell they weren't the source of his current mood.

He turned off the road onto a paved path, and she realized they were at the bluffs. The spot where they'd shared their first kiss, right here on his motorcycle. He cut the engine, and the night fell heavy and silent around them. They were hidden from sight from the road, stars winking overhead as the forest rustled around them.

Emma took off her helmet and slid off the bike, turned, and swung around in front of him, facing him, her fingers fisted into his jacket.

"Emma." His voice rumbled through her fingers.

"Kiss me," she whispered.

He groaned, yanking her into his lap as his lips crashed into hers. His kiss was explosive, lighting her up like a stick of dynamite. Her knees hooked over his thighs, bringing her hips against his. His hands gripped her ass, pressing her closer, rocking her against his erection.

They kissed, touching and teasing, until she was about to combust. Beneath her fingers, Ryan's muscles were so taut she could have bounced a penny off him. She reached between them and unbuttoned his jeans, pushing down the zipper. His cock pressed into her fingers, thick and hot. Her body throbbed as she stroked him, feeling him grow even harder beneath her touch.

Ryan swore roughly, thrusting his hips into her hand.

He fumbled with the button on her jeans, shoving them down her hips. She sucked in a breath as the night air met her overheated skin. Ryan reached into his back pocket, and then he was rolling on a condom.

Sex on a motorcycle. It sounded so exciting that her whole body was humming with anticipation. The reality? Slightly less glamorous. No matter how she positioned herself above him, her jeans were in the way. She laughed as they fumbled in the moonlight, struggling frantically to bring their bodies into alignment.

"Emma," he breathed against her neck, his arms tightening around her. She felt him smile against her skin. "How do you do that?"

"Do what?" she asked.

"You make me laugh," he said. "I'm so hard for you right now I might just explode, and there's a hole in the wall of my living room where I punched my fist through it. And . . . you take it all away."

She absorbed that information, grateful to the night for hiding the love that had to be stamped all over her face. "I'm glad."

"I can take anything with you in my arms." He pressed his lips to hers with another kiss that stole her breath.

"Did you really punch a hole in your wall?" she asked when they'd come up for air.

"Yeah."

"You want to tell me why?"

"Not while we're in this position." His hands came down to palm her bare ass. His cock strained against her belly, and her skinny jeans were still bunched around her hips like a damned chastity belt.

"I hate these jeans," she whispered.

"I fuckin' love them. They're sexy as hell, but right now, they are not my favorite thing." He smiled against her lips.

"I have an idea." She reached down and rolled the condom off him.

Ryan let out a groan of defeat.

"Hold that thought," she said, pressing her palm against his cock. She hitched her jeans back into place, then slid off the bike and knelt beside him.

"Emma—" he growled.

"Stay right where you are," she whispered. She leaned in, licking the bead of moisture that had gathered at the tip of his cock. He swore, and his cock jerked against her tongue. She took his head into her mouth, licking and sucking. His hands fisted in her hair.

She tilted her head and took him all in. Her position was awkward, with one shoulder wedged against the side of his bike, her knee braced against the pavement, but as she looked up and saw him looking so sexy and badass on his bike, his head thrown back, eyes closed, it was so worth it. It was the most erotic thing she'd ever seen.

She slid him in and out of her mouth, finding the tempo he needed. He swore, the sounds coming from this throat growing increasingly desperate as she worked, until he stilled with a hoarse, "I'm going to come."

She increased the suction with her mouth, and boy, did he ever. His whole body tensed as he came in a series of hot spurts that she swallowed, reveling in his guttural cry as he lost control.

He slumped forward, his arms shaking as he cradled her. "Fuck."

She slid to her feet and climbed back onto the bike in front of him. "Better?"

He hauled her up against his chest and kissed her senseless. "Baby, that was so much better than you could ever know."

"Good," she murmured against his lips. She'd helped him physically, but emotionally? That might be a much harder job.

* * *

"You working tomorrow?" Ryan nuzzled his face into Emma's hair, breathing in her fresh scent. They'd made it back to her place after their little rendezvous on the back of his bike and he'd fucked her senseless here in her bed. Funny how his need for her never seemed to lessen. If anything, it grew stronger each day.

She shook her head in answer to his question. "You?"

"Not 'til noon."

"You want to stay?" she asked, her arms tightening around him.

"Yeah." He wanted it more than anything. "But I may need to make a run for some food. I've been hungry all damn day."

"You missed lunch," she murmured.

"And supper."

"Oh wow." She sat up. "You are hungry, then. I think I have steaks in the freezer. We could toss them on the grill?"

"Sounds great." He climbed out of bed and started pulling his clothes back on.

Emma did the same. She went into the kitchen while he went out onto her patio to start the grill. By the time he had it nice and hot, she had the steaks thawed and seasoned. "I threw a couple of potatoes in the oven, too."

"Steak and potatoes. You know the way to a man's heart." He had no idea where those words came from, but he'd blame it on being famished.

Emma gave him a funny look but said nothing.

They didn't talk much while they cooked, and while he was still somewhat tongue-tied over what he'd just said, the silence didn't feel uncomfortable. Once he'd devoured enough food to fill the aching void inside him, he sat back with a satisfied sigh.

Emma slid closer, her shoulder bumping into his. "You want to tell me about it now?"

"Yeah." He did, too. "Trent's parents came to see me tonight."

"And it didn't go well."

"No. And then I lost my cool, which was stupid."

"You're only human, and they've been awful to you." She ran a hand down his back. "You did wait until after they'd left to punch your fist through the wall, though, right?"

He choked on a laugh. "Yeah."

"Good." She smiled, but it looked sad. "I'm sorry. I thought this would be your chance to finally set things right with them."

"Yeah. I was hoping that, too." And now he felt only a bone-deep weariness. "Trent's an adult now, legally. They can't stop him from visiting, but I hate for the kid to feel like he has to choose between us."

"They never should have kept you apart," she said softly.

"No." In that word, he felt all the pain come crashing down on him, the pain of being an eleven-year-old kid all alone in the world, of being an eighteen-year-old who'd aged out of the system with nothing to show for it. No home, no family, no place in the world. The pain of all the years he'd spent searching for Trent, when all it would have taken was one phone call from the Lamars to set it all right.

* * *

Emma was still in bed when Ryan left the next morning. They'd been up late, *really* late, and she wasn't feeling in any hurry to move. She rolled over, replaying in her mind the naughty things they'd done on his motorcycle. Ryan pushed her outside her comfort zone, except he didn't—because he was never the one pushing. She pushed herself out of her comfort zone when she was with him, and she liked that. She *really* liked that.

She liked everything about being with him, and she wasn't even trying to deny—to herself at least—that she was in love with him. Nope. She was all in, but she was a big girl. She'd always carried a torch for Ryan, and she could continue to bear it after they broke up. *If* they broke up. Because she wasn't an idiot. This thing between them wasn't just sex.

He'd come to her last night when he was hurting. He'd opened himself to her, let her comfort him. They'd shared things, done things, that spoke to a much deeper connection.

Would he ever be ready or willing to admit it? She didn't know. For now, she was content with things the way they were. They'd only been together a few weeks, after all, and Ryan was still adjusting to a more stable life here in Haven.

If she got accepted at the University of Georgia, then it would be time for them to have a serious talk about their future together. Otherwise...

With a sigh, she climbed out of bed, sending an offended Smokey stalking off in the direction of the living room. Already naked from her mostly sleepless night with Ryan, she headed straight for the shower.

Her reflection in the bathroom mirror stopped her. Her tattoo had gone through an icky, scabby phase while it healed, but now...now it looked...wow. She touched it with a smile. It was pretty and sexy and feminine. She loved it even more than she'd thought she would.

The poppy represented both her work and her love for her brother. It reflected so much about her, but it was private. No one had to see it unless she showed them. Yeah, she loved it. It was perfect.

With a happy smile, she stepped into the shower. Now that it had healed, she could take hot showers again. Long, hot showers. Or soak in the tub. Both sounded good, but right now her stomach was instructing her to hurry so she didn't linger too long beneath the shower's hot spray. Instead, she hopped out, dressed in a white tank top and jeans, and headed for the bakery. She was starved, and only one of Carly's cinnamon buns would do.

"Hey there, stranger," Carly said with a wide grin when she walked in.

"Hey yourself." Emma snagged a seat at the counter.

Carly set a cup of coffee and a plate with a cinnamon bun in front of her with a smile.

"Am I that predictable?" she asked. "Yeah, I am, and I don't even care."

"Nothing wrong with knowing what you want," Carly said. "So how are things with Ryan?"

"Good." She sipped her coffee with a happy sigh. "Really good, actually."

"You do have that happy glow about you," Carly said, eyeing her up and down.

"That might be partly due to what you're feeding me," she said around a mouthful of cinnamon bun.

"Aw, you're sweet, but this looks like more of a man-made glow."

"The glow of someone who..." She lowered her voice, giving a sly glance around her. "Gave a blow job on a motorcycle last night?"

Carly's eyebrows lifted. "You naughty girl, Emma. That sounds technically...awkward."

She giggled. "It was a little bit, but it was also amazing."

The bell above the door chimed, and she and Carly looked over to see a tall, slender brunette enter. Emma straightened in her seat. "Good morning, Mrs. Lamar."

The woman glanced at her, seeming at first not to recognize her, but after a moment's pause, she walked over with a polite smile. "Emma, right? And please call me Kate."

"Yes. Thanks, Kate." Emma motioned for Kate to take the seat beside her.

"What do you recommend?" Kate asked.

"The cinnamon bun, definitely. Carly's cinnamon buns are pretty much the best breakfast food ever created."

Kate glanced at Emma's plate. "That does look good."

"It's delicious."

Carly smiled from the other side of the counter. "I should hire her to work for me. Would you like to taste a sample?"

"No, thank you," Kate said. "I'll take Emma's word for it. Two cinnamon buns, please. One for here and one to go. For my husband," she added, glancing at Emma.

"Are you guys enjoying your time here in Haven?" Emma asked.

Kate nodded. "It's a lovely town."

"Your son's a great kid. We've all enjoyed having him here."

The older woman's expression was pained. "It's not that I object to him being here exactly...but he should be in college right now. Instead he's here, playing around, riding zip-lines and DJ'ing in a club. He's headed down the wrong path."

"And no one has tried to convince him of that more than Ryan," Emma said quietly.

"Excuse me?" Kate gave her a sharp look.

"Ryan didn't get to go to college, you know. He couldn't afford it so he just worked his ass off to make up for it, and he's done well for himself. Really well, I think. He doesn't like the club thing any more than you do, and he's been riding Trent hard about getting back into college. He doesn't want his brother to make a mistake he'll regret later on."

Kate was silent as Carly set a plate with a cinnamon bun on it in front of her.

"Coffee?" Carly asked.

Kate nodded. "Please."

"I actually warned him to back off," Emma said. "I told him if he pressured Trent too hard about it, he'd push him away."

"I didn't know," Kate murmured.

"He's really a great guy, you know? He had a crap start in life, but he made something of himself anyway. He's kind and generous and one of the most hardworking people I know. Trent's lucky to have him as a big brother, Kate. And you should support that, instead of trying to drive a wedge between them."

"But the tattoos...and the motorcycle..."

"What about them? Spend a little time with him, and you'll see. Give him a chance."

"You love him," Kate said, giving her an assessing look.

"Yeah, I do," Emma said softly.

On the other side of the counter, Carly dropped a plate with a crash and a muffled swear.

"Don't even pretend you didn't hear what I just said." Emma shook her head with a smile. "But don't you dare repeat it either."

Carly straightened with a shit-eating grin and mimed zipping her lips.

"Ryan doesn't know?" Kate asked.

"This thing between us is...well, to say it's complicated is cliché, but we've been friends most of our lives, and this new step is well...new. He's nowhere near ready to hear or say those words yet."

"I see," Kate said. "Well, we don't leave until tomorrow evening. I don't suppose he'd have an opening for a rock climbing lesson in the morning?"

Emma couldn't contain the smile that creased her cheeks. "You'd have to ask him, but on a Monday morning? I'm guessing he could fit you in."

Kate nodded briskly. "We'll just see about that."

CHAPTER SEVENTEEN

*R*yan stood inside the front office, watching as Kate climbed out of the Lamars' gray rented Lexus. Gary drove off, leaving her standing there in black leggings and a jacket. Dressed to climb. He'd hardly been able to believe his ears when she'd called to ask if he could fit her in for a lesson this morning. After the way they'd left things the other night, he'd never expected to hear from either one of them again.

Ryan picked up the bag with their gear and stepped outside. "Good morning, Kate."

She met his gaze, her gray eyes steady and flat. "Good morning, Ryan."

Since she didn't seem eager to rehash their argument—or to apologize—he decided to stick strictly to business. He wanted her to have a good time on the rock, but he was done trying to forge a relationship with her. "Great morning for a climb."

"Yes," she said. "It is."

"Right, then. Let's get going." He led the way down the path into the woods with Kate beside him. The morning was brisk and alive with spring, birds twittering and squirrels leaping from branch to branch overhead.

"It's really peaceful out here," she said after they'd walked in silence for a few minutes.

"Yeah. There's really nothing quite like it."

"I've never climbed outdoors."

"You're in for a treat then. This is a whole different ball-game than an indoor wall. A bit trickier, but so much more worth it. When you get to the top, you get to look out over the forest, not down at the gym floor."

"I think I'll like that," she said with a hint of a smile.

They arrived at the rock face, and Ryan was encouraged by the excitement on her face. He opened his bag and helped her get geared up in the harness and helmet. They didn't talk about anything other than the business at hand while she started to climb. The rock intimidated her at first. He could tell. Her movements were timid and stiff, and she fell several times before she made any progress.

But after a little while, her prior experience seemed to come back to her, and she began to climb with more confidence. She had an advantage over Emma during her first lesson in that Kate already knew how to keep her weight in her feet and her body flush with the rock, thanks to her time spent on the indoor climbing wall.

Forty-five minutes after she'd started, she climbed over the top.

"Wow," she said as she stared out over the landscape before her.

Ryan stayed put at the bottom of the rock, one hand on the belay rope, and let her enjoy the moment. She sat up there for several minutes, her expression quiet and pensive.

When she looked down at him, she looked like she had something to say.

He just wasn't sure he wanted to hear it. "Something else up there, isn't it?"

"It sure is."

"I've climbed indoors, too, but it just isn't the same once you've done this," he said, raising his voice slightly to carry to her thirty feet above his head.

"No, I don't imagine it would be."

"The view from up there gets in your blood. Nothing else will do," he said.

"Ryan—"

"Yes, ma'am?"

"You've done your best. I know that." She stared out at the treetops behind him.

He didn't say a word, had nothing left to say on this topic.

"And so have I. I've always tried to do what's best for Trent."

Ryan was silent for a long moment, but his tongue finally got the better of him. "You ever consider that the best thing for Trent might be getting to know his brother?"

"No," she said faintly, the word almost lost in the chasm between them. "But maybe I should have."

* * *

Emma held an unopened envelope from the University of Georgia in her hands. It was thick. Really thick. She'd never done this before, but she remembered her friends in high school saying that a thick envelope was good news.

Good news. Her stomach cramped, and her heart raced. Suddenly, she wasn't sure what she wanted the letter to say.

Attending the University of Georgia had been her dream

for so long. When she'd first graduated high school, she'd have given anything, *anything* for the chance to go to college. To truly learn her trade. Oh, how she wanted a diploma to frame on her wall, something that said she'd made it.

But did she still need that diploma? Was it worth the mountain of debt that would come with it in student loans and leaving behind all her friends—and Ryan—in Haven?

She smacked herself on the forehead. What in the world was the matter with her? This was her dream!

She ripped the envelope open, sliding the papers inside onto her palm.

Congratulations. We're extremely pleased to extend an invitation to the University of Georgia's Landscape Architecture Program...

She'd done it. She'd gotten in.

Despite the fact she'd been having mixed feelings a moment ago, she realized she was smiling. Actually, she felt like jumping up and down. She must have made a sound because Smokey gave her a disgusted look and headed in the direction of the closet.

Emma pulled out her phone and dialed Ryan. His phone rang until voice mail picked up, which meant he was probably either with a client at Off-the-Grid or on his bike. She hung up, knowing he'd call when he saw that he'd missed her.

Needing to share her news with someone, she snapped a picture of the acceptance line at the top of the letter and texted it to Gabby. Moments later, her phone rang.

"Oh my God!" Gabby said. "Congratulations."

"Thanks."

"I'm so proud of you. For the record, I never had any doubt that you would get in."

Emma laughed softly. "Well, for the record, I had plenty

of doubt, but I'm glad I got in. I'm relieved. I'm really excited."

"I bet you are. Did you tell Ryan yet?"

"I called, but he didn't answer."

"He's going to be so proud of you, too. We should get everyone together and go out tonight to celebrate."

Emma felt herself grinning like a fool. "Actually, that sounds really fun."

"Great. You tell Ryan. I'll rally everyone else. See you tonight."

Emma hung up and stared at the letter in her hands. Gabby was right. Ryan would be proud of her. Would any part of him want her to stay? Or would he just feel relieved that their relationship had a clear end in sight without a messy breakup?

The little tug she felt in her chest was definitely all about him. It was her poor heart cracking at the thought of leaving him behind. But she wouldn't let it break. Nothing was going to ruin this for her, and no man was going to derail her dreams.

Chin up, she brought her laptop into the bedroom and curled up in bed to browse apartments in Georgia. A half hour later, she heard the sound of a motorcycle approaching. Not necessarily Ryan, but...

She hurried to the front door, where indeed his Harley came into view at the bottom of the hill, winding its way up to her driveway. He pulled in and killed the engine, giving her a wicked smile. "Lookin' for me?"

She nodded, motioning for him to follow her inside. She handed him the letter from the University of Georgia, watching as his expression went from guarded to ecstatic. He grabbed her and spun her around, a huge smile on his face. "Holy shit. You did it!"

She nodded, wrapping her arms around him.

"I am so fucking proud of you, babe."

"Thank you. I can't quite believe it."

"If anyone understands how much this means to you, it's me," he said, his expression earnest. "Kids like Trent...they get college pushed on them so that it feels almost like an obligation. For you and me? It was the impossible dream. And now you're living it."

"I am." She pressed her face against his neck.

"You're going places."

"Sometimes I wish they weren't such faraway places," she whispered.

"Yeah, me, too." His voice sounded a bit gruff. "But Georgia's not so far away. You can still visit, and we'll come see you, too."

"Yes."

They were quiet for a few beats, just clinging to each other while she tried to think of a way that leaving him behind in Haven didn't totally suck.

"We're going out tonight to celebrate," she said.

"Yeah?"

She nodded against his neck. "I don't know the details yet, but Gabby's rounding everyone up."

"Sounds good to me. I've got some business in town this afternoon, was on my way there when I saw your missed call. I'll come by and pick you up later?"

"Okay."

He pulled back to look into her eyes. "Not that I ever doubted you'd get in, but seriously...congratulations. This is great news."

Her eyes grew misty. "Thanks."

"I've got to run, but I'll see you soon, okay?" He pulled her in and kissed her, hard, then headed for his bike.

Emma watched him go, her emotions tumbling like a

whirlwind inside her. Maybe she was feeling a little home-
sick about leaving them all behind—Ryan especially—but
she wasn't going to let it ruin her celebration tonight or her
plans for the future. She was going to get her degree and
start her own landscape design company. And hopefully the
rest of her life would fall into place behind it.

* * *

Ryan pulled up in front of Emma's apartment a few hours
later and cut the engine. She walked out her front door,
dressed in snug jeans and a blue jacket, her eyes wide.

"What's this?" she asked, eyeing his new ride.

He swung out of the cab and grinned at her. "We needed
a way to move equipment and gear around the property, and
I knew a guy selling a truck."

"So you bought a pickup truck?" She ran her hand over
the hood.

"Sure did. What do you think?"

"I like it. It suits you, I think." She glanced over at him,
her lips curved in a soft smile.

"The bike suits me better, but it sure doesn't help me
move lumber across the property to make repairs on the zip-
line platforms."

"I think there's room in your life now for the bike *and*
the truck." She was still smiling, and he got the feeling she
was talking about something more than just moving lumber.
But okay, yeah, it had been frustrating that he couldn't drive
Trent anywhere. Ryan wasn't a lone wolf anymore. Sometimes a man needed a passenger seat.

And a truck bed.

He glanced at the empty truck bed, then at Emma. "Are
you thinking what I'm thinking?"

"We might need to christen it at some point," she said with a wink.

"I think that's a definite."

She giggled as she walked around to the passenger side. "So I hear we're meeting everyone at The Drunken Bear."

"That's the plan. Ethan and Gabby will be coming late after he finishes coaching the swim team at the high school."

He cranked the engine and drove them into town. Climate control was nice and all, but he missed the rush of riding on his bike. Holding Emma's hand as he drove through town was pretty nice, too, though. Maybe she was right. Maybe there was room for both vehicles in his life.

"This worked out well for tonight," she said after he'd parked. "I love riding with you, but it really does a number on my hair." She ran her fingers through its blond lengths.

"Don't get too used to it," he said, leaning in for a kiss. "I don't plan to drive the truck all that much."

"Didn't think you would."

They walked down the street together and found Trent standing outside The Drunken Bear, busily texting on his phone.

"Hey, Trent," Emma said, "I'm so glad you could make it."

He looked up with a smile. "So you're going to college, huh?"

She threw her head back and laughed. "Ironic, right?"

"Yeah," Trent said. "It really is."

"It's never too late," she said, hooking her arm through Trent's as the three of them walked inside The Drunken Bear.

They were seated at a table near the window. Emma ordered a Celtic Sunrise—a house special with Irish whiskey,

Grand Marnier, orange juice, and a splash of grenadine. Ryan wasn't big on mixed drinks, but this one wasn't half bad. He'd tasted everything on the menu when he started tending bar here. Tonight, though, he stuck with beer. Trent ordered a Dr Pepper.

"I do think it's cool that you're doing this," Trent said.

"That mean you're going to re-enroll in the fall?" Ryan couldn't help asking.

Trent shrugged. "Still thinking about it."

Emma pressed her hand over his. "You've got plenty of time."

"So you're moving to Georgia?" Trent asked.

"Yeah." She glanced at Ryan.

"That's a bummer," Trent said.

Tell me about it. Ryan was still smarting over that information himself, even though he ought to be thanking his lucky stars because this gave him an easy out with Emma before things got any more complicated between them than they already were. A clean break.

"Well, if you're ever in the Atlanta area, look me up," Emma told Trent with a smile.

"I will."

"So you guys have been really busy at Off-the-Grid lately, huh?" Emma said.

"Booked solid on the weekends and doing decent business during the week," Ryan said. Now that the weather had warmed, business had definitely picked up, and he expected it to keep growing as they headed into summer. This would be their first full summer in operation, and if things kept going in the direction they were going, they were in pretty good shape.

"And how are things at the club?" Emma asked Trent.

The kid's eyes lit with real excitement. "Sweet. I've got a

regular gig there now on Tuesday nights. Iris has really been awesome. I'm learning so much."

Emma leaned forward with a conspiratorial grin. "So if I came by one Tuesday, would you introduce us?"

Trent's eyes rounded. "Uh..."

Ryan grinned.

Trent glanced between them. "Yeah, sure."

"We're really proud of you. You know that, right?" Ryan told him.

Trent ducked his head. "Thanks."

They kept on like that, talking about all the things going on in their lives, and it felt really good. He, Emma, and Trent shared such an easy rapport together. It was hard to imagine not having either of them in his life, yet they were both going to leave Haven in the coming months. Sure, he'd still see them from time to time but not like this.

And he didn't like it one fucking bit.

Emma whispered something in Trent's ear, and the kid almost fell off his chair, doubled over in laughter. She winked at Ryan.

He just shook his head. "Yo, you better watch it, you two."

"Or what?" She raised an eyebrow in his direction.

"Or I'll start whispering some things of my own."

Trent shook his head with a grin. "You guys are weird."

"Family's supposed to be weird, right?" she said with a laugh.

"Yeah." Trent's head bobbed, a wide grin on his face.

The door opened, and Mark stepped inside. He slipped his shades into the pocket of his jacket and scanned the room until he spotted their table. He walked to them and put a hand on Emma's shoulder. "Congrats."

"Thank you." She gave him a warm smile.

Mark took the seat next to Trent, then glanced at Ryan. "Saw the new truck. Should come in real handy."

"Yeah. I'll drive it tomorrow so we can get lumber out to that platform in back."

"Great."

Mark ordered a beer, and the conversation turned to Off-the-Grid's upcoming obstacle course race, the Adrenaline Rush. It wasn't too much later when Ethan and Gabby arrived. They ordered a fresh round of drinks for everyone.

Emma leaned in to whisper in Ryan's ear, "This is great, right? It almost feels too good to be true."

* * *

Emma was feeling pretty giggly by the time she'd polished off her third Celtic Sunrise. She'd eaten dinner, too—fish 'n' chips because they were delicious here—or else she'd probably be on the floor already from the amount of alcohol she'd consumed.

"I booked us spa treatments on Saturday afternoon," Gabby said, polishing off her own Celtic Sunrise. "I figured we'd need some pampering after I drag you around with me all morning looking at wedding dresses."

"That sounds perfect. I can't wait to help you try on dresses."

Gabby got a dreamy look on her face. "I have no idea what I want. I guess we'll just see what looks right once I start trying them on."

"We're going to have so much fun," Emma said. "I see you in something kind of light and flowing. Flowers in your hair."

Ethan leaned in, a big smile on his face. "I think Emma just nailed it."

Gabby swatted at him playfully. "Shh, you're not supposed to know anything about my wedding dress."

"I can as long as the dress is still hypothetical."

"Not if you want to keep your manhood intact," Ryan joked.

Ethan flipped him the bird. "If fantasizing about my wife-to-be in her wedding dress threatens my manhood, then I'm happy to take that risk."

Emma noticed that Trent had retreated from the conversation, busy texting on his cell phone. Whether the wedding conversation had gotten too boring for him or his girlfriend was just distracting him, she wasn't sure. "You playing at the club next Tuesday?" she asked him.

He nodded. "Yeah."

"Cool. I'll see if any of my friends want to stop by with me. It's a lot of fun dancing and listening to you play."

"Thanks. I think I'm going to head out. Congratulations again." The sheepish look on his face made Emma pretty sure he was sneaking off to meet up with his girlfriend, but she couldn't say she blamed him.

"Thanks, Trent. I'm so glad you came out with us to celebrate."

"Any time." He said his good-byes to the rest of the table and headed out.

"I think he's meeting up with Iris," Ryan said, watching him go.

"Me, too. He seems really into her lately."

"Yeah." And Ryan didn't look too pleased.

"So what's the plan, Emma?" Gabby asked, butting back into the conversation. "When do you think you'll be leaving us to head off to Georgia?"

"I think I'll probably leave after the memorial opens. That will give me time to get settled in an apartment and find a part-time job before classes start."

"I'm already planning my first visit," Gabby said with a smile. "Girls' night out in Atlanta."

"Definitely." She glanced over at Ryan, who'd gotten suspiciously quiet.

Would he visit? Or would it be a final good-bye?

CHAPTER EIGHTEEN

*E*mma and Gabby collapsed in a fit of giggles. Their attendant at the Ivory & Lace Bridal Boutique had served them flutes of champagne as they browsed the aisles of dresses. Consequently, they were both feeling rather silly by the time they settled into the dressing room to actually try them on.

Their attendant, a cheerful brunette named Eliana, bustled into the room with an armload of gowns, hung them up, and went back for more.

"Wow," Gabby said softly. She reached out to run her fingers over the beaded bodice of the gown closest to her. "I can't believe I'm really doing this."

"I know." Emma took another sip of champagne. "It's pretty great."

"Thanks for coming with me."

"I'm so glad you invited me." She and Gabby hadn't known each other very long, not even a year, but they'd become really close.

"This is everything," Eliana said as she hung up the last of the dresses they'd picked out for Gabby to try on. "I'll be just outside if you need any assistance. The sample sizes will be too big for you, but I can pin them to give you a better idea of how the dress would look in your size."

"Thanks," Gabby said with a smile.

Eliana left, closing the door behind her.

Gabby gestured to the rack of dresses. "Where do I start?"

"Let's start big." Emma reached for the Cinderella-style ball gown she'd insisted Gabby try—just for the fun of it since they both knew it wasn't Gabby's style. "Try this one on for fun, and then we'll get down to business."

"Sounds like a plan." Gabby stripped to her underwear, and Emma held the poufy gown open so that she could step into it. It was strapless, white satin with intricate beading across the bust and a ridiculously full skirt. She zipped it, then grabbed one of the pins Eliana had left behind to clamp the extra fabric so that it didn't fall down.

"Wow." Emma grinned widely as she caught Gabby's reflection in the mirror. "You look like a princess."

"Like I've just stepped out of a Disney movie," Gabby agreed, her eyes glossy. She ran her hands over the front of the skirt, then twirled in front of the mirror. "I never would have picked it, and I'm not going to walk down the aisle in it, but just seeing it on me is like something out of a fantasy."

"Let me get a picture." Emma grabbed her cell phone and snapped a few shots of Gabby showing off her best princess pose.

After that, Gabby tried on dress after dress. If they deemed it a contender, they'd leave the dressing room and let Eliana pin it properly so that Gabby could preen in front of the big mirrors outside. Emma got teary several times watching her friend try on dresses.

They made it through the first rack with a handful of contenders but none either of them felt sure was "the one." Emma couldn't stop admiring one of the dresses she'd picked out for Gabby. It had little pink flowers made of rhinestones sewn together with beads across the bodice and a simple, flowing white chiffon skirt.

"It's beautiful," Gabby commented as she stepped out of the dress she'd just tried on. "But it's not me. It's *you*."

"What?" Emma yanked her hand back from the dress.

"You should try it on."

"But I'm not getting married." Emma reached instead for the next dress on the rack, an off-white gown with a delicate lace bodice, cap sleeves, and a long, flowing skirt edged in lace.

"Yet." Gabby winked as she slipped into the dress. "Because you and Ryan...*oh*." Gabby looked in the mirror, and her eyes welled with tears.

"This is it," Emma said breathlessly, pressing a hand to her chest. "This is the one."

"Yes." Gabby just stared at her reflection as Emma zipped her up. The sample gown was a few sizes too big, but the lace added a classic yet feminine touch that was *so* Gabby, and the long, flowing skirt was reminiscent of the bohemian skirts she wore almost daily.

"Let's go show Eliana," Emma said, lifting the lacy train to follow Gabby out of the fitting room.

Emma and Eliana helped Gabby up onto the little pedestal in front of the bank of mirrors so that she could see herself from every angle. The dress looked even more perfect out here. The creamy color complemented Gabby's pale complexion and caramel brown hair, and the cap sleeves and lace accents suited her style perfectly.

"This one," Gabby said, twirling in front of the mirrors. "It's perfect."

"Oh, I agree," Eliana said, bustling behind Gabby to spread her train out and show the dress in its best form. "It is absolutely stunning on you."

"It's you, Gabby. I don't think you'll find anything more perfect if you tried on a hundred more dresses," Emma said, feeling a lump in her throat to see her friend in her wedding dress.

Gabby preened in front of the mirrors for a few more minutes before making her decision final. Eliana moved in to take measurements and then there was a ton of paperwork to make it all official. Gabby's dress would arrive in four months, just in time to get it ready for her October wedding.

When everything had been taken care of, Emma and Gabby retreated to the fitting room.

"I don't know about you, but I'm glad I booked us at the spa this afternoon. This was exhausting," Gabby said.

"Yes." Emma stepped behind her to unzip the dress. "But worth it. I'm so happy for you. This dress is perfect."

"It really is." Gabby ran a hand over the lace bodice. She stepped out of the dress, and Emma hung it back up while Gabby got dressed. "There's one more dress to be tried on before we leave, though."

Emma turned in confusion. "What?"

Gabby held up the dress Emma had been admiring earlier, the one with the pink, beaded flowers across the bodice. "I promise I'll never tell anyone, least of all Ryan, but will you try it on? For me?"

"Oh no. I really shouldn't." Because what if she loved it? A wedding was nowhere on her horizon.

"Just for fun," Gabby said. "Come on." She lifted the

dress from its hanger and spun it so that the chiffon skirt twirled around her legs.

"All right. Just for fun. No pictures." She pointed a finger in Gabby's direction.

Gabby pouted.

Feeling slightly ridiculous, Emma slipped out of her T-shirt and shorts and stepped into the dress. Gabby zipped it up and clipped the back, as Emma had just done for her.

"Open your eyes, silly," Gabby said from behind her.

Emma hadn't even realized she'd closed them, but now she peeked through her lashes at the mirror. And gasped.

"Wow," Gabby said, one hand pressed to her mouth.

Yeah. *Wow.* It was perfect. The pink flowers added a splash of color, and the chiffon skirt was delicate and feminine, but not too dressy. It would be perfect for a mountain-top wedding.

"When you get engaged," Gabby said, "you've got to come and try on this dress again."

"Maybe." Emma resisted the urge to twirl in front of the mirror the way Gabby had. Because she wasn't getting married, and this was craziness.

"We'll come back here and pick out a whole room full of dresses for you to try on just like I did today," Gabby said. "But I bet this is the one."

Emma let herself fantasize for a moment about the vision Gabby had put in her head, of her walking down the aisle in this dress. Of Ryan waiting for her at the other end, looking so dashing in a tux...She was so busy daydreaming she didn't even notice Gabby holding up her cell phone until it was too late.

Click.

"I said no pictures!" Emma felt her cheeks flush hot.

"But we need to be able to remember which dress it was,"

Gabby said with a shrug and a grin, leaning over to take a picture of the tag. She straightened and snapped several more pictures of Emma in the dress before she could stop her.

"You could have just written it down!" Emma scrambled out of the dress and hung it up before Gabby got any more carried away.

"What fun would that be?" Gabby said, not even trying to hide the smug look on her face. "Okay, lunch. And then to the spa."

Two hours later—after a sushi lunch and hot stone massages—Emma and Gabby lay soaking side by side in tubs fed by Haven's famous natural hot springs. Emma sank lower in the water, letting it work out any last kinks in her muscles.

"So great," she said, eyes closed and totally blissed out.

"Mm-hmm," Gabby said from beside her. "I do this about once a month."

"Really?"

"Yep. It sure has been good for my soul."

Legend said that the natural minerals in Haven's hot springs could calm your soul. Emma's soul didn't generally need calming, but these last few months were a different story. She'd been tied up in knots ever since the night Ryan had given her a ride home from The Drunken Bear. The night her friends had dared her to shake things up, and boy had she ever.

* * *

Spring in Haven segued into summer in a frantic rush. Artful Blooms always saw a surge in business once the weather warmed up, and although Lucas and Mary would be retiring in just a few months, business hadn't yet started to taper off. The memorial had been installed last week, and Emma spent most mornings working on the gardens that would surround it. It would officially be unveiled on July first, just over two weeks away.

She'd barely seen Ryan this week either; he was so busy at Off-the-Grid. Busy was good, though, for both of them. Busy kept her mind off things, including the fact that she'd put a deposit on an apartment outside Atlanta last week. Leaving Haven felt so bittersweet, but she was a believer that everything happened for a reason. Hopefully, in this case, it meant big things were waiting for her in Georgia.

As for Ryan? He couldn't leave Haven, not now that he had Off-the-Grid here. She'd be more than willing to try a long-distance relationship, but only if he was ready to make a commitment. She wasn't going to let him rip her heart slowly to shreds by coming home to Haven over school vacations so that they could have casual sex.

Nope. She needed a commitment or a clean break.

She sank her hands into the warm earth, pressing into place one of the many dazzling red poppies she'd selected for the memorial gardens. She scooped fresh potting soil over the roots and sat back, dirty hands on her knees. She still had dozens of poppies to go, but already she could see her vision starting to unfold, and it was *perfect*.

"It's going to be amazing," Ryan said from behind her.

She looked over her shoulder, surprised to see him standing there, hands shoved into the pockets of his jeans. "What are you doing here?"

"Saw you as I was driving home. Thought I'd stop by and see how the memorial was coming along."

"It'll be finished this week."

He came to stand beside her. "These red flowers remind me of your tattoo."

"They're the same. Red poppies."

"You told me they represent fallen troops."

"Yes." She touched the flower she'd just finished planting. "Derek's birthday is next week. I haven't been to visit him in a while. Thought I might go."

"His grave?"

She nodded. She visited Arlington National Cemetery every few years. It was a special honor that he was buried there, but sometimes she wished he were here in Haven, beside their mom, where she could visit him more often. Of course, that wouldn't matter soon anyway...

"I haven't been in a while either," Ryan said. "Mind if I tag along?"

"I'd like that." She stood and let him pull her into his arms. "I know he would, too."

Ryan's brows furrowed, but he didn't say anything.

Stubborn man. "He would. You know that, right?"

* * *

No, Ryan wasn't so sure about that at all. He had a good idea Derek might turn over in his grave if he caught Ryan and Emma fooling around together in DC. But it had been too long since he'd visited his friend's grave. He could clear his schedule at Off-the-Grid for a few days next week and go with Emma. He owed his old buddy that.

"You got plans tonight?" he asked.

Emma nodded. "Girls' night."

"In that case, I'll see if I can convince Trent to stay home from the club and hang out with his boring big brother." He cracked a grin.

She laughed. "Who'd have thought anyone would ever call you boring?"

"Not me."

"You're settling down," she said.

It's what he'd come home to Haven for. He'd wanted to leave his nomadic, hell-raising lifestyle behind. But to hear Emma say it? While she was looking at him with those big, blue eyes that seemed to see right into his soul? He had the sudden, irrational need to take off on his bike, go in some seedy bar somewhere for a cheap beer and...*no*. Even in his imagination, he couldn't fathom picking up some random chick and sleeping with her the way he used to. "I'm the same guy, Emma."

"Just with a pickup truck so you can take your brother out for burgers, a business that's one-third yours, and the first girl you've ever dated long enough to call her your girlfriend." She tipped her face up to his, still smiling, but there was an edge to her words.

An edge that sliced deep into his chest. "That sounds awfully—"

"Domesticated? It's okay, Ryan. Your secret is safe with me."

"I—"

"Sh." She pressed a finger to his lips. "Don't say anything stupid right now to ruin the moment, okay? I promise I'm not fishing for anything more from you. I'm leaving town in a few weeks anyway."

"I wish you weren't." The words just slipped out, and he immediately wanted to take them back. "But I mean, I'm glad, too. You're chasing your own dreams for once, and I'm so happy that you are. It's just...I'll miss you."

"Me, too." Something incredibly sad slipped across her features. "It doesn't have to be good-bye, though."

"What are you saying?"

"I'm saying we'll talk more when the time comes." Her gaze never wavered from his. "But in the meantime, think about what you want. Really think, Ryan."

And without elaborating, she dropped to her knees in front of the memorial to resume planting flowers.

Rather than ask what she meant—because he wasn't sure he wanted to know—he took a step back. "Let me know about next week, and I'll shift my schedule around."

"Okay. Bye, Ryan."

"Bye." He strode across the commons and down Main Street, not slowing until he'd reached his front door.

"Someone chasing you?" Trent asked with a smirk, leaning over the railing from the second floor.

He dodged Trent's question with his own. "You looking for me?"

"Yeah." Trent waved some papers at him. "I did that ancestry test you suggested, and I just got the results back."

Ryan gestured for him to come in. "So what's the verdict?"

Trent bounded down the stairs and followed him into his condo. "I'm half Korean."

"Just as you suspected." Ryan smiled as he went to the fridge for a couple of Cokes. He tossed a can to his brother. "Feel good to know for sure?"

Trent nodded, popping open the can. "It really does. I've been looking for Korean communities around here but haven't found any yet. I'd like to get to know more about my culture."

"That's great. Modern science rocks, doesn't it?"

"Yeah. There's a pretty big Asian community back home," Trent said, looking down at his soda.

"You given more thought to re-enrolling at Missouri College?"

Trent shrugged.

"You know I love having you here. I want you to stay. But I also want you to go back to college. Don't waste the opportunity to get an education."

"When I'm ready." Trent squashed the empty soda can between his fingers. "I have an opportunity here, too, that I don't want to waste. I'm spinning tunes once a week. That's a pretty big deal at my age."

Ryan drew a deep breath. "Yeah, it is. And I'm so friggin' proud of you. I am."

"Don't worry, bro," Trent said, and Ryan's chest tightened at the endearment. He used it often with Mark and Ethan, but on his actual brother's lips... Well, it was pretty fucking amazing.

"I'm young." Trent tossed his can in the trash and headed for the door. "I've got time. I'll figure it all out eventually."

He *would* figure it out. Ryan was sure of it. Trent was motivated and hardworking, in the areas that interested him anyway. Passion like that, it took people places. The real question was... would Ryan figure his own shit out? Because Emma was leaving town in a few short weeks. Trent would have to go back to Missouri soon, too. Ryan was losing his newfound family, and he had no idea what to do about it.

"Hey, you want to stick around?" Ryan asked. "Maybe order a pizza, watch the game?"

"Um." Trent stopped by the door, indecision written all over his face. "Yeah, okay. Sure."

"Great." Ryan had no clue what to do about the future, but right now, he was going to keep his family close and, like Trent, hope he'd figure the rest out eventually.

CHAPTER NINETEEN

*E*mma and Ryan arrived in Washington DC a little after four o'clock on Tuesday, the day before Derek's birthday. The six-hour ride had left them both restless so, after checking into their hotel, they went for a walk around the National Mall to stretch their legs.

"I remember coming here on an eighth grade class trip," she said, glancing over at the Smithsonian Air and Space Museum as they walked past. "It was my first time in Washington DC, and I was so friggin' bored the whole time."

"Terrible age to take kids on a trip like that, really," Ryan said with a smile.

"Seriously. All anyone cared about was going to Busch Gardens on the last day."

"I cut school the whole week, and no one even noticed," he said.

"You didn't go to DC?"

"At fourteen, I was much more interested in securing

contraband beer and cutting class than learning how our government works."

And probably he'd had no one to pay for the trip for him, Emma realized with a twinge of regret. She remembered that her mother had had to take a payment plan from the school system to send her and her brother, but she wouldn't hear of letting them miss out on the trip. "So have you been here other than for Derek's funeral?"

He nodded. "Came back a few years later to pay my respects when I was passing through, looking for work."

"So you've never really played tourist here?"

He gave her a mock-serious look. "Playing tourist is not really my thing."

She nudged her shoulder against his. "Cut it out. We've got to hit a few of the landmarks while we're here. And"— she glanced back at the museum they had just passed— "we've got to go into the Air and Space Museum."

"Museums aren't my style, Em," he said, but there was a twinkle in his eye.

"It's free, and it's really cool. Come on." She led the way toward the entrance. Thirty minutes later, Ryan had discovered the flight simulators and dragged her inside the "fighter jet," which actually turned a full three hundred and sixty degrees when you flipped the plane.

Emma shrieked as he flipped them upside down. Her feet hung suspended in front of her, her hair dangling above her head. Ryan was laughing like a kid as he fired at the enemy plane on the simulation screen in front of them without making any attempt to right their plane.

Finally, she reached over and grabbed his control, swinging them out of their barrel roll.

"You're no fun," he said with a smile.

"I'm lots of fun, but whoa...head rush."

They rode in the flight simulator four times, until Emma begged for mercy. After they left the Smithsonian, they walked by the Capitol Building then went in search of dinner. They ended up at a little hole in the wall Chinese restaurant that served some of the best kung pao chicken she'd ever tasted.

"Okay, you're right. Being a tourist is fun sometimes," Ryan said as he popped half of a fortune cookie in his mouth.

"If it involves hanging upside down in a flight simulator?" she asked with a giggle.

He shrugged. "Always wanted to fly a plane."

"Not sure I'd let you fly me anywhere in a real plane."

"Yo, watch it." He pointed his fork at her, then winked. "You'll pay for that later."

She smiled, then sobered. "I'm glad you came with me for this."

His smile faded, too. "So am I."

* * *

Ryan woke to near darkness in the hotel room, but the clock on the table beside the bed said it was a few minutes past eight. Sunlight illuminated the edges of the thick curtains covering the window. Emma slept beside him, naked beneath the covers, her legs entwined with his. He hooked an arm around her waist, drawing her closer.

She murmured in her sleep, pressing her ass against his cock. *Torture.*

But she looked so peaceful that he wasn't about to disturb her. Instead, he closed his eyes and fantasized about all the things he wanted to do when she woke up. Somewhere after taking her against the wall beneath a scorching hot shower, he must have dozed off because, the next thing he knew, he jerked awake. The clock read nine fifteen.

Emma's hips moved restlessly against his, and she whimpered in her sleep. His cock was painfully hard, as if he'd done nothing but dream about sex for the past hour, which was probably true.

If he wasn't mistaken, she was dreaming about sex, too. She moaned, her hips occasionally bucking against the sheets. With a sigh, she rolled to face him. Her eyes were closed, her body draped against his. She kept moving, still lost in her sex dream and rocking against him until, with a cry, she went still. And her eyes popped open.

"Mornin'," he said, his voice deep with sleep and arousal.

"What in the…" Her blue eyes were wide, her cheeks flushed.

"Did you just come in your sleep, sweetheart?"

She sucked in a breath then laughed. "I think I did. And I think you helped."

"I'd say I was more of a spectator," he said with a laugh of his own.

Her cheeks turned pink. "That's maybe a little embarrassing."

"Are you kidding? It was sexy as hell."

She reached down and wrapped her fingers around his aching cock. "Maybe I can return the favor?"

"I wouldn't say no to that offer." He closed his eyes, unable to contain a groan as she slid her hands up and down his cock. She kept her movements painfully slow at first, and he fisted his hands in the sheets, desperate for more. He pumped his hips against her, increasing the pace, too far gone to hold back.

She tightened her grip and stroked faster, harder, until all he could feel was the friction of her skin on his and the need rising like a tidal wave inside him. He swore as he broke, coming in several hot spurts against her belly.

"Fuck." He clutched her against him, his body still tingling with aftershocks.

"Not a bad way to wake up," she said softly.

"Not bad at all."

They finally made it out of bed—where he indeed took her against the wall in the shower—then dressed and headed out for food and some more sightseeing before they visited Arlington National Cemetery.

They got bagels and coffee and walked past the White House, the Washington Monument, and the Lincoln Memorial. Despite his usual dislike of sightseeing, he had to admit this was pretty cool. So much history here. And really, the truth was, he seemed to enjoy anything if Emma was at his side.

They had a late lunch at an outdoor café then found a flower shop where Emma picked out an arrangement to bring to Derek's grave. Their festive mood had sobered somewhat by the time they hopped on the Metro, which took them under the Potomac River to the cemetery.

Emma didn't stop at the welcome center for a map. Instead, she struck out down the network of paths and roads through the cemetery by memory. The sheer size of the cemetery was humbling. Row after row after row of fallen service members, as far as he could see in every direction.

Large trees grew amid the tombstones, and the green grass beneath their feet was meticulously tended. Birds called overhead. Along the edges of the field, flowers bloomed brightly. It was reassuring, somehow, to see nature so alive here, a visual reminder that life went on, even in the face of such enormous loss.

Emma slid her hand into his and squeezed. She had on a

blue sundress, which had seemed fun and flirty while they were playing tourist but took on a more somber look now. She led him down a row of graves and stopped before the white tombstone bearing Derek's name. She bent to place the flowers in front of it. He hooked an arm around her shoulders as they stood together in front of Derek's grave.

He had such a vivid memory of standing beside her like this ten years ago at the funeral. She'd been so stoic that day in a black dress meant for someone much older than her seventeen years, refusing to let her tears fall until after the crowd had left. It had been just the two of them then, too. She'd sobbed on his shoulder, and he'd promised he would always be there for her.

He'd promised Derek he'd never sleep with her. Maybe she was right when she said that Derek hadn't been looking this far into the future when he'd warned Ryan away from her, but standing here right now...

He felt like the worst kind of asshole.

Coming here with Emma today had been just the wake-up call he needed, a solid slap in the face to remind him of what Derek had sacrificed. Of the promise Ryan had made. Of all the reasons he never should have taken her in his bed.

A funeral was in progress on the other side of the cemetery. Emma leaned into him, glancing in that direction. "I hate what those people are going through right now."

"Yeah."

"You never could have convinced me of it at the time, but the heart really does heal," she said softly. "It doesn't hurt nearly as much now."

"I'm glad." He knew what she meant. The pain of losing his mom had faded, too. It would never go away altogether, but visiting her grave felt almost peaceful now.

"Thanks for coming here with me."

"I'm glad I got the chance." Still feeling as though Derek was looking down on him from somewhere up high, he dropped his arm from Emma's shoulders. It was for the best she'd be leaving town soon.

Because deep down, he knew she should never have been his.

CHAPTER TWENTY

$\mathcal{E}$verything seemed to be happening in fast forward after they got back to Haven. Emma was working long hours, between putting the finishing touches on the memorial garden and handling her other projects with Artful Blooms. Everything had to be finished this week.

Because next week... next week was all about packing up and leaving Haven. Something she'd looked forward to for so long. But now that the time had come, it only made her feel sad. She'd made such great friends here. Not until last year, when Gabby came to town, had she truly had a *best* friend. But Carly, Mandy, Jessica, and so many others were important to her, too. She'd miss them all. Not that she couldn't keep in touch with them from Georgia, but it wouldn't be the same as dropping by each other's places and going out for drinks on a whim.

And Ryan. She fell more in love with him every day. Should she tell him before she left town? Give him the chance to make this thing between them real? She was awfully afraid he'd push her away no matter what. He was a loner, a man who didn't do relationships, and he still harbored some guilt about that stupid promise he'd made to Derek a million years ago.

Was it better to leave town under the guise of remaining friends and nurse her broken heart privately or to tell him everything and probably still leave town brokenhearted but with their friendship hopelessly shattered as well? She wasn't sure yet. The decision would probably involve a girls' night out and plenty of alcohol.

Smiling at the thought, Emma stood, brushing dirt from her knees. In front of her, the memorial garden rippled like a sea of flames as a breeze danced through the poppies and over the reflecting pool behind them. The memorial itself stood about ten feet in front of her, its semicircular design inviting visitors to step into its embrace as they located the names of their loved ones.

It was beautiful, exactly as she'd imagined it, maybe even better. She'd never been more proud of something she'd designed. It felt so right that this would be her last project here in Haven.

"It looks phenomenal," Mary said from behind her.

"You think?" Emma turned, not having heard her boss approach.

Mary nodded, walking forward to stand next to Emma. "I knew you'd do us proud when we chose you to lead this project, and you certainly did not disappoint."

"Thank you. That means a lot." Mary and Lucas had taught her everything that she knew, and she admired them both so much.

"You must be so excited about your big move."

"Not as excited as I thought I'd be," Emma admitted as she and Mary walked to one of the benches beside the garden and sat.

Mary looked surprised. "No?"

Emma rested her elbows on her knees and stared at the red poppies still swaying in the breeze. "This has always been what I wanted, and I mean, it still is. I just didn't expect to feel so sad about leaving."

"Well, of course you do." Mary nodded briskly. "It's always hard to leave home."

"It's not just that." Emma drew a deep breath and blew it out. "It probably sounds strange, but I always felt kind of lonely here. That was one reason I set my sights on Georgia for architectural design school. I wanted to start over somewhere new."

"Oh, Emma." Mary turned to look at her. "I had no idea."

"I had lots of friends, but none of them felt like family, not until this year anyway. And now I do have people I love, and I'm leaving them all behind."

"Ryan," Mary said softly.

Emma nodded, her throat tight. "And Gabby. And our whole little group. They're the closest thing I've had to family since losing my mom and Derek."

"That certainly complicates things," Mary agreed.

"But with you guys retiring, this was my chance to spread my wings," Emma said. "And I don't regret it. It's time for me to start working toward owning my own landscape design business. That's always been my ultimate dream, you know?"

Mary looked thoughtful. "Yes, and you're right. It's time for you to make that dream come true."

* * *

Friday morning dawned bright and clear. Perfect weather for the memorial opening ceremony. Emma put on a purple dress and matching sandals. She added a little bit of curl to her hair when she blew it dry, and tried out the shimmery pink lipstick she'd bought last week and had been looking for an excuse to wear.

She met Ryan at the commons. So many people had already gathered for the ceremony: Ethan and Gabby, Mark, Trent, Jessica, Carly, Mandy, and pretty much everyone else she knew in town. Lucas and Mary stood near the memorial, chatting with the mayor.

"It looks amazing," Gabby said when she caught sight of Emma. "I can't wait to get a closer look after the ceremony's over."

"Thanks."

Ryan leaned in to give her a kiss. "So proud of you, babe."

Behind him, Mandy and Carly gave Emma a big thumbs-up, grinning from ear to ear. Emma mingled with her friends until Lucas and Mary motioned for her to join them up front. Terrence Clemmons, the mayor of Haven, greeted her with more warm praise for the project.

A podium had been set up in front of the memorial, and Mayor Clemmons stepped behind it now. "Good morning, everyone."

A hush fell over the crowd. Emma stepped closer to Lucas and Mary, feeling somewhat self-conscious there behind the podium instead of out in the crowd with the rest of her friends. She ran her hands over the front of her dress nervously. Ryan caught her eye from across the crowd. He smiled, and everything inside her relaxed.

"Thank you so much for joining us on this beautiful morning," Mayor Clemmons continued. "We are thrilled to unveil the new memorial gardens here in Haven, honoring all the fallen servicemen and -women from Pearcy County,

North Carolina. The memorial and its gardens will serve as a place for us to reflect on the sacrifices they've made for our country. It's a place to pay our respects but also a place to honor the many brave men and women who've fought for our freedoms. We hope you'll come here to learn their names. And we hope you'll come to sit and enjoy the beautiful gardens that have certainly added a welcome splash of color to our downtown area."

The crowd broke into applause.

When they'd finished, Mayor Clemmons continued. "The team at Artful Blooms Landscape Design has really done a top-notch job in designing these gardens for us, and we'd like to give special thanks to owners Lucas and Mary Pratt, who'll be retiring this fall. They've provided many beautiful, functional, and dynamic designs for our town over the years. We'd also like to recognize Emma Rush, who designed the gardens you see here today."

He gestured toward her, and Emma felt her cheeks burn as the crowd applauded loudly. Mary gave her shoulder a squeeze.

"Emma's own brother, Derek Rush, is memorialized behind us."

Unexpectedly, she felt tears pressing at the backs of her eyes. *I miss you, Derek.*

Mayor Clemmons spent the next ten minutes reading the names of every serviceman and -woman memorialized here. "And now, a moment of silence as we remember those who've made the ultimate sacrifice to protect our great country."

Emma dipped her head, staring down at her purple sandals and remembering the day Derek had graduated from boot camp. He'd looked so dashing in his freshly pressed uniform, so young, so enthusiastic about going into service. Without money for college, joining the Marines had been

Derek's ticket out of town after their mother died. He'd served two years, and from his letters and her visits with him during that time, she knew he'd never regretted his decision. He was proud to serve his country, and he'd died doing what he loved.

After their moment of silence, Mayor Clemmons invited everyone to stay and enjoy the festivities. They'd hired a bluegrass band to play over on the commons, and there was plenty of food and refreshments ready to be served.

Emma accepted congratulations from the mayor and several other people standing nearby before she gratefully lost herself in the crowd, finding her way over to her group of friends. She slid in next to Ryan.

"Here's the lady of the hour," Ethan said, toasting her with a plastic cup of something pink and frothy.

"Fruit punch?" Gabby held out a cup toward Emma.

"Thanks." She accepted it and took a grateful swallow. Her throat had gotten awfully dry up there with the whole town watching.

"You did great," Ryan said, giving her a squeeze.

"I just stood there," she said with a laugh.

"Well, you looked great standing there," Carly said. "And I can't wait to get a closer look at the memorial. My grandfather's on there."

"And my uncle," Jessica said, stepping into their circle. "I didn't realize until this morning that you'd designed the new memorial garden, Emma. I stopped by to look at it and find my uncle's name yesterday."

"Thank you." Emma gulped the rest of her punch. "I appreciate it, guys."

"We need to do this again later today," Gabby said, holding up her plastic cup, "but with real drinks."

"Agreed," Carly said.

"Yeah, that sounds great." Emma nodded. "Will you join us, Jess?"

Jessica glanced to the right, and her smile vanished. Emma followed her gaze and saw Mark staring back at Jessica, his face a blank mask, as usual.

"Please?" Emma added.

"Yeah, sure," Jessica said finally, tearing her gaze from Mark's. "I'll stop by for a drink. Just let me know when and where."

"Will do."

They made their way over to the memorial. Ryan still had his arm around her shoulders, such a comfortable and familiar weight. She turned to look up at him. "You working this afternoon?"

"Actually, I had a cancellation. Why?"

"Let's go to the bluffs," she said.

His brow furrowed. "Em—"

"The weather's great, and I'm leaving town next week. It's now or never."

"You really want to jump?"

She nodded. "I really do. It'll be a huge rush. And if you know a spot where I could do a little climbing on the way up, that would be even better."

He finally smiled, his cocoa eyes crinkled. "All right. It's a date then."

"Yay." She leaned into him, a burst of excitement skittering through her belly. Jumping from the top of the bluffs sounded a little bit terrifying and a whole lot awesome. It had been so off limits to her when she was a kid, wanting to tag along with Ryan and Derek. It seemed somehow fitting that she jumped at one of Derek's favorite spots after honoring him here today.

She and Ryan stood in the middle of the semicircular

memorial, looking at all the names engraved. A steady stream of people moved around them, talking quietly and touching the names of loved ones. A few people had tears on their cheeks.

"You seeing this?" Ryan asked softly.

"Yeah." Her throat had gotten painfully tight.

"You've created something really beautiful here."

"Well, to be fair, the idea for the memorial was Mayor Clemmons and the Town Council's."

"But it could have been stuffy and boring. You've made it modern and colorful. It's a nice place to visit, maybe even sit and hang out for a while." He spoke with such pride that the lump in her throat grew even tighter.

"Thanks." She turned to look at the gardens, the people walking through it and sitting on benches. It really had turned out well.

"Ryan!" A man approached, his hand out.

Ryan took it and shook. "Yo, what's up, man?" He introduced Emma to Steve Fields, one of his rock climbing students.

"You got a minute?" Steve asked Ryan.

"Sure. I'll catch up with you later, Em." Ryan excused himself, and the two men walked off, talking about a climb Steve was planning next month.

Emma headed toward Carly, who was standing alone beside the memorial, texting on her phone.

"Excuse me," a woman's voice said from behind her.

Emma glanced over her shoulder and saw a tall, slender woman in her late forties.

"You're Emma Rush, right?"

"That's right," she said with a smile.

"I'm Angela Davenport. I'm the owner of the Silver Springs Lodge."

"Oh...Ms. Davenport, it's a pleasure to meet you." Emma had heard plenty about the Silver Springs Lodge. It was a fairly large new hotel being built in Silver Springs. Some people thought it was *too* big, but the general consensus was that it would be good for local business. Emma agreed.

"Please call me Angela," she said, extending a hand.

Emma took it and shook. "I've heard a lot about the new lodge. It sounds very exciting."

"Thank you," Angela said. "I was actually hoping to invite you out to the site on Monday morning to show you around."

"Really?" Emma hid her confusion behind a sunny smile. "That sounds lovely."

"I'm so impressed with the new memorial gardens. I'd love to hear more about your work."

"Oh, well, thank you."

She and Angela exchanged business cards and said their good-byes. Emma wasn't really sure what that was about, but she was curious to get a sneak peek at the new hotel. She mingled at the memorial until the crowd had died down, and then she snuck off to get ready to go to the bluffs with Ryan. *Finally.*

* * *

Ryan pulled into Emma's driveway just past two o'clock. Before he'd even switched off the bike, she had appeared on her front porch, wearing jeans and the blue jacket she usually wore when she rode, a backpack on her shoulders.

She hurried over and leaned in to place a kiss on his lips. "I can't wait."

He smiled against her lips. "I can tell."

She unclipped the spare helmet and swung onto the bike behind him as if it was second nature. So confident and sexy. He loved that.

And he couldn't wait either. He hadn't been in favor of bringing her out to the bluffs at first, not to jump anyway, but he'd done it enough times to know it was fairly safe. The water at the base of the cliffs was close to fifty feet deep, a straight drop. And Emma was a strong swimmer, had been since they were kids.

She slid her arms around his waist, and he pointed the bike out of town, roaring over the winding roads outside Haven. Emma's hands rested over the waistband of his jeans, as distracting as ever, but it was a familiar distraction now. Something he was both used to and not because he didn't think he'd ever completely get used to the way Emma had rocked his world.

He pulled into the entrance to the bluffs and parked.

Emma leaned closer. "Both times we've been here together, we've made out on your bike."

They'd done more than make out on his bike the last time they were here. His dick hardened at the memory, which was not at all comfortable given that he was straddling a bike, wearing swim trunks under his jeans.

Emma tossed her backpack, helmet, and jacket on the asphalt beside them, then swung around in front of him. "Just doesn't seem right if we don't keep up the tradition," she whispered as she lowered her mouth to his.

Who was he to complain? He drew her in and kissed her, slow and fierce. By the time they'd come up for air, they were both panting for breath, and Emma's eyes had that glazed, unfocused look she got when she was really turned on.

"You are so damn sexy," he murmured, nibbling his way down her neck.

"Not sure how sexy I'll be when I'm flailing around in the air on my way to the lake," she said, gasping as he licked a sensitive spot on her throat.

"Oh, trust me, that will be sexy, too." He laughed softly, fingering the hot pink bikini strap peeking out from beneath her shirt. "You ready?"

"Heck, yes." She slid off the bike, a gleam of excitement in her eyes he hadn't seen since that first night he'd given her a ride.

"Okay then. I think I remember a spot you can do some climbing on the way up, but we'll go easy since we're not in our climbing shoes."

"Sounds good to me."

He swung off the bike and adjusted himself with a grimace as Emma giggled.

"Sorry about that," she said. "I'll help you with it later."

"I'll take you up on that." He stowed their jackets in one of his saddlebags. Then they headed for the path that led to the top of the bluffs. "What's in the backpack?"

"Towels, mostly."

"Okay." He changed course and led them down a path to the water's edge. The cliffs towered over their heads.

"Wow, it's a little intimidating from down here," she said, looking up.

"It won't be after you've jumped. Leave the backpack here."

"Good plan." She set it beneath a tree near the water. "Okay, let's do this."

They hiked away from the water, beginning their winding ascent to the top. He was pretty sure he remembered a spot they could do some low-key climbing, but it had been a long time since he'd climbed here so he wasn't sure he knew the way.

As it turned out, he didn't, but they stumbled upon another spot that worked out even better than the one he'd been thinking of. The rock face was about fifteen feet high, with a gentle incline and plenty of knobs and ledges for hand- and footholds. He sent Emma up ahead of him so that he could help her out if she got in a jam, but with quiet concentration, she zoomed straight to the top.

"Wow," she said as he climbed over the top beside her. "That was awesome."

"You just kicked ass on that rock face," he said.

"Thanks. It felt really good. Maybe I'll climb it again if we come back up." With a smile, she got to her feet and led the way back to the trail.

He was hot and sweaty by the time they'd reached the top, more than ready for a dip in the sparkling blue water below. The view from up here never failed to get his adrenaline pumping, the way the world just dropped off all around them. Fucking awesome.

"Hoooly shit," Emma whispered as she looked down.

"Not too late to change your mind."

She glared at him. "How often have you known me to back down from a challenge?"

Hmm. "Never."

"Right. So anything I need to know before I jump?" She reached up and yanked her T-shirt over her head.

"What?" Because he was staring at her breasts, perfectly cupped in a hot pink bikini top, and he'd all but forgotten where they were and why they'd come here.

"Pervert." She giggled as she shimmied out of her jeans, revealing a matching pink bikini bottom that was *holy shit* hot. And her tattoo...

He shucked his clothes and drew her in for another kiss, and okay, an excuse to feel her up in that itty-bitty bikini.

"Ready?" she whispered against his lips.

"Shoes," he said. They'd both worn old sneakers today to jump in. He'd jumped barefoot before, but the water hurt like a bitch when you hit. Better that they wear shoes.

She slid hers on and laced them up tightly while he did the same. "Anything else?"

"You want to stand a few feet back from the edge, get a running start, and jump as big as you can," he said. "Keep your body straight in the air, arms above your head, toes pointing toward the water."

"Got it." She walked to the edge and looked down, and then she just stood there, oddly silent.

He put a hand on her shoulder and felt the tension running through her. "It's better if you don't look too long. Just spot your landing, and then go if you're going."

"I'm going, all right." But her voice was soft, lacking the bravado she'd sported a few moments ago.

He took her hand. "Together?"

She looked up at him with a smile. "Yeah. I'd like that."

They backed up to the tree line. "Ready?" he asked.

"Three. Two. One. Go!" She ended on a shriek, already sprinting for the edge.

CHAPTER TWENTY-ONE

*E*mma screamed as she leaped. Out of the corner of her eye, she saw Ryan jump beside her. Her stomach did a barrel roll as she dropped, and some last-second instinct had her squeezing her eyes shut just before...

Splash.

The water smacked her toes and slammed up her nose, and then it had swallowed her whole. She went down, down, down, her ears popping the whole time. For a moment, she hung suspended in the water. She opened her eyes to a deep blue haze and the shadowy image of Ryan below her to her right. She looked up at the surface sparkling above her and started kicking.

She broke the surface with another splash, laughing and spluttering and gasping for breath. Ryan popped up beside her, treading water with one hand while he swiped water from his eyes with the other.

"That was awesome!" she shrieked.

"Yeah, it was," he said, a wide grin on his face.

"I want to do it again."

Now he was laughing at her, kicking toward the spot where they'd left her backpack. She followed, gliding through the water behind him. It had felt shockingly cold when she first went in, but now that her body had adjusted, it wasn't bad at all.

He climbed onto the rocky shore, reaching out a hand for her. She gripped it and hauled herself up onto the rock beside him. Before she'd realized what was happening, she was in his arms, her body plastered to his, and he was kissing her like a man possessed.

"You were sexy as hell jumping off that cliff," he murmured against her lips.

"It was even more fun than I thought it would be." She wrapped her arms around his neck and kissed him back.

"This part's pretty fun, too."

Yep. They were dripping wet and completely entwined, their skin slipping together with a delicious friction that warmed the last chill of the water.

"This part's not fun, though." Ryan adjusted himself in his trunks.

She giggled. "Sorry."

"Don't be," he said, his voice all low and rough. "I'm not."

"Well, in that case..." She leaned in and kissed him again. His tongue slid against hers, igniting a fiery need inside her. She needed this moment, this man, this life. How could she give it all up next week?

"Emma," he rasped, pulling back, "we'd better get going if we're going to hike back up."

She grumbled a little in protest, and Ryan hauled her in for one more blistering kiss. His cock pressed against her, so deliciously hard inside his swim trunks. She really wanted to help him out with that problem, but yeah, she wanted to jump again, too.

"Not going to be as much fun in wet, squishy sneakers," she said, sliding them off one at a time to empty as much water out of them as she could.

"Maybe not, but it beats climbing back up barefoot."

"Is that what you and Derek used to do?" she asked.

He nodded with a smile. "Tore our feet up pretty bad. Never brought towels either."

"See? We girls think of everything."

"You do," he agreed. "Definitely an improvement."

She wondered if he meant that, or if a part of him wished it were still her brother out here with him, racing their way to the top, barefoot and soaking wet.

He stepped closer and took her hand, as if he'd read her mind. "It's different. Derek and I were here to out-daredevil each other. It was wild and reckless. Fun, sure. But it's really great sharing it with you, too. I love sharing this kind of shit with you."

The look in his eyes made her heart turn over in her chest. *Gah.* He didn't mean...but... "I love sharing it with you, too." She pressed her lips to his again then led the way back to the path.

This climb was a little different, wearing nothing but swimsuits. She wasn't self-conscious in her bikini, especially not with Ryan, but okay, she wasn't exactly sorry that their slippery, wet sneakers meant they had to forgo any rock climbing this time because she could only imagine what kind of view he'd have gotten following her up the rock face...

"Best afternoon we've spent together in a long time," she said, sliding her hand into his.

"Agreed." He looked over at her with an easy smile on his face.

They hiked together in comfortable silence, coming out once more at the top of the rock. Their clothes lay right where they'd dropped them.

"I guess we should have just hiked up in our swimsuits the first time. Now we're going to have to come back for our clothes at the end."

"Don't mind," he said with a shrug.

"Me either." She walked to the edge and peered down. Beside her, Ryan looked like a god in nothing but low-slung green board shorts, his skin bronzed and glistening, all his tattoos on display. "I should spend more time with you in a swimsuit," she said, sliding into his arms.

"Sounds like a great idea to me."

She slid her hands over his tattooed biceps. "I want to spend more time with you, Ryan."

"What are you saying?" A guarded look came into his eyes.

"I don't know. Let's just not think of me leaving next week as a good-bye, okay?" She grabbed his hand and yanked. They sprinted together to the edge of the rock, and as she leaped out into the air, she whispered under her breath, "I love you."

* * *

Ryan surfaced with a splash, feeling oddly disoriented. He could have almost sworn he heard Emma say...

But that was ridiculous. Wasn't it?

She floated nearby, watching him from those bright, blue eyes.

"What was that about up there, about not saying good-bye?" he asked.

"I just...I used to think I wanted to leave Haven behind and start over somewhere else, but now I'm not sure I do."

"But your degree..."

"I had this crazy thought just now." She kicked her feet, floating closer. "What if I don't need a degree after all? Maybe I could just start my own landscape design firm here in Haven and hope for the best."

His stomach had gone all tight and cramped. "Emma, this is your dream. Don't you dare give it up because of—"

"You?" she said, her eyes sad. "I wouldn't give up my dream for anyone, Ryan. Don't worry. But sometimes dreams change. Sometimes once you start chasing them, you realize those dreams represented who you were ten years ago, not who you are today."

He stared at her, completely blindsided. "What are you saying?"

She looked away. "I don't know, really. I'm just having some second thoughts."

"You have to go to Georgia," he said. Because he'd known Emma forever, and she'd always wanted this chance. She'd planned and saved for years for this opportunity. And no matter what she said, he had an uncomfortable suspicion that part of her current change of heart had to do with her feelings for him. Because they'd been together awhile now, and *fuck*, what had he been thinking?

This wasn't casual, not for either of them, and now he was about to derail her future.

No way. He couldn't live with himself.

"You need to go," he said again. "Try it. If it doesn't feel right, drop out. But you should give it at least a semester. You've worked too hard for this chance to let it slip away, Emma."

"A semester. I like that plan." She started kicking toward shore.

He swam behind her, totally distracted by the flashes of

pink from her bikini through the water. She pulled herself out onto the rock, wet and glistening and so fucking gorgeous. He hauled himself out beside her and pulled her into his arms.

"How did we get here, Ryan?" she asked softly, her lips pressed against his neck.

"I don't know." His voice sounded gruff because he knew what she was asking. How had they gone from friends, to friends with benefits, to *this?* Because this felt like something he was terrified to put a name to. It felt like whispered confessions as she leaped off the cliff. It felt like things he had no business thinking about, not with Emma.

She'd never been his, not really. They'd just been fooling around. Having fun.

And now her lips were on his, and he was kissing her until all the madness in his head stopped, until all he could think about was the way she tasted and the feel of her wet skin on his. Her hands were on his back, her fingernails skimming over his skin, driving him mad. He dropped his left hand to the red poppy on her hip, as soft now as the rest of her.

"I packed something else in my backpack," she whispered.

"What?" He hardly dared hope.

"Condoms."

"Is that so?" His cock surged against the confines of his trunks.

"You haven't properly scandalized me until you've had me outside in broad daylight," she said with a wicked grin.

"And you want to be scandalized, do you?"

"I do." Her hands slid inside his trunks, squeezing his ass.

"Well then, I'd better give the lady what she wants." He glanced around, spotting an area behind the rock that was sheltered from view of the path in the unlikely event anyone else came along. He bent and spread out the oversized yellow towel Emma had packed for him.

She came up behind him, a foil packet clutched in her palm. She tossed it onto the towel and gripped him through his trunks. He hissed out a breath as she slid her palm up and down his length, working him into a frenzy.

"Strip," she whispered.

Too turned on—and captivated—to object, he kicked off his soggy sneakers and shucked his trunks. He spun to face her. Emma was staring at him like he was a lollipop and she needed a sugar fix.

"You really have no business being so sexy," she said. "It's just not fair to the female species. How could I resist doing this?" She gripped him in her fist. "Or this?" She sank the fingernails of her other hand into his ass.

He quivered beneath her touch, his dick painfully hard.

She stroked him, hard and fast, then released him and gave him a shove toward the towel. He dropped to it and sheathed himself in the condom, then looked up at her. She looked like a goddess in that hot pink bikini, the red tattoo peeking out on her hip. Just looking at her was almost more than he could bear right now; he was so hard for her, so desperate to lose himself inside her.

She shimmied out of her bikini bottom and climbed into his lap, rocking against him with a needy little whimper. He captured her mouth with his, reaching between them to tease her with his fingers, to drive her as mad as she'd driven him.

She lifted her hips so that his cock pressed against her entrance, and he clutched at the towel beneath him.

"So good," he ground out. "More."

"Like this?" She sank onto him, taking him all the way in.

"God, yes."

"I can't get enough, Ryan," she whispered, then she kissed him, her hips pressed to his, his dick fully nestled in her tight, hot body. Their tongues tangled, thrusting desperately against each other while she held herself still in his lap.

He was on fire, burning for her, and it was the most exquisite form of torture.

She pushed him down flat on his back, looking so fucking beautiful astride him, and then she began to move. She leaned forward so that her hair fell in a blond waterfall over his chest, tickling and teasing him. He thrust up into her as she finally let herself go, riding him with wild abandon. Her eyes were closed, but he kept his open, not wanting to miss a moment.

Her head was thrown back now, her face bathed in the look of arousal he'd come to know as she grew closer and closer to her release. He pushed back his own need so that he could watch her move, watch as she bucked her hips harder and faster against his, panting until, with a cry, she convulsed around him.

He'd been so caught up in watching her that the next thing he knew, his own orgasm slammed into him, drawing a feral cry from his throat as he came. It was a good damn thing he was already lying flat on his back because he wasn't sure he could move, let alone stand, right now. He drew her against his chest and held her tight until he'd caught his breath.

"I think bad has been good for me," she said, her breath tickling his chest.

He managed a hoarse laugh. "Yeah."

"Really is a shame that our clothes are on top of that rock, though."

"It really is." Even more of a shame that he'd have to put on his cold, wet trunks to climb up and get them.

"Next time, we hike in our suits and leave our clothes down here."

Next time. "Yeah." He lay there for several minutes, just holding her. Then he got to his feet and climbed into his wet trunks and soggy sneakers. "Still worth it," he said with a wink.

"Totally." She tugged her bikini bottom back on and reached for her sneakers.

"You stay here." He picked up her pink towel and draped it over her shoulders. "I'll be right back."

* * *

Four hours later, Emma was seated at a table surrounded by her friends, halfway through her second beer, and today was definitely right up there as *best day ever*. She plucked a nacho from the half-demolished platter on the table in front of her, earning a heated look from Ryan as she licked cheese sauce from her finger.

"So have you started packing yet?" Carly asked, snagging a nacho for herself.

Emma shook her head. "I've been too busy this week with the memorial, but next week, work will start winding down for me." She caught Ryan watching her intently. Maybe she'd said too much earlier. She wasn't even sure where it had come from because she was still committed to moving to Georgia. Her emotions had gotten the better of her for a few minutes there after they jumped, but she wasn't giving up on her dream.

Ryan was right. She had to go for at least a semester. Even if she didn't finish her degree, she'd learn valuable skills she could use in her future business. And chances were, once she got there, she'd find the enthusiasm to stay.

The one part she was no longer sure about was what happened after graduation. She'd planned to stay in Georgia, but if Ryan was willing to make a go of a long-distance relationship, she'd happily move back to Haven after she graduated. In fact, even if they broke up, she might come back here after she earned her degree.

Because the people she loved most in the world were sitting around this table with her tonight, and she couldn't imagine leaving them all behind forever. They were her family, and Haven was her home.

"Hi, guys. Sorry I'm late."

Emma looked up to see Jessica standing beside their table. "You're not late. We're still on appetizers. I'm so glad you could come." She motioned toward the only empty seat at the table...right next to Mark.

Ouch. That was awkward, but no way around it now.

Mark glanced at Jessica, his eyes dark and unreadable.

Hers weren't. They flashed with anger, but she sat, casting a warm smile at Emma.

Sorry, Emma mouthed to her. Jess and Mark hadn't exactly been on speaking terms since he dumped her in high school, but that was ten years ago now. It seemed like enough time had passed that they could handle being civil to each other here tonight.

Jessica shook her head, letting Emma know it was okay. "So I hear you're leaving us next week?"

Emma nodded. "Lucas and Mary are retiring so I'm going to take the chance to get my degree, maybe open my own landscape design firm when I graduate."

"That's great," Jessica said, pointedly not looking at the tall, silent, scarred man beside her.

"We need to squeeze in another girls' night out before you go," Gabby said from across the table. "Jessica, would you like to join us?"

"Yeah, sure. I'd love to." Jessica's beer arrived, and she took a long sip.

Emma sighed into her own beer. "We finally have this awesome girls' night out group, and now I'm leaving."

"You'll meet new people," Gabby said. "You told me yourself you're a social butterfly."

Yeah, but this was the first time she'd had such a group of *close* friends. "You're right. I'll make new friends. And I'll be back to visit so often you guys will get sick of me."

"Not sure that could ever happen," Gabby said with a grin.

Their food arrived, and conversation became more scattered as they ate. Ryan and Ethan were talking about a big group of zip-liners they were taking out the following morning while Gabby shared wedding details with Emma, Carly, and Jessica between bites of her shepherd's pie.

Emma soaked it all up, the big table full of friends laughing and talking. Jessica had her hands in the air, telling Carly a story Emma hadn't caught the beginning of, but it involved someone walking in on a guy jerking off in one of the spring-fed hot tubs at the spa, and Carly was laughing so hard that tears leaked from her eyes.

"And then he was like—" Jessica flung an arm up to imitate the guy, and her elbow caught the handle of her beer mug, sending it flying. Jess's beer shattered on the tile floor with a crash that silenced conversation across the restaurant.

All eyes were on their table.

Mark popped out of his seat and hovered over Jessica, his brow bunched in concern. "You okay?"

"Yeah, just…klutzy." Jessica's cheeks were red with embarrassment.

"It happens." Mark gathered several napkins from the table and placed them over the puddle of beer on the floor. The waitstaff arrived a few seconds later to clean everything up.

Jessica still looked mortified after they'd left, her hands clasped tightly in her lap.

"Seriously, Jess," Emma said. "We've all done it."

"Maybe not in such spectacular fashion," Ethan added with a grin, ribbing her.

"How about a toast?" Emma suggested, after Jessica's beer had been replaced. "To great friends and spilled beer."

"Here, here." All around the table, hands lifted mugs of beer into the air.

"And to you, Emma," Gabby added. "May this be your year to shine in whatever direction life takes you."

*C*HAPTER TWENTY-TWO

*T*heir first zip-lining group of the day canceled last minute so Ryan, Mark, and Ethan seized the opportunity to walk the property together, finalizing the course for the upcoming Adrenaline Rush. They'd held the team-based obstacle race for the first time last summer as part of the grand opening for Off-the-Grid, and it had been such a success they'd decided to make it an annual event.

"I think we should add a mud obstacle this year," Ethan said, leading the way down the path toward the stream.

"You really want to make a mud pit out here?" Mark asked.

Ethan shrugged. "Simple enough to fill it in afterward."

Ryan lunged upward to grab an overhead branch, swinging for a moment before jumping back onto the trail. "You got a spot in mind?"

"Maybe the field behind the ropes course."

"Yo, we paid Artful Blooms to reseed that field for us a couple of months ago. Not a good investment to dig it up."

"Oh yeah." Ethan looked thoughtful.

"Could use the area behind the second zip-line platform," Mark suggested.

"That might be perfect," Ethan said. "It's mostly mulch, and it tends to get muddy anyway."

"I like it," Ryan said. "We definitely need to switch some things up this year, keep the course interesting and unpredictable."

"I agree," Ethan said.

They spent the next hour walking and talking, coming up with new ideas and deciding which bits of last year's race they could repeat. They headed back toward the main building just in time to get ready for their next zip-lining group.

"So you're really going to let Emma move to Georgia next week?" Ethan asked, smiling like a cocky bastard.

"Let her? It's not my job to tell her what she can and can't do."

"No, but don't you think you guys ought to have a chat? You know, about feelings and all that mushy shit?"

Ryan wanted to punch the cocky grin right off Ethan's face. "Feelings?"

"Bro, you can't just let her walk away without fighting for her."

Ryan tripped over a tree root and almost fell flat on his face. "Of course I can. This thing between us was always short term. It's just casual."

"Just casual, huh?" Ethan glanced at Mark. "You hear this shit?"

"Seem to recall having the same conversation with you not so long ago," Mark commented drily.

"That's true," Ethan said. He turned to Ryan, his expression gone serious. "There are photos on Gabby's phone of Emma in a wedding dress."

Ryan damn near fell on his face again. "Say what now?"

* * *

Emma spent Saturday evening finishing up the summer landscaping at Off-the-Grid. She'd brought in several lavender asters to brighten up the walkway area and the flower bed beneath the sign. They were hardy and should flower on and off all summer long.

The guys needed low-maintenance, especially after she left town. Another wave of homesickness hit her as she imagined someone else here tending their landscaping, adding new flowers to the bed she'd built.

But no matter. They were just flowers, after all.

She'd just finished up and put her tools back in her car when she spotted Trent headed down the path toward the ropes course, cell phone in hand. She jogged after him. "Hey, Trent."

He turned, swiping a lock of hair out of his eyes with a smile. "Hi, Emma."

"How's it going? You made any plans for the summer?"

"Iris is going to LA to try her luck. There are a lot of opportunities there, DJ'ing and music and all that." He looked over at Emma, a defiant look in his eyes. "I might go with her."

"Have you talked about it with Ryan or your parents?" she asked cautiously, knowing Ryan would hate this idea. His parents would, too.

"I mentioned it to Ryan. He's not a fan," Trent said with a shrug.

"Well, you're old enough to make your own decisions, but that doesn't mean you shouldn't listen to some advice, too."

"Guess not."

"I've had a lot of people giving me their advice about

my move to Georgia," she said. They had reached the ropes course. Since Trent didn't seem to be working at the moment, they sat side by side in a couple of the tires that were part of the obstacle course. She kicked her feet, swinging gently back and forth. "You want to know the truth?"

"Sure." He kicked off next to her and swung.

"I don't really want to go."

"No?" He turned to look at her.

She shook her head. "I dreamed about it for so long, but now that I'm doing it, I don't know... it doesn't feel right."

"So you're dropping out like I did?" He was grinning now.

"Actually, no. I talked it over with Ryan and decided I have to go, at least for a semester. You're never too old for advice, you know." She nudged at him playfully as he swung past.

"The truth is, I don't really know what I want out of life," Trent said. "I'm just, I don't know... restless."

"I hear you. You're a free agent right now. You can go anywhere and do anything you want. But if you always go chasing after the next shiny thing to catch your eye, someday you might end up regretting the people and opportunities you left behind."

"You don't think I should go to LA."

She laughed. "I didn't say that. But why *do* you want to go? Just because of Iris? Do you really think there are DJ opportunities there for someone your age that aren't here in Haven?"

"It sounds exciting," he said. "And yeah, I do think there are a lot of opportunities. I mean, with Hollywood and everything. How could I pass that up?"

"There are also a lot of people vying for those opportunities. And it's crazy expensive to live out there. How are you going to support yourselves while you look for work?"

Trent didn't say anything, just swung back and forth, staring at the ground.

"We're opposites right now, you and me," she said thoughtfully. "You want to leave your family behind and head off in search of adventure, which is exactly what I thought I wanted to do. And right now I'd give anything to stay home with you guys."

"Because of my brother?"

She smiled over at Trent again. "You're awfully wise for eighteen. Yes, your brother is a big part of it."

"You love him?" Trent asked.

"Yeah," she said softly. "I do."

"Does he know?"

It was her turn to shrug. Had Ryan overhead what she said when she jumped yesterday? If he had, he hadn't let on. "Do you love Iris?"

"Yeah," he said fervently.

Ah, young love. "Well, Trent, I think you have to follow your heart. Don't let Ryan or anyone else guilt you into doing what they think is best for you."

"Then I should go to LA."

"I said follow your heart, not follow the girl," she said with a laugh. "You have to really listen to what it's telling you, and don't make your decision tonight. Think on it."

"Ryan and my folks really want me to go back to college."

"Yeah, and it's not a bad idea. Take it from someone who's learned the hard way, it's a lot harder to go back to school at twenty-seven than when you're fresh out of high school. Getting an education now will provide you with so many more opportunities later on."

"You're easy to talk to," Trent said thoughtfully.

Emma felt something warm and light fill her chest. "Thanks. So are you."

* * *

Ryan stormed down the path toward Off-the-Grid's main building. His chest felt like it might burst, so many emotions churned inside it. Hurt. Fear. Anger. He'd been passing by the ropes course when he heard Emma and Trent talking. He hadn't meant to eavesdrop, but he couldn't help overhearing her encourage Trent to go running off to LA, which was about the worst idea ever.

And then she'd said she loved him.

He'd almost convinced himself he hadn't heard her whisper those words yesterday as they jumped at the bluffs. But she had. And then she'd told Trent she didn't want to go to Georgia anymore. And *fuck*. Hadn't Ethan told him just that morning he'd seen pictures of Emma in a wedding dress on Gabby's phone?

She was about to give up her spot in landscape design school for him, the spot she'd worked so damn hard to earn. He couldn't let that happen.

Because *dammit* . . . she meant too much to him. She was one of the most important people in his life, and he'd never forgive himself if he derailed her dreams and her future because of him. He swung at the nearest tree, swearing a blue streak as its rough bark bruised and scraped his knuckles.

He couldn't seem to catch his breath, and there was something in his eyes, goddammit. He swiped at the dampness on his cheeks furiously with his good hand as he continued his wild march through the forest, headed for his bike.

He clenched his jaw, forcing back the hurt so that anger took over. Trent was going to chase his good-for-nothing girlfriend to LA, and Emma had encouraged him to do it. The kid had no money saved up, no job waiting. It was a recipe for disaster.

Dammit. It was exactly the kind of thing Ryan would have done at eighteen. Which was exactly why it was such a terrible idea. And now, thanks to Emma, he'd have to work even harder to get Trent to see reason.

How dare she butt into his and Trent's business like that? This should have stayed between him and his brother. He definitely shouldn't go over to Emma's place spoiling for a fight, which was exactly why he was going to do just that.

Because this thing between them had to end. Tonight.

* * *

Emma heard the bike coming and went to her front window. She watched as Ryan pulled into her driveway and sat, his face expressionless, staring at her front door.

He looked . . . hurt. Maybe even angry.

She opened the door. "Is everything okay?" she asked, motioning him to come in.

He got off the bike and stood facing her. "No."

A feeling of dread coiled in her stomach. "What's happened?"

"I overheard you and Trent earlier." He spoke without emotion, his expression hidden behind his mirrored sunglasses.

What had he overhead? Oh God, she'd told Trent she loved him . . . "Oh. Okay—"

"Don't." He put a hand up to stop her. "I can't believe you told him it was okay to go to LA."

Oh, *that's* what he was all bent out of shape about? She scowled at him. "You must not have listened very well because that's not what I said, and not nearly all we talked about."

"You know how I feel about this, Emma. He's eighteen, for Christ's sake. He's not even old enough to drink a beer, and you think it would be okay for him to take off across the country with this woman he hasn't even introduced us to?"

"You can't stop him any more than I can. The best thing you can do right now is to support him."

"That's bullshit," he growled. "He needs some sense knocked into that thick skull of his before he makes a huge mistake."

"Ryan," she said, her voice gone soft, "why are we arguing about this?"

"Because..." He paused a moment, looking uncertain. "Because you shouldn't have meddled in my family business with Trent."

Ouch. She took an involuntary step backward. She didn't know how to respond because she wasn't sorry for a single word she'd said to Trent. "Excuse me?"

Ryan met her gaze, but instead of warmth and laughter, she saw only cold, hard anger reflected in his eyes. "You heard me."

"Yeah, I did." She folded her arms over her chest and glared up at him. "And I think *you're* the one overstepping here, Ryan, if you think you have the right to tell me who I can and can't have a friendly conversation with."

"You should have backed me up."

She stepped forward and jabbed a finger against his chest. "You honestly think I don't have your back? Don't be such an ass."

"We let this go too far, Emma. I never meant to end up

here." He looked down at the handlebars of his bike. "But it's done. It ends tonight."

She flinched, as hurt mixed with anger inside her, swelling into a big ball of emotion in her chest. "Just like that? We had our first fight so now you're breaking up with me?"

"We always said we'd go back to being just friends when the time came. And the time is now." His voice sounded flat, distant. Cold.

"That's just…what the actual fuck, Ryan?" She didn't know whether to cry or punch him.

"What did you expect?" he asked, looking genuinely confused.

"Too much, I guess." Tears pricked behind her eyes, and she blinked them back, desperate to hold on to her anger until he had gone.

"Well, there you go." He shoved his hands into his pockets, pinning her in that dark, angry gaze. "You wanted me to help you be a little bit bad, right, Emma? You wanted a hot fling with a guy like me, but I'm not—"

"Stop right there," she cut him off. "Fuck you, Ryan. Good-bye."

CHAPTER TWENTY-THREE

*E*mma woke on Sunday with a sore heart and puffy eyes. She still didn't know exactly what had gone wrong with Ryan because surely he hadn't dumped her just because she'd encouraged Trent to follow his dreams.

And if he had...if their relationship meant that little to him? Well, then screw him. And good riddance.

She buried her face in the pillow, wishing she never had to get out of bed and face reality. Smokey hopped onto her back and curled up for a nap, making Emma laugh. "That's really not comfortable for me, you know."

But Smokey was purring contentedly, and her familiar weight felt comforting right now. Smokey might hate her temporarily when she uprooted their lives and moved them to Georgia, but Emma had never been more grateful for the kind of unconditional love offered by her pet.

Ryan was such a pigheaded idiot...

Fresh tears welled in her eyes. Well, she hoped she didn't see the stupid jerk again before she left town because she might just give him another piece of her mind, and she'd never been particularly eloquent when she was mad...or hurt.

Since today was her day off, her *last* day off before she wrapped up her work with Artful Blooms later this week, she dozed off again with Smokey still asleep on her back. When she woke up, it was nine thirty, her back was sweaty beneath Smokey's toasty form, and she had to pee. Reluctantly, she rolled out from under her cat and went into the bathroom.

And then she decided to do something pretty unheard of for her...she decided to spend the whole day in her pajamas in bed. She loaded up a marathon of *Gilmore Girls* on Netflix, rooted around in the freezer for her emergency ice cream, and settled in for the duration.

The relationship between Rory and Lorelai reminded her so much of her relationship with her own mother. This show had always been one of her favorites. She laughed. She cried. She ate way too much ice cream. She snuggled a lot with her cat. Then she slept.

And by the time Monday morning rolled around, she felt ready to rejoin society. She was still hurting, still emotionally fragile, but life went on, with or without the man she loved. She'd always known she would probably lose him, although she'd never imagined he'd dump her in such a frustratingly unexpected way.

She took a much-needed shower and debated what to wear to her meeting with Angela Davenport at the future Silver Springs Lodge. She wanted to look nice, but she also had to go to work after. Finally, she decided on a pair of khaki cargo pants and a blue top.

She hopped in her car and drove to Silver Springs. The hotel site was on top of a hill with lovely views of the mountains surrounding it. Such a prime location must have cost a pretty penny. Emma didn't know much about Angela Davenport other than that she wasn't from the area. This seemed like an unusual project for an outsider. Emma's curiosity was piqued.

She parked in the construction lot beside a string of other vehicles and got out, looking around for Ms. Davenport. She spotted the older woman coming out of the construction trailer and headed in that direction.

"Emma, I'm so thrilled you could make it," she said, walking over with her hand outstretched.

Emma took it and shook. "Of course. You have a beautiful location here, Ms. Davenport. I can't wait to see the lodge once it's finished."

"Call me Angela, please," she said. "Let me show you around the building site to give you a feel for it, and then I'll show you our mock-up of the finished product."

"That sounds great," Emma said, still having no idea why she was here but curious all the same.

Angela led the way across the construction site. Already the skeleton of the hotel was in place, beams and pipes and a whole lot of upturned earth. Emma's eyes took in all the exposed red clay, already visualizing bushes, flowers, and walkways around the building.

"The lodge will face this way," Angela said, indicating the sweeping valley in front of them. "Many of the rooms will have balconies overlooking the valley. We're going for a very 'mountain retreat' feel here. We'll have lots of amenities on-site for our guests to pamper themselves as well as a network of hiking trails into the mountains and down to the valley. I also have plans for an extensive garden area off to the side here." She gestured toward the right-hand side of the property, where a large plot of land lay open and undisturbed, flanked by the valley on one side and forest on the other.

Emma imagined winding paths lined with lush flower beds. Benches for guests to sit, relax, and enjoy their surroundings or even read a book. Maybe flowering bushes along the outer edge to create a "hidden garden" feel.

It would be breathtaking.

Angela brought her to the construction trailer to show her mock-ups of the completed lodge. The garden area had been filled in with the most basic rendering of flowers and bushes.

"It needs fleshing out, obviously," Angela said with a smile.

"It will be beautiful," Emma told her. "The lodge looks amazing. It should be a great addition to the area once it's open."

"You might be wondering why I've brought you here," Angela said, giving Emma a shrewd look.

She smiled. "I did wonder, yes."

"Well, I was very impressed with your work on the new war memorial. I've gotten the chance to know Lucas and Mary Pratt while I've been in town, and they speak very highly of you. If you haven't figured it out yet, I'd like to hire you."

Emma's mouth popped open. "Hire me?"

Angela nodded. "I'd be so pleased if you would design and maintain our gardens for us. It's very important to me to work with local professionals wherever possible. I'm from a small town myself, although on the West Coast. I've opened a string of hotels across the country, but not a chain. Each are independent, unique, and tailored to their surroundings. I like you, Emma, and your work is vibrant and exciting, yet reflective of the local flair."

Emma's mind was reeling. Designing the gardens for this

lodge? That was a big job. *Whoa...* "You got all that from seeing the memorial gardens?" she asked faintly.

"And from talking with Lucas and Mary. They were kind enough to show me some of your other work."

"Wow, Angela. I'm really flattered."

"I'm not sure if you have room in your schedule for a project of this size. Construction on the lodge is moving along quickly, and we hope to be open for business by the end of the year so I'm afraid I'd be monopolizing a lot of your time between now and then."

"I'll...well, I'm sorry. Lucas and Mary must not have mentioned that I'm leaving town next week. I've enrolled in the University of Georgia's landscape architecture program."

"Ah," Angela said. "I didn't know. My loss then."

"If I weren't leaving town, I would jump on this project in a heartbeat. It's exactly the kind of work I want to do." Emma felt a crushing sort of sadness settle over her that she wouldn't get this chance. "I'll be sure to stay here when I visit."

"That's very kind," Angela said. "Well, I wish you the best of luck in your new endeavor."

Emma stayed for a few more minutes, talking with Angela, then walked back to her car in a haze of mixed emotions. That, right there, had been her dream job. Exactly the kind of project she wanted to work on. As she drove back over the winding roads to Haven, a niggle of doubt began to work its way through her.

What if she stayed? What if she opened her own landscape company now, sans degree, took this job, and made a go of it?

Was that totally crazy?

She picked up her phone and dialed Mary. "Why didn't

you tell her I was leaving town?" she asked after filling Mary
in on her meeting with Angela Davenport.

"Where are you?" Mary asked.

"Almost in downtown."

"I'm at the bakery. Swing by, and let's chat."

"Okay." Emma drove down Main Street and parked at the
commons near the new memorial. The red poppies made her
smile every time she walked by, although today her smile
was bittersweet. She entered the bakery and waved at Carly,
spotting Mary at a table near the back.

"Your usual?" Carly called out.

"That would be awesome. Thanks." Maybe a coffee and
a cinnamon bun would help her sort out this crazy-confusing
morning. Really, the last two days had been such a roller
coaster. At this point, she had no idea which end was up.

"So," Mary said when Emma had sat across from her, "I
want to tell you a few things, and I'm not sure how you're
going to feel about them."

"Okay," Emma said, a vague sense of unease settling in
her stomach. Carly swung by with her coffee and cinnamon
bun, and she took a welcome sip of the hot brew.

"When we first started planning our retirement this year,
Lucas and I had talked about passing Artful Blooms on to
you," she said.

"What?" The coffee mug nearly slipped from Emma's
fingers. She set it on the table with a clunk.

"You're our protégée. We're both so proud of you, and we
knew Artful Blooms would be in great hands with you. In
fact, that's why we originally chose you to lead the memorial
project. We were grooming you to take over for us. But then
you told us you'd enrolled in college and wanted to start a
new career for yourself in Georgia, and we were thrilled for
you, Emma. We didn't want to hold you back. You're right

in thinking that there are opportunities for you there that you just won't find in a little town like Haven."

Emma had no idea what to say.

Mary lifted her coffee cup and took a sip. "But after our conversation last week, I realized we'd made a mistake in not at least extending our offer to you. Artful Blooms' customers adore you and would love to continue working with you. Designing the gardens at the Silver Springs Lodge is the kind of project that could help really put you on the map around here. Truthfully, I'm not sure full-time college is your best investment right now. Sometimes when you've got momentum like this, it's best to grab it by the horns and run with it."

"Wow." Emma took another sip of coffee, her insides gone strangely numb.

"Here's another idea for you to consider," Mary said, placing her coffee cup back on the table. "A degree is a definite asset, especially in owning your own business. There are a number of online universities these days, geared toward students like yourself, men and women who've already entered the workforce. You could work toward a business degree in the evenings while still doing the work you love during the day."

Was Mary right? Maybe she could do as well, or better, getting a business degree online while she kept up her landscape design work. Not only that, but she could stay here in Haven, with the friends who'd become her family.

Her heart had been nudging her in this direction for the past few weeks, and now she had a real reason to stay, even if staying meant living in the same town as Ryan without having him in her life.

* * *

Ryan cut the engine and climbed off his bike, praying he didn't run into anyone on his way in because he was not fit for company right now. He'd been pissed off ever since he broke up with Emma, and a couple days to stew over it hadn't helped.

He'd been an idiot, plain and simple. He had no idea if they'd manage to salvage their friendship after this, but did it even matter when she was leaving town anyway? Now he'd think of her every time he rode on his bike or visited the bluffs. Hell, even the rock face at Off-the-Grid. Every aspect of his life had been infiltrated with sweet, sexy, amazing memories of Emma.

She'd torture him from afar without even knowing she was doing it.

He missed her so fucking much already, and she hadn't even left town yet. Dammit all to hell. How had he let this happen?

He'd just shoved the key in his front door when he heard someone coming down the stairs, dragging something heavy. It scraped and thumped down each step. Had to be Trent. Mark never made that much noise.

He turned to see Trent round the corner above him, dragging an enormous suitcase. *Fuck.* "You're really going to LA? Just like this? Were you even going to say good-bye?"

Trent shook his head, a lock of hair falling over his eyes. "I'm going home."

Home? "What?"

Trent shoved his suitcase down to the landing and shook his hair back from his eyes. "Iris dumped me. Are you happy now?"

Ryan stared, noticing for the first time that his brother looked as wrecked—and as pissed at the world—as Ryan himself felt. "I'm sorry, man. I'm real sorry to hear that."

"Whatever," Trent said, dragging the suitcase in the direction of his car. "This place blows. I'm going home."

"You're going back to Missouri?"

"Yeah, I am."

Ryan followed him. "Yo, don't leave like this, Trent. At least stay the night. You shouldn't start a long drive this late in the day."

"You're as bad as Mom and Dad!" Trent wheeled on him, dark eyes snapping as he unleashed all his hurt and anger on Ryan. "Stop telling me what to do. Just leave me alone."

Ryan stepped back as his brother's words clawed at him, ripping at his heart. "I'm sorry, Trent. I just wanted to help. Don't leave like this. Please."

"Whatever," Trent said again, sliding into his car and slamming the door behind him. "I don't need your help or anybody else's."

The engine roared to life, and Ryan watched helplessly as his brother drove away.

Just leave me alone.

Those words hurt like a motherfucker. He'd lost Emma, and now Trent, and suddenly it felt like all the color had been sucked out of his life. He stormed into his condo, slamming the door behind him. Next thing he knew, he'd punched another hole in the wall, and now his fist hurt like a motherfucker, too.

* * *

Emma lifted her cotton candy martini and gulped from it. Tonight's girls' night out had changed from going-away party to "Ryan dumped me" commiseration to "dream job here in Haven" celebration. When Gabby offered to drive,

Emma had jumped at the chance because she had no desire to stay sober enough to drive herself home.

Nope. She was getting trashed tonight.

To eliminate any chances of running into the guys—or really just Ryan—they'd taken their party to Jazzy's Martini Bar in Silver Springs, and the change of scenery was just what Emma needed. Rowdy's and even The Drunken Bear held too many bittersweet memories for her to handle right now.

"To Emma's new job," Carly said, raising her glass.

"And staying in Haven," Gabby added.

They all clinked glasses. Seated around a bar-height glass table with her were Jessica, Gabby, Carly, and Mandy. The best friends a girl could hope for.

"It still hasn't sunk in that I'm not leaving," she said. "It's been such a rock in the pit of my stomach for the last few weeks, dreading the move but knowing I needed to stick with the plan I'd set in motion."

"Seriously, though, I can't believe you're taking over Artful Blooms. That's such an amazing opportunity," Carly said.

Mandy raised her eyebrows, and Emma winked at her. After she'd left Mary at the bakery, Emma had called Angela Davenport to accept the Silver Springs Lodge project, then driven straight to Mandy's apartment. They'd spent the rest of the afternoon putting together a business plan.

"About that," Emma said. "Artful Blooms is actually going to be a joint partnership. Mandy and I are going in fifty-fifty."

"What?" Gabby's smile grew impossibly wide. "That's so awesome!"

"Yep." Mandy nodded enthusiastically. "It's a dream come true for both of us."

"We make a great team, and I'm going to work toward my business degree online in the evenings," Emma said. "With the clients the two of us already have, the Artful Blooms name behind us, and the upcoming project at the lodge, we should be in good shape."

"I've heard a lot of buzz about the Silver Springs Lodge," Jessica said. "It should be a great way to get your names out."

"Have you told Ryan?" Gabby asked, sipping from her lemontini.

Emma gave her a look. "Are you kidding? I haven't seen him since he dumped me, and I don't expect to...not for a while anyway."

"I still can't believe he did that." Carly scowled. "The big jerk. Because you offered his brother some advice?"

"I don't think that's why he did it," Gabby said with a shake of her head. "Not the only reason anyway."

"I'd love to think you're right, but..." Emma broke off with a shrug.

"The man's thirty years old, and he's never had a real relationship with a woman," Gabby said. "You guys were in over your heads almost before you started sleeping together. I think there's a decent chance he panicked and bailed before you left town."

"Well—" Tears pooled in Emma's eyes, and she took a furious sip of her martini. "It doesn't really matter because he was such an ass about it. I don't know if I could forgive him even if he asked me to, which I have no reason to believe he will. So..."

She finished off her martini, and Mandy signaled to the bartender to order her another.

"I'll try my best not to make things awkward for our group." Emma stared into her empty glass. "It's inevitable we'll be around each other since we share the same circle of friends. Eventually I'll be ready for it, but I'm not there yet."

"Perfectly understandable," Jessica said.

"Does he know you're in love with him?" Carly asked quietly.

Thankfully, the waitress placed another cotton candy martini in front of Emma at that moment. She took a fortifying gulp before she answered. "I think he might."

"Maybe I'm just an optimist after the way things worked out for Ethan and me," Gabby said, "but I think Ryan has real feelings for you, too. He just has no idea what to do about it."

Tears threatened again. Emma waved a hand in front of her face. "Enough about Ryan. What else is new?"

"I heard the guys might be adding a mud obstacle to this year's Adrenaline Rush," Gabby said.

"Bring it," Mandy said, lifting her glass.

"I could do without mud," Gabby said. "But count me in, and this year, I'm crossing the finish line." Last year, Gabby had fallen from the climbing wall and sprained her ankle, ending her race early.

"You joining us on Team Flower Power this year, Jess?" Emma asked.

Jessica, who'd been rather quiet so far tonight, swirled her glass thoughtfully. "I'll think about it."

"You sound like I did last year," Gabby said with a conspiratorial smile.

"It's really a lot of fun," Mandy said. "Team Flower Power seriously kicks ass."

"It's true," Carly said with a nod.

Jessica shrugged, taking a sip of her martini. "Sure, why not?"

"If I can do it, you can," Gabby said. "I actually made

them change the date this year so that the Adrenaline Rush comes after our wedding. Otherwise, I was afraid I'd be getting married on crutches or, at the very least, all covered in scrapes and bruises."

"Smart thinking," Mandy said with a laugh.

By the time Gabby drove her home that night, Emma was completely sloshed and feeling *much* better about life in general. She staggered through her front door, poured herself a tall glass of water, then went into her bedroom to change into pajamas. She climbed into bed and turned on *The Late Show* to keep her company until she dozed off.

A motorcycle roared up the road outside, and she walked to her bedroom window out of habit. The bike kept going, continuing up the road and out of sight. Of course it wasn't Ryan. He wasn't coming, not anymore.

CHAPTER TWENTY-FOUR

$\mathcal{R}$yan had been riding the empty, winding roads outside Haven for hours, trying desperately to calm the chaos tumbling around in his brain. After Trent left, he'd called the Lamars to let them know what had happened, and Kate had promised to stay in touch when she heard from him. At least he was finally on speaking terms with them. That had to count for something. Ryan gunned the engine and let the beast beneath him roar. As he rode by Emma's apartment for the third time, he realized he had a problem.

The fourth time? He had identified the problem. It was Emma, but she wasn't a problem. She was the solution to his problem, and he'd been too stupid to see it. He hadn't been with another woman, hadn't even *looked* at another woman in almost a year. Emma had been in his head almost since he returned to Haven, long before he slept with her. He kept pushing her away because of the promise he'd made Derek, but he'd also promised to look out for her, and what better way to look out for her than to be *with* her?

Before he realized where he was headed, he found himself parking the bike in front of the town commons. The flowers Emma had planted rippled in the breeze, their vivid red color muted to a steely gray under the cover of night. He walked to the memorial and stood there, squinting to pick out Derek's name on the darkened stone surface, illuminated only by the faint glow of a nearby streetlight.

"Wish I could have this conversation with you in person," Ryan said. More than anything, he wished he could get his buddy's blessing on what he was about to do. "But I need to believe that you'd be okay with this because I promise you I'm going to do anything and everything I can to make Emma happy if she'll give me another chance."

He stood there with his hands shoved into his pockets, staring at Derek's name on the memorial. The memorial that Emma had designed. She'd brought so much color, so much *life*, to this formerly barren part of the commons.

So much color to his life.

Ryan had no fucking clue how to make a relationship work, let alone a relationship with a woman as incredible, as sweet and funny and vibrant and beautiful, as Emma. She was leaving town in a few days, but it didn't matter. If she was willing to give him a second chance, they'd find a way to make this work. Hell, he loved riding his bike. He'd ride to Georgia once a week if he had to, just to see her.

He stepped closer to the memorial, touched his fingertips to Derek's name, and took a silent oath to make his buddy proud, to take care of Emma the very best way he knew how. Then he strode back to his bike and pointed it toward her house.

This time, when he rode by her place, he pulled into the driveway and parked. He checked the time on his phone and cringed. It was one thirty in the morning. On a Monday night. As usual, his timing was all wrong.

So he just sat there staring at her front door, wondering

what she was doing. Sleeping, no doubt. In the buff? In some kind of sexy nightie?

In answer to his question, the front door opened, and she appeared in the doorway, squinting out at him. She wore short pink sleep shorts and a matching tank top, her hair wild and messy around her face as if she'd just rolled out of bed.

He'd woken her in the middle of the night. He was such an asshole. He ought to leave now. Instead, he took off his helmet and swung off the bike.

"Ryan?" She blinked at him as if not entirely sure she wasn't dreaming.

"Yeah. Sorry. I didn't realize how late it was."

She scrunched her nose, looking adorably confused. "What are you doing here?"

"I've been riding. Thinking." And hell, there was no going back now. "Can I come in?"

She pulled herself up taller, crossing her arms over her chest, a wary look in her eyes. "No."

He dragged a hand through his hair. "Fair enough. I have a few things to say if you're willing to listen."

"I don't know, Ryan." She stared at him, her blue eyes full of hurt and distrust. "I think...I think I'm still too angry." Her voice caught, and he felt like someone had just stomped on his chest.

He'd done this to her. *Goddammit.* "I came to apologize."

"It better be a good one or else I might really lose it." She planted her hands on her hips.

"Christ, Emma." He fumbled his helmet, and it hit the pavement with a crash. He was absolutely terrified he was going to fuck this up and lose her forever. Maybe he already had. "I'm going for the biggest apology of my life here, up to and including groveling. Begging. Whatever you ask, I'll do it."

Her eyes widened. "Okay, come in."

She turned, motioning him to follow her inside, and staggered slightly.

He grabbed her shoulder, steadying her. "You okay?"

"Yep, just...still feeling the effects of girls' night." A smile flickered on her lips, and he realized she was tipsy, if not drunk. At one thirty on Monday night, or Tuesday morning, or whatever the hell day it was.

She stepped backward out of his grasp and stood there in the middle of her living room, just watching him.

"Emma, I sure as hell hope you're sober enough to remember this because I have some pretty important things to say."

She swallowed hard but said nothing.

"I'm so fucking sorry for everything I said the other night. I was a total asshole for taking my frustration with Trent out on you. You were right. I was too hard on him. He left. He's moving back home with his parents."

Her mouth formed an "oh," and her eyes welled with sympathy.

"But that wasn't why I broke up with you. I did that because I'm a coward. I was scared of what's happening between us...and, Emma, I was terrified you were going to give up your dreams to stay here in Haven because of me."

She opened her mouth to speak.

"Wait, let me get this all out before I lose my nerve." He let out a rough laugh, scrubbing a hand over his jaw. His hands were all over the place. He had no idea what to do with them. And then he looked at Emma.

The expression on her face cracked his heart wide open.

He loved her. He'd always loved her. Granted, he'd loved her in a purely platonic way until recently, but now? Now he loved her with every fiber of his being, and there was nothing platonic about it. "So I'm here to beg for your forgiveness on the condition that you promise you won't derail your plans for me. If you can find it in your heart to forgive me, we'll make it work, Emma. I'll ride out to Georgia as often as I need to."

Tears spilled over her eyelids, splashing down her cheeks. "You can't derail my plans because I already did that myself. I'm staying in Haven. I'm taking over Artful Blooms with Mandy, and I'll get my business degree online in the evenings."

He wanted to pull her into his arms and kiss her senseless, but she hadn't forgiven him yet. "That's amazing. You'll be running your own landscape design firm four years earlier than you thought."

"And I'll be living out my dream right here in Haven." She smiled softly. "So I'm staying, and it has nothing to do with you. Is there anything else you wanted to tell me?"

"One more thing." He drew a deep breath and took her hands in his. "I love you."

"What?" More tears were sliding down her cheeks now.

He had no idea if he was doing this right, but now that he'd said the words out loud, he'd never felt more exposed. He'd overheard her confessing her love for him, but she'd never said it to his face. "I'm in love with you, Em. I've always loved you, even when you were just Derek's pesky little sister. You've always felt like a part of my family, in a totally non-incestuous kind of way—" He grimaced. *Shit.* He was terrible at this.

Emma dissolved in a fit of giggles, tears still pouring down her cheeks, reminding him that she was borderline drunk. *Jesus.*

"It wasn't until a few months ago that I realized we could be more than friends, and Em, we are so much more. So damn much. You're all I can think about. You make me laugh at the weirdest fucking moments. Like right now." He choked on a laugh, his throat gone tight. "And when we're making love. Nothing feels right when we're not together. I can't imagine ever being with anyone else. Please tell me we still have a chance together."

She flung herself in his arms, her arms around his neck, laughing and crying, her forehead pressed against his. "I've always loved you, too, Ryan. Since we were kids. Never anyone else. You're it for me."

Relief pulsed through him, making him dizzy. "I am absolutely crazy for you."

"And this thing between us is crazy-good." She hiccupped, her chest heaving as she smiled through her tears.

"Yeah, it is." He crushed his lips against hers, desperate to taste her after two long days without her. They kissed for a long time, and he felt whole in a way he never had before. He'd been a lone wolf for a long time, too fucking long. Now he had Emma, the woman he loved and wanted to spend the rest of his life with. He had Trent, because he was going to go after the cocky-ass kid and smooth that over, too. And he had the rest of their circle of handmade family. If this was what settled felt like, he wanted more.

"Will you stay?" she asked, her dewy eyes glazed with desire—and maybe still alcohol.

"I don't see where I have a choice," he said, fighting a smile. "In case you have trouble remembering any of this in the morning, I'd better be here to remind you."

"I won't forget. But I might ask you to tell me again in the morning just for fun."

"Gladly." He carried her toward her bedroom. He'd happily profess his love for Emma every day for the rest of his life.

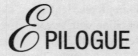

$\mathcal{E}$PILOGUE

Two Months Later

$\mathcal{E}$mma stared at the plastic stick in her hand. She gave it a little shake, as if that might somehow change the plus sign to a minus. Because yeah, she was two weeks late and right now she felt like she might hurl, but *pregnant?*

She leaned forward and rested her elbows on her knees until the spinning sensation in her head had stopped. This was *so* not part of her plan right now. She and Mandy had just taken over Artful Blooms. She was knee-deep in the Silver Springs Lodge project and a few weeks into her first semester of business school.

She didn't have time for a baby right now. *A baby.* Her eyes welled with tears. Holy crap. She and Ryan had made a baby together. That was…amazing…and terrifying…and wonderful.

How would he react? They'd only been together a few months. Their love was still so new. They'd never even mentioned marriage, let alone starting a family. Something warm grew in her chest, spreading through the panic clutching at her insides.

A baby. Her and Ryan's baby.

She let out a shaky breath, tossed the pregnancy test in the trash, and walked outside to her car, unable to wait another moment to tell him. She drove straight to Off-the-Grid and parked, still in somewhat of a daze.

"Hey, Emma," Ethan called, waving as he walked toward the zip-line course.

"Is Ryan around?" she asked.

"He's down by the ropes course fixing a loose board."

"Thanks." She walked briskly down the path until the ropes course came into view.

Ryan sat straddling the top of the climbing wall, hammer in hand. A huge smile covered his face when he saw her. "Hey, Em. What's up?"

"I've got something to tell you, but you might want to come down from there first," she said, anxiety knotting in her stomach.

Ryan's smile faded. "Everything okay?"

"Yeah, just come down. Please."

He dropped to the ground and walked to her, taking her hands in his. "You're shaking. What's wrong?"

"I'm..." She sucked in a breath. "I'm pregnant."

Ryan was silent for a beat, his expression hidden behind his mirrored lenses. Then his arms were around her, her body crushed against his as he spun her around, kissing her like crazy. "No shit?" he said as he lifted his head.

She nodded, her heart pounding against her ribs. "I just took a test. We've been careful, but—"

"So this is what they warned us about in all those sex ed classes in high school," he said, but he was grinning widely, his arms still warm and tight around her.

"I guess. It's the worst possible timing." Tears welled in her eyes. "With work, and school, and you and I just…"

But Ryan was shaking his head. "Remember that night at the commons? We were eating cupcakes, and we talked about how the best things in life are the ones we never saw coming. This is one of those moments, Emma. This might be the biggest moment in our lives."

"Really?" She dabbed furiously at the tears spilling over her cheeks.

He released her, and she took a step back. He reached down and pressed his hand against her stomach. "A baby. *Our* baby. I don't know when it happened, but I know it's amazing."

"Our baby," she whispered, resting her hand over his.

"I bet it was that night a few weeks ago when we christened the back of the truck." He was still grinning, and if she wasn't mistaken, tears glistened in his eyes, too.

"That was quite a night." She laughed through her tears, remembering how they'd made love in the bed of his truck, a pile of blankets beneath them, a blanket of stars overhead.

"Emma," he said, his voice gone low and serious.

"Yeah?"

He walked to the edge of the clearing and bent down. When he came back, she saw that he had a flower in his hands, one of the red poppies she'd planted there last month. He went down on one knee in front of her, and everything spun out of balance…

"This isn't how I imagined doing this, but then again nothing between us has ever gone the way I thought it would. I thought you were just my friend, but I was wrong. I love you more than I ever knew it was possible to love anyone. We haven't talked about it, but I've known for a while I want to spent the rest of my life with you and start a family together."

She pressed a hand to her mouth, too overcome to speak.

"And there's nothing I'd love more than for you to say you'll marry me."

"Yes." Her voice was a hoarse whisper, her throat painfully tight. "It's what I want, too, more than anything."

He took her left hand in his and wound the stem of the flower around her finger, creating a makeshift ring. She stared at it, that beautiful red poppy nestled on her finger as a symbol of Ryan's love and their future together. It was more perfect than any ring he could have given her.

"I love you so much, babe." He stood and pulled her into his arms. "I can't fucking wait to marry you and start our life together."

Neither could she.

* * *

Four weeks later, they stood on a grassy overlook at the bluffs. Not the top. Emma'd had some ideas, but Ryan had won out as the voice of reason. They simply couldn't ask their wedding guests to hike to the top of the bluffs, and neither was he about to let his pregnant wife-to-be climb up there in her wedding dress.

Emma stood before him now, wearing the same dress Ethan had seen photos of on Gabby's phone. It had little pink flowers across the front and a long flowing skirt, and Ryan could hardly draw breath she was so fucking gorgeous.

Mark stood in front of them, looking awfully damn official in a black suit, their vows in his hands. He'd gone and gotten himself ordained for the occasion. Ethan, Gabby,

Trent, Carly, Sam, Mandy, and Jessica rounded out their little wedding party.

"By the power vested in me by the State of North Carolina, I now pronounce you husband and wife," Mark said.

Emma leaped into his arms with a kiss that set his heart ablaze with love. For their future, and their family, and a lifetime of happiness. Everyone rushed in to congratulate them.

"I still can't believe you beat me to the altar," Gabby said in mock anger, tears streaking her cheeks.

"I can't either." Emma's giggles were mixed with her own tears. "But we'll be doing this again for you and Ethan in just a few weeks."

Trent stood beside Ryan, tugging at the ever-present beanie on his head. "Congrats, you guys."

"Thanks, man." Ryan clapped his brother on the back. "So glad you're back."

Emma flung her arms around Trent. "I'm so happy to have you as my brother-in-law."

Trent had come back to Haven last month and was taking classes at the local community college, working toward his degree at his own pace while still DJ'ing once a week at The Music Factory. He and Emma often commiserated about homework.

"Can you believe it?" Emma whispered in Ryan's ear, her arm going around his waist.

"I'm afraid to blink sometimes. So much has changed."

"Yeah." She was beaming, the happy glow in her cheeks the only visible sign of the baby who'd jump-started their happily ever after. "When I said I wanted to shake things up this year, I had no idea what I was starting."

"This may be the wildest ride of all." He leaned in to kiss her. "I'm absolutely crazy for you, today and always."

"Me, too," she whispered against his lips. "Me, too."

Please turn the page for a preview of
Can't Forget You.

Available Winter 2017

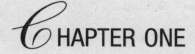

CHAPTER ONE

*J*essica Flynn picked her way along the grassy roadside. To her right, the forest beckoned, wild and beautiful. The timing wasn't perfect, but after eyeing this undeveloped tract of land next to her spa for years, it had finally been put up for sale. And now it was going to be hers.

She rubbed at the headache squeezing her temples, remembering—belatedly—that she'd meant to take some ibuprofen before she headed out to meet with the realtor. Oh well, too late now. And actually, now that she was away from the hustle and bustle of the spa, she realized her whole body hurt, a deep ache in her joints and a shivery sensitivity on her skin that felt an awful lot like she was coming down with something.

Which was just friggin' great. Half her staff had been out with the flu already this month, and she was booked solid with client appointments for the rest of the week.

But first things first...

About ten yards ahead, a white SUV sat in the gravel

driveway beside the For Sale sign. As she approached, the vehicle's front door opened, and a balding, middle-aged man stepped out.

"Ms. Flynn?" he asked.

"Yes."

"I'm Gordon McDermott." He stuck out a hand, and she shook. "You said on the phone you own the adjacent property?"

"That's right," she said. The Haven Spa was her baby, the culmination of years of sweat, tears, and dreams. And once she'd bought this additional land, she was going to expand the spa into a minimalistic resort.

"Then he must own the property on the other side." Gordon nodded toward a man standing at the end of the gravel driveway, his back to them.

Jessica's spine stiffened as if it had turned to steel. He was tall, lean, and muscular, his black hair close-cropped, hands shoved into the front pockets of his jeans. She'd know that profile anywhere.

Mark Dalton, the first man to own—and break—her heart. The man she couldn't get within five feet of without wanting to kick him in the shins for being such a jerk when they were teenagers. And unluckily for her, he was also one of the owners of the property on the other side of this one.

He turned, and their eyes met. His were the color of rich espresso, sizzling in their intensity. His bronzed skin was marred by a vicious scar that slashed his right cheek, the only visible reminder of the accident that ended his Army career. "Jess," he said, his voice deep and a little scratchy.

"Mark." Her hands clenched into fists. Figured he and his friends would have their eye on this property, too. Well, she'd just have to outbid them because she'd been dreaming about expanding the spa for a lot longer than they'd been giving zip-line tours over at Off-the-Grid Adventures.

"I take it you two already know each other?" Gordon said, looking pleased.

She and Mark both nodded, eyeing each other warily.

"Great. Well, as you may have heard, the property owner, Randy Wexler, passed away unexpectedly a few months ago, and his family is looking to sell this property as quickly as possible to settle up his estate. My impression," he said, raising his eyebrows for emphasis, "is that he left behind quite a few bills that need paying."

"That's sad," Jessica said. "I wonder why he never got around to building anything out here?"

"He'd owned this property for decades, hoped to someday retire and build his dream home here," Gordon said. "Unfortunately, he waited too long to make it happen. Naturally, the family is thrilled that we already have not one, but two, interested buyers for the land."

"I bet." Jessica eyed Mark again. He still stood near the end of the gravel driveway—the driveway that Randy Wexler had envisioned leading to his dream home but instead dead-ended into the forest beyond.

Mark, never one for casual conversation, said nothing.

"As you both know, there's a little over forty acres out there, all undeveloped. The property is zoned residential, but with businesses on both sides, I wouldn't anticipate a problem having it rezoned commercial."

Mark cocked an eyebrow. She'd heard that the guys had had quite a time getting their property rezoned to allow Off-the-Grid to open, but in the end, it had worked out. And the realtor was right—with businesses on both sides, rezoning was a no-brainer.

"You mind if I have a look around?" Mark asked.

"Not at all. Take your time. I imagine you both are familiar with where the property lines lie," Gordon said, gesturing toward the forest before them.

"Thank you," Jessica said. "I'd like to poke around a bit, too." She'd already done some snooping on her own, but she couldn't pass up the chance to openly explore. This land wrapped around behind the spa, and since no one used it for anything, she'd occasionally hiked through, daydreaming about little cabins with private hot tubs nestled in the woods.

Mark walked to the end of the driveway then turned and looked back, as if waiting for her to catch up. *Dammit.* She'd been planning to strike out on her own. Well, maybe she could feel him out for how serious he and the guys were about buying. "I didn't know you guys were interested in more land," she said as she fell into step beside him—well, kind of beside him. She'd left a few feet of space between them for good measure. Any closer and she might wind up wanting to strangle him. Because if she looked too deeply into his cocoa eyes, the memories threatened to swamp her. So many stolen kisses and whispered promises. This was the man she'd thought she might spend the rest of her life with, right up until he dropped her like a bad habit when he enlisted in the Army.

Mark kept his eyes on the leaf-strewn ground before them. "We've been talking about adding a mountain bike course. Ethan says there are some hills back here that would be perfect."

A mountain biking course? She wasn't opposed to the idea except for the fact that this property bordered her spa on two sides, and she wasn't sure she wanted adrenaline-seeking men and women racing past her natural spring-fed hot tubs whooping and swearing while her clients were trying to relax and unwind. "Why can't you build that on the land you already own?"

"Hills on our side are too rocky. Perfect for climbing, not biking."

"So you're pretty serious then? About buying?"

His eyes flicked to hers, just for a moment, and he nodded. "You looking to expand the spa?"

"Yes," she said and left it at that. Her headache was getting worse, and *ugh*, she really felt lousy. She was going to be so pissed if she had to go home from work early today.

She and Mark walked in silence for a few minutes, crunching over the bed of leaves and pine needles that carpeted this part of the woods. Birds twittered overhead, darting through the colorful foliage. Here in Haven, North Carolina, fall had officially arrived, bringing with it a chill on the breeze and a kaleidoscope of color in the trees.

October had always been her favorite month, what with the foliage, cool air, fresh apple cider, and Halloween, which was arguably her favorite holiday. Yeah, fall rocked, especially out here in the Smoky Mountains, where Mother Nature really got a chance to put on a show. It was almost enough to take her mind off the stabbing pain behind her eyes and the vicious ache in her bones that intensified with every step she took.

Mark started toward a steep incline to the left, and she seized the opportunity to part ways. "I'm headed this way." She gestured to the right, toward the flatter area she'd been scoping out for her spa cabins. "I'll see you back by the road."

He paused, and those dark eyes met hers again, burning right through her. He nodded and turned away, hiking toward the hillside. She turned away, too, before she caught herself doing something stupid like watching his very fine ass as he walked away.

* * *

Mark Dalton grabbed the rock and pulled himself up. It didn't compare with the rock face they used over at Off-the-Grid, but he'd never say no to a new rock to climb. His right knee ached as he moved, stiff and tight in a way he'd never fully get used to.

He pulled himself over the top of the rock and stood, finally allowing himself to look in the direction Jess had gone. She was nowhere to be seen.

Just as well.

Since he'd returned to Haven, she'd made it clear she didn't want anything to do with him. Not that he blamed her. It was just his dumb luck that he still wanted her something fierce. In the eleven years since he left Haven—and Jess—behind, no woman had ever come close to what he'd had with Jess. They'd shared something intense, something *real*, that he'd never felt with anyone else.

But that was in the past. These days, he'd gotten so used to the occasional random hookup that he'd come to prefer it. He enjoyed being on his own. Always been a loner. Probably always would be. No doubt his fantasies about Jess were better off kept as just that…fantasies.

Pausing, he surveyed the hilly area where he, Ethan, and Ryan had talked about building a mountain bike course. The terrain out here was ideal, lots of gentle slopes and steep drops. The three of them had opened Off-the-Grid Adventures together last year, offering zip-line tours, rock climbing, survival skills classes, and the like. The whole thing had been Ethan's brainchild, but it sure had been the right thing at the right time for Mark.

After he'd been blown half to pieces in Iraq two years ago, his knee was too messed up to return to active duty so he'd been stuck drilling new recruits at Fort Jackson during Basic Combat Training. It didn't fucking compare to being out in the field, busting drug deals or securing hostile territory with his Special Forces team.

Now, for the first time in his adult life, he was a civilian. Finally starting to come to terms with it, too. There was something reassuring about the peace and quiet of the woods after spending so much time in a war zone. The creatures here weren't capable of evil. They just did their thing and lived their lives. Not so different from him these days.

Movement snagged his attention out of the corner of his right eye. Instinct had him reaching for the weapon he no longer carried. Exhaling slowly, he glanced over his shoulder. He moved more quietly than most hikers and often surprised wildlife out here in the woods. Sure enough, about two hundred feet away, a black bear and two cubs ambled through the trees. One of the cubs paused and looked back at him, then kept walking.

No cause for alarm. Bears were pretty common out here and rarely bothered people unless people bothered them first. Mark watched as they made their way through the woods, headed roughly in the same direction Jess had gone. And *that* he didn't like.

Unable to help himself, he doubled back. No doubt Jess knew how to handle herself around bears as well as he did, but the duty to protect was too deeply ingrained in him to ignore.

The bear and her cubs had ventured far enough ahead to be out of sight now, but he could still hear their feet crunching through the bed of fallen leaves and twigs that covered the ground and the mama bear's occasional snorts as she called to her cubs. They weren't exactly stealthy, nor did they need to be. They ruled these woods, and they knew it.

He veered to the right in the direction he'd last seen Jess. It wasn't hard to follow her tracks. The leaf bed here was still damp from yesterday's rain, and the imprint of her shoes showed easily. He found her sitting on a tree stump, staring into the trees as if completely lost in thought.

Yep, that was Jess. He stopped and shoved his hands in his pockets to watch her. So damn pretty. Her brown hair hung just past her shoulders. A shaft of sunlight brought out its gold undertones. Probably daydreaming about her plans for expanding the spa. Not wanting to interrupt, he stood back and waited for her to notice him.

After a few moments, she stood and headed in his direction. About two steps before she walked right into him, she let out a little shriek and clutched her chest. "Oh my God, Mark. You almost gave me a friggin' heart attack."

He bit back a smile. "Sorry."

"If you have to do your whole Army stealth thing out here, at least give a girl a heads-up, huh?" She frowned at him, her brown eyes flashing as she brushed past him and kept on walking.

"Didn't mean to sneak up on you."

"Why are you over here anyway? I thought you were checking out the hills for your mountain biking course."

"Saw a family of black bears headed your way," he said, falling into step behind her.

"And you thought I was just some helpless female who needed your protection?" She glared over her shoulder at him.

Nope, Jess was definitely not helpless.

"Well, for your information, I've seen plenty of bears out here over the years," she said. "They don't bother me a bit. I'm perfectly capable of taking care of myself."

"Got it." Knew it was true, too. And he also knew he'd do

the same thing again, for any hiker out here, male or female, but especially for Jess.

Neither of them spoke as they walked back toward the entrance to the property. Silence was his preferred method of communication, but this silence buzzed with a tension that made his scalp prickle with misgivings. Whichever of them ended up buying this land, they were going to be neighbors, and it would make things a hell of a lot easier if they could get along.

Beside him, Jess rubbed at her forehead. All the color—and the anger—seemed to have drained out of her.

"You okay?" he asked.

"Fine," she muttered, but now that he was looking at her up close, she didn't look fine. She was pale, her movements jerky as if she were in pain.

"Jess..." He touched her arm, hoping to get her to slow down, and *Jesus H. Christ*. "You're burning up."

She jerked her arm away from his touch. "Am I?"

"Hold up a minute here." He reached for her again, and this time she stopped, letting out a weary sigh.

"I might be coming down with the flu. Half my employees have had it already this month."

He pressed a palm against her forehead, frowning. "You're running a high fever. Have you taken anything?"

She shook her head. "I will as soon as I get back to the spa."

"Let me take you home."

She started walking again. "No, thanks."

"You can't go back to work like this."

She let out a frustrated groan. "I know that. Much as it kills me to cancel on my afternoon clients, I can't see as I have any choice. Not good for business if I infect them with my germs, is it?"

He walked beside her, still watching her closely. "Are you limping?"

"Will you cut it out? My joints hurt. I'm sick. I'm going home, I promise."

But she didn't complain when he offered his elbow to lean on, and that spoke volumes. They lapsed back into silence, making their way through the woods. A few minutes later, they rounded an outcrop and found themselves face-to-face with the bear and her cubs, not ten feet in front of them.

Jess gasped, her grip on his arm tightening.

The mama bear had been sharpening her claws on a tree trunk while her cubs climbed the tree. She turned her head at the sudden human intrusion then lunged in their direction, slapping her front paw against the leaf-covered ground as she blew loudly through her nostrils.

Mark raised his hands in the air, beginning to back away. "Easy, girl. We didn't mean to sneak up on you."

"Holy shit," Jess whispered, yanking on his arm. "Shouldn't we run?"

"Nope," he said, walking backward away from the bears while still facing them, keeping his body between Jess and the agitated mama. "She's just bluffing. We startled her. She's telling us we're too close to her and her babies."

"No friggin' kidding."

"No need to get upset." He lifted his voice to carry to the bears. "Easy does it."

Mama bear slapped the ground again, huffing loudly.

"Why are you talking to her like that?" Jess hissed in his ear. "You're pissing her off!"

"We're making sure she knows we're not prey, but we're also respecting her wishes and getting out of her space." He kept his voice calm, level, and loud enough for the bears to hear.

Mama bear continued to huff and snort, eyeing them warily until they'd backed out of sight into the surrounding trees. Only then did Mark finally turn around, leading Jess briskly through the trees in the direction of the road, keeping his ears tuned for any sound from behind them.

"Holy shit," she said, looking paler than ever.

"She didn't want to fight us. It was just a warning. You should take my survival skills class sometime," he said, glancing at her.

"I'll think about it."

He took that as a no.

They reached the road a few minutes later, and she lifted her hand from his arm, tucking it around her waist. "Thanks for waiting while we poked around," she said to Gordon McDermott.

"You two see everything you needed to see?" the realtor asked.

"Yep," she said. "And then some," she added with a small smile in Mark's direction.

He nodded. "We'll be in touch with our offer."

"So will I," Jess said, her expression hardening.

They said their good-byes, and Gordon climbed back inside his SUV.

"I'll walk you to your car," Mark said to Jess because she didn't look entirely steady on her feet.

"No, thanks." She started off in the direction of the spa, walking quickly.

He fell into step beside her anyway.

She frowned up at him. "You know, maybe some women swoon for your macho style, but I'm not one of them."

"I noticed," he said drily, wishing her words didn't burrow their way under his skin and stick there like some unwelcome parasite.

"So, bye then." She waved a hand in his direction, picking up her pace.

He didn't argue, just kept walking beside her.

She muttered something under her breath, glared at him, and kept walking. She wasn't limping anymore, but he wasn't sure if she was feeling better or just being stubborn and putting on a brave face so that he'd leave her alone.

The latter, apparently, because when the spa finally came into view, her shoulders slumped and her relief was palpable. She ran a hand through her brown hair and gave him another pointed look. "Okay, thanks for walking with me. I can take it from here."

"Jess . . . let me drive you home."

Now that she'd stopped walking, she looked like she might topple over if a strong breeze gusted against her. "I'm going inside to finish up a few things first. I'm fine."

"You're not fine, and I'm not taking no for an answer."

"Stubborn man," she mumbled. "Well, I'm going inside to finish up. You can wait here if you really want, but knowing you're out here is not going to make me rush."

On the contrary, she'd probably dawdle just to spite him, but he didn't care. She was in no shape to drive herself home. So he stood to the side of the entrance, hands in his pockets, and waited. Eight years in the Special Forces had given him plenty of experience waiting. He could stand here all afternoon if he needed to.

He didn't much like the idea of going up against Jess to buy this property, but there didn't seem to be any way around it. She was certainly going to do her best to snag it for herself, and there was no way the guys would want to back down so they would, too. May the best man—or woman—win.

Thirty minutes later, she came out the spa's front doors,

her purse and another larger bag slung over her right shoulder. And it was a good thing he'd waited because she looked even worse than when she'd gone in.

She stopped in her tracks and gawked at him. "Oh my God. Have you seriously been standing here this whole time?"

He nodded.

"Well, I...I figured you'd leave. I forgot how stubborn you are when you get an idea in your head, but for the record, I'm perfectly capable of driving myself home."

"Jess." He stared at her, frowning. "Stop arguing and let me drive you home."

"Fine." She huffed in annoyance and led the way toward a black Kia Sportage parked around back. She was limping again, moving more slowly than she had during their earlier hike. The doors unlocked with a beep, and she walked to the passenger side. "How's this going to work anyway? How are you going to get back?"

"I'll call someone to pick me up at your place."

She pointed a finger in his direction. "I'm not inviting you in, just so you know."

"Fair enough." He slid behind the steering wheel and texted the one person at Off-the-Grid most likely to be goofing around on his phone this afternoon: Ryan's teenage brother, Trent. Sure enough, Trent replied right away. "Trent's going to swing by and get me."

Jess leaned back against the seat and closed her eyes. "Okay...207 Riverbend Road."

"Got it." He started the engine and pulled out of the lot. Jess was quiet during the drive. He might have thought she was sleeping except for the lines of tension creasing her brow. Ten minutes later, he turned into the driveway of her little brown-paneled house, parked, and shut off the engine.

Her eyes opened, bright with fever, and she gave him a pinched smile. "Thanks for the ride, and you know ... saving me from bears." Then her usual attitude flared to life, and her eyes narrowed. "But I'm still going to outbid you on that land."

ABOUT THE AUTHOR

Rachel Lacey is a contemporary romance author and semi-reformed travel junkie. She's been climbed by a monkey on a mountain in Japan, gone scuba diving on the Great Barrier Reef, and camped out overnight in New York City for a chance to be an extra in a movie. These days, the majority of her adventures take place on the pages of the books she writes. She lives in warm and sunny North Carolina with her husband, son, and a variety of rescue pets.

Rachel loves to keep in touch with her readers! You can find her at:

RachelLacey.com
Twitter @rachelslacey
Facebook.com/RachelLaceyAuthor

A SMALL-TOWN BRIDE
By Hope Ramsay

Amy Lyndon is tired of being "the poor little rich girl" of Shenandoah Falls. In her prominent family, she's the *ordinary* one—no Ivy League education and no powerful career. But when her father tries to marry her off, she finally has to stand up for herself, despite the consequences. Cut off from the family fortune, her first challenge is to find a job. And she's vowed to never rely on another man ever again, no matter how hot or how handsome.

Fall in Love with Forever Romance

HOLDING FIRE
By April Hunt

Alpha Security operative Trey Hanson is ready to settle down. When he meets a gorgeous blonde in a bar, and the connection between them is off the charts, he thinks he's finally found the one. But after their night together ends in a hail of gunfire and she disappears in the chaos, Trey's reasons for tracking her down are personal...until he learns she's his next assignment. Fans of Rebecca Zanetti and Julie Ann Walker will love the newest romantic suspense novel from April Hunt!

THE HIGHLAND DUKE
By Amy Jarecki

Fans of *Outlander* will love this sweeping Scottish epic from award-winning author Amy Jarecki. When Akira Ayres finds a brawny Scot with a musket ball in his thigh, the healer will do whatever it takes to save his life...even fleeing with him across the Highlands. Geordie knows if Akira discovers his true identity, both their lives will be jeopardized. The only way to protect the lass is to keep her by his side. But the longer he's with her, the harder it becomes to imagine letting her go...

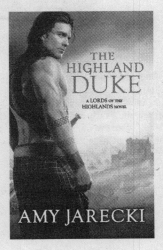

Fall in Love with Forever Romance

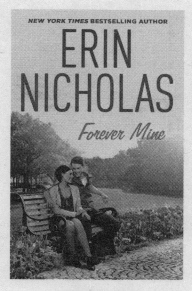

FOREVER MINE
By Erin Nicholas

The newest book in *New York Times* bestselling author Erin Nicholas's Opposites Attract series!

Maya Goodwin doesn't believe in holding back. Ever. As a cop, she never hesitated to throw herself into harm's way to save someone. As a doctor, Alex Nolan knows all too well that risks can have deadly consequences. So Maya—daring and spontaneous—is the exact opposite of who he's looking for. But he can't resist exploring their sizzling attraction, even though falling for Maya might just be way too hazardous for his heart.

CRAZY FOR YOU
By Rachel Lacey

Emma Rush can't remember a time when she didn't have a thing for Ryan Blake. The small town's resident bad boy is just so freakin' hot—with tattoos, a motorcycle, and enough rough-around-the-edges sexiness to melt all her self-control. Now that Emma's over being a "good girl," she needs a little help being naughty...and Ryan is the perfect place to start.